GW00384428

REDCAP RUNS AWAY

REDCAP
RUNS AWAY

by

RHODA POWER

Illustrated from drawings by
C. WALTER HODGES

JONATHAN CAPE
THIRTY BEDFORD SQUARE
LONDON

FIRST PUBLISHED 1952
REISSUED 1971

JONATHAN CAPE LTD
30 BEDFORD SQUARE, LONDON, WCI

ISBN 0 224 00503 0

PRINTED IN GREAT BRITAIN
BY LOWE AND BRYDONE (PRINTERS) LTD, LONDON
BOUND BY G. AND J. KITCAT LTD, LONDON

CONTENTS

ILLUSTRATIONS

This
book is for
JUDITH STEELE

PREFACE

THIS is a story of fourteenth-century England, just before the Black Death, when minstrels roamed from town to village, along highway and byway, entertaining knights and ladies, townsmen and peasants, with songs, music and stories.

When you have read this book, if, like Redcap our hero, you have enjoyed the minstrels' tales and want to know something more about them, read the note at the end.

REDCAP RUNS AWAY

I

REDCAP AND THE WISE WOMAN

*In which Redcap hears of a runaway uncle and Janet tells
the story of the abbot's jackdaw*

T HERE was an old woman in the village, older than
anyone else. She looked as old as the tree which had
been struck by lightning when Redcap was a baby. She
had been old when his grandfather was a child and she remembered things that no one else knew about.

Twin wisps of white hair hung down over her eyes and when
they tickled her wrinkled face or prevented her from seeing
clearly, she thrust out her lower lip and blew them out of her
way with a queer whistling sound as though she were talking
the language of the wind. Her back was humped and her neck
skinny as a plucked chicken's and she always carried a gnarled

stick, cut from an oak bough, which served her as a third leg, for she was lame and could only shuffle along slowly.

She lived inside the wood where the villagers gathered sticks for their fires and the swineherd drove the pigs to root for acorns. People would come to see her if a child was sick or if they had aches and pains of their own, and she would brew a mess of herbs for them in a big black pot and stir it, round and round, with a spoon made from the bone of a cow's leg, while her black cat waved its tail and a tame jackdaw perched on her shoulder and screeched with wide-open beak.

Most people called her "the wise woman" but if a horse sickened and was unable to work or a calf died for no apparent reason, the owner would mutter that someone had cast the evil eye on his beast and would look in the direction of the forest and whisper the word "witch", but it was never more than a whisper for people were afraid of witches and believed them to be friends of the devil himself. The priest said that old Janet was harmless and a good woman, who crossed herself whenever she passed the church door. And how could a friend of the devil make the sign of the Cross and come to no harm? She was wise and not wicked, yet it was strange that when she stood still and looked up into the sky, far above the tree tops, her bleary old eyes seemed to clear and become bright blue with little spinning points of light in them like tiny stars. It was then that she spoke very quickly and said "This or that will happen", and sure enough, as time went on, it did happen and people remembered what she had said.

Redcap met her one day when he had slipped away from his father's forge while the smith was dozing in the doorway after a dinner of hot pease porridge. He expected Redcap to wake him if anyone came with a horse to be shod or a tool to be sharpened. But Redcap was tired of waiting and had crept round to the back of the smithy without waking his father and darted like a hare into the wood to idle away his time whittling sticks and making them into whistles.

The croak of a jackdaw startled him and he saw old Janet

among the trees with the black cat behind her waving its tail and the bird perching on her head.

Old Janet looked first at him, then up to the tree tops at a patch of sky and her eyes twinkled.

"If you're here till sunset, Redcap," she said, "the shoe will follow behind you. You'll not see it but you'll feel it coming. So you had better be off."

Redcap looked bewildered. "Shoes don't move of their own accord," he said.

"No," said the wise woman.

"And when people walk shoes go with them, they can't go behind, so I don't know what you mean," said Redcap.

"Time will show," said old Janet, "but I'm warning you."

Redcap grinned. "I like finding things out," he said, "so I'll stay here till sunset. And anyhow, I'm barefoot and I've never had any shoes, at least not real leather ones. Father has a pair," he added confidentially. "The soles are made of cowhide, double, and hard as iron. He wears them to church. Mistress Janet —"

She ruffled his red hair with her skinny old hand and smiled. "What now?" she asked and sat down on the trunk of a fallen tree, lowering herself with little gasps and groans. "What now, Redcap?"

The small boy sat at her feet and looked up. "Mistress Janet, do you always know what's going to happen?" he asked. "I don't mean making jokes about shoes and things, but real things about people?"

"Sometimes," said old Janet. She poked him in the ribs with her stick. "This very minute I know what you're going to ask me. You want an adventure and you are going to ask me whether you'll have one."

Redcap chewed a fallen leaf and looked at her, his brown eyes wide with wonder. "I'm always wanting to know," he said, "but it's no use asking anyone. The priest says God sent us an adventure when He gave us life so wherever we are we're having one, but he's different from me and I can't talk to him.

Then there's mother. She says, 'Wait till you're a man and who knows what will happen.' And father —"

He paused and frowned, his face growing discontented and his eyes clouding.

"What does father say?" asked old Janet.

"He says all I need is to learn to be a smith and a good one. He says we've all been smiths for hundreds of years — his father and his grandfather and his great-grandfather and it's adventure enough to do the day's work. And just because I've red hair —"

"Ah," said old Janet, "just because you've red hair — what does he say about that?"

"He says no one else has it in the village and just because I've red hair I needn't want to be different in other ways. A smith I was born and a smith I'll become if he has to hammer it into me."

Old Janet picked up her cat and stroked it till it closed its eyes and purred and the purring was like distant music, the gentle thrumming of a minstrel beating a quiet tattoo on a little drum.

"I know John Smith, Redcap," said Janet, "and his hand will never be too heavy on you. He's a gentle peaceable man but he'll argue a boy must be whipped now and then. Maybe he's right, maybe he's wrong, but he'll bring you up in the way you should go, and wherever you are you'll come back to it."

She stopped stroking the cat and looked up at the patch of blue sky above the trees and her eyes seemed to clear and the light in them sparkled and spun. "There's always one redhead in the Smith family," she said, "there always has been and there always will be and they're never the same as the others. The dark haired stay where they're put and the fair haired do as they're told but the red haired must follow a secret flame even though it's a Will-o'-the-Wisp."

Redcap did not understand. Old Janet often seemed to be saying things that had no meaning. "I shan't follow a Will-o'-

the-Wisp," said he. "Father says it's a little fire that dances in the bogs and leads men to death."

"Ay, a little dancing fire that leads those who are lost on and on, because they think it's the light in a home and they're tired of wandering."

Redcap looked uneasy. "Do you mean if I have an adventure, I'll get lost," he asked.

Old Janet did not answer for a minute. She peered up at the sky as though she could see behind the clouds. "You will go a long way, Redcap," she said, "over hills and valleys, into strange cities, but remember, however far the feet may wander, the heart remains. You will freeze with cold and burn with fever. You will be cuffed and scolded till you cry yourself to sleep. But for every evil there's the hidden good, and you have only to look for it and the day that you find it will bring a red-haired smith singing to the village."

Old Janet struggled to her feet, thrust out her lower lip and blew a wisp of grey hair from in front of her eyes, and the eyes were no longer blue and sparkling but the dim tired eyes of a very old woman.

"The sun's going down," she said.

Redcap glanced quickly over his shoulder and the wise woman chuckled.

"I don't see a shoe behind me," said the little boy.

"I said you would feel it," said Janet.

"I don't feel a thing," said Redcap, "and I'm coming home with you. I may, mayn't I? I've time before supper."

"Time never waits," said Janet, "you must do what you think is best." And with the cat waving its tail behind her and the jackdaw on her head, she hobbled farther into the wood.

Redcap trotted along beside her, thinking of what she had told him. Her words seemed to have promised an adventure but when would he have one and how? Would he really go far away and see strange cities?

"Mistress Janet," he began.

"Don't talk to me, Redcap, while I'm walking, for my breath

runs short and I can't answer you. Wait till I get to the house."

She wheezed and stood still for a minute and the jackdaw flew from her head on to her shoulder, opened one eye, and began to peck the little wooden crucifix which hung around her neck on a piece of knotted string.

"Nay now, Jacky, now Jacky!" she said, "that's holy. There was a jackdaw who stole what was holy long ago, and you know what happened to him. Stop it, bad bird!"

Redcap pricked up his ears. This sounded interesting. Old Janet was always saying things which made him think that her head was full of stories, and if ever a boy loved a story, it was Redcap.

"What was that jackdaw, Mistress Janet?" he asked.

"It's a tale I had from your uncle. I'll tell you when we sit down, Redcap. Open the door for me and blow up the fire. When the sun begins to go down, my old bones get chilled."

They had arrived at a little hut made of wooden logs with a roof of sticks, twigs and moss smeared with dried mud. There was no chimney but a small hole through which the smoke escaped from the fire, which was smouldering on a large flat stone, set on the floor in the middle of the room.

Redcap kicked a log and poked a handful of sticks and chips under it, then lay with his right cheek on the ground and began to blow till the sparks reddened and the sticks caught fire and there was soon a warm red blaze which made old Janet's shadow dance and tremble as though it were now more alive than she was herself.

Redcap looked around to see if she had anything new, but the room was always the same, the earth stamped hard and flat like the floor in his mother's cottage, the walls streaked with smoke, and black cobwebs hanging from the ceiling. But it was cosy. A bundle of straw, where old Janet slept covered by a coarse grey blanket, lay in the corner, a stool was drawn up by the fire, just near enough for Janet to reach the big black pot which hung from a chain on a hook in the roof. On a rod across one corner of the hut two moleskins were drying, a piece of

THERE WAS SOON A WARM RED BLAZE

bacon and a pig's trotter hung side by side and next to them was an old grey cloak lined with rabbit, mole, squirrel and weasel skins sewn together into a sort of patchwork. There were seven apples on a shelf, and in a row beside them an earthenware jar full of nuts, a jug, a cup carved from a piece of wood, and made smooth by much rubbing, a wooden plate and a knife with a sharp steel blade. Like all the village women, old Janet spun her own wool and her distaff and spindle were propped against the wall under the shelf.

"Take an apple, Redcap," said the old woman, "and pull my stool a little farther from the fire. Red Eric your great-uncle made it for me when he was little more than your age."

'I didn't know I had a great-uncle, Red Eric," said the boy.

"You mightn't," said old Janet, "for he left this village before your father was born and never came back but once."

"Why did he go?" asked Redcap, for people were not in the habit of leaving the village except to carry eggs or vegetables to the nearest town and they always came back to till the fields and bring in the harvest and live the same kind of life year after year. "Why did Red Eric go away, and why was he called Red Eric, and what did he do when . . . ?"

"Hey, hey! One question at a time," said Janet putting her skinny old hands up to her ears. "You chatter more than Jacky when he wants to be fed."

Hearing his name Jacky flew from Janet's head where he had been perching and alighted on Redcap's shoulder and crouched there with his beak stroking the little boy's neck.

"Red Eric," said Janet, "was your great-uncle, the very spit of yourself when he was nine. His hair was a flame and his temper was hot and he carried a heart in him like a live coal. When he was joyful, his eyes flickered like a fire and when he was sorrowful, they died down like ashes. He could sing like a thrush, the way you do, Redcap, and his voice well nigh charmed the heart from the body."

"What did he sing?" asked Redcap.

22

"The songs the priest taught him and some of the songs that you yourself sing. I always knew when he was coming to see me for I'd hear his voice carolling in the woods —

> A woman is a gladsome thing,
> They do the wash and do the wring!
> Lullay, lullay she doth thee sing
> And yet she hath but care and woe.

Old Janet's voice reached a note too high and it cracked so that she began to cough and wheeze. When she had recaptured her breath, she finished the song to the end, stirred the pot and began to talk again.

"Red Eric came to me one day with that stool and I could tell by the way he looked over his shoulder that he didn't want anyone to hear him. 'Here's a goodbye present, Janet,' he said. 'Where are you going, Red Eric?' I asked, but he wouldn't tell. He just shook that red head of his and looked as solemn as an owl. 'I don't like a present that means "goodbye for ever", Red Eric,' I said, 'and I see by your eyes that you're going away for a long time.' 'I'll come, one day, with a "good morning present",' he said, 'one day when I've had an adventure.' He went to the door and peered out. Then he came back, gave me a hug and was gone. I think he was fourteen or fifteen years old at that time, but I never saw him again till a red beard had grown on his chin and his eyes looked wise but merry."

"Where had he been?" asked Redcap.

"Away and away till his feet were sore and you could count the ribs in his body, but his head was full of music and tales fell from his lips like drops of rain from the sky."

"Did he bring you a good morning present?" asked Redcap.

"He brought me Jacky one night and was gone the next morning."

"Is Jacky so old? Is that why he looks so feeble?" asked Redcap.

"There's no knowing how old he is," said Janet, "but he was

young and spry when your great-uncle brought him and said, 'Keep your eye on him, Janet, he's a thief like the abbot's jackdaw.' "

Redcap's eyes sparkled. He spat the core of his apple into the fire, put on another log and leant against Janet's knee with the jackdaw still on his shoulder.

"Great-uncle told you about the abbot's jackdaw, didn't he?" he coaxed, "and you'll tell me, Mistress Janet, won't you? I love stories."

"You'd wheedle the tongue out of my old mouth, wouldn't you, Redcap?" she chuckled, "and you'll get what you like from me, for you're the spit and image of your great-uncle who ran away to the minstrels."

"Is *that* what he did?" said Redcap.

"Ay, he joined the wandering singers and tale tellers and that's how he learnt about Jacky's ancestor, the abbot's jackdaw."

"Tell it, please tell," begged Redcap, and the firelight made his eager eyes flicker like little flames.

Old Janet put her hand on his head and began to talk and as she spoke the walls of the hut seemed to fade and Redcap felt himself carried away to a stone monastery where monks lived and worked and prayed, for this is the story that the minstrels told to Red Eric, and Red Eric told to Janet and Janet told to Redcap.

"Long long ago," said old Janet, "there was an abbot who lived as a man of riches, feeding on the fat of the land, with grandeur and comfort on all sides, unlike the monks of his house who were simple folk, eager to do the will of God.

"One of these monks, who loved all living creatures, cherished a tame jackdaw which he fed with his own hand, enjoying its antics and teaching it to dance, with spread wings and up-lifted claws, so that the abbot himself could not resist laughing.

"One day the abbot, who delighted in good company, held a feast for some princes and great lords. The long table was spread with linen as fine as a spider's web and the goblets from which the sweet wine was drunk were of gold and of silver, marvellously chased with figures of men, beasts and flowers. Certain monks, who were serving-brothers, waited at the table and brought in platters of fish cooked with white sauce, fine bread, pigeon pie, and deer's meat and fruits from the abbot's garden.

THE ABBOT'S JACKDAW

"After Grace had been said and a blessing asked of God, all the guests made merry, talking and laughing together as they ate, while the jackdaw perched on the back of the abbot's chair, its little black eyes darting this way and that.

"The meal was a long one and every man ate his fill until the fruit and the sweetmeats were finished and the last cup of wine drunk. Then three monks came to the table, one carrying a silver basin, another a silver jug and the third a towel of fine linen. Each guest in turn put his hands into the basin and water was poured over his fingers, which were sticky from the fat and gravy on the bones of the meat.

25

"The abbot pushed back his loose sleeves, drew the glittering ring from his middle finger and placed it on the table while the monks washed his hands and dried them carefully with the towel. When this was finished, he rose from his chair and led the way to his own private garden where cushioned benches were set for himself and for his guests.

"Now it happened that when the guests were gone, the abbot glanced at his hands and saw that his favourite ring was not on his finger. He sent for a brother and told him to bring the ring from the table where he had put it when his hands were being washed.

"The monk did his bidding but returned saying, 'My Lord Abbot, the plates and dishes have not yet been cleared from the table, for the serving-brothers are at prayer, but the ring is not there.'

"'Then,' said the abbot, 'I pray you return and look again for I remember that I did not put the ring back on my finger when my hands were dry.'

"The monk obeyed, but search as he might, he could not find the ring and he returned to the abbot and said again, 'My Lord, the ring is not there.'

"The abbot rose from the bench where he was seated and said, 'Follow me and we will look together for I think that your eyes are at fault.'

"Back to the hall they went and made a thorough search, but seek as they might, the ring was nowhere to be found.

"Then the abbot's face grew red and his eyes flashed. 'There is a thief among us,' he said. 'When the serving-brothers have come from their prayers, send them to me!'

"But neither the serving-brothers nor the men who brought the water for the guests and for the abbot to wash, knew anything of the ring. And so, because the monks seemed to be innocent, the abbot began to suspect his guests who lived in the cities near and far from the abbey, and he sent for all the parish priests and bade them give notice in the churches that the abbot's ring had been stolen and that until it were found no one could enter a church to hear the word of God.

"The parish priests did as the abbot had told them, raising their right hands and saying, 'The sins of this thief shall find him out for he shall be accursed when he rises in the morning and when he goes to bed at night. He shall be accursed in his waking and in his sleeping, in his eating and in his drinking, in his walking and in his sitting, in his work, in his play, and in all that he does and wherever he is.'

"The people who heard these words knew that terrible things would happen to the thief who had stolen the ring, for the abbot's curse was a strong curse and he who was guilty could not escape.

"They went from the church, troubled in spirit and crossing themselves, praying that the thief would soon bring back the ring, for they were all unhappy if the church doors were closed against them.

"A week passed and still the thief did not appear, nor was the ring found. The brothers in the monastery remained in good health and none of the abbot's guests seemed to suffer from the curse. The townspeople, too, went about their business and were none the worse, sorrowful only because they could not go to church.

"Another week passed, another and yet another and still the ring was not found and no one near or far suffered.

"Only the tame jackdaw seemed to ail. It turned away from the titbits which were offered to it at table. After a while it could scarcely caw or croak and remained hunched in a corner with its wings drooping. As time went on, it began to moult and the feathers around its neck grew damp and the two little black eyes which had once been so bright grew dim as though a blue veil had been drawn across them.

" 'What ails the little creature?' asked one of the monks. 'What has become of all his gay antics and friendly caws?'

" 'He is little more than a skinful of bones,' said another. 'Why should he sicken so suddenly?'

" ' 'Tis as though a curse had fallen upon him,' said a third.

"A curse! One of the monks standing near the abbot, who was seated in his chair among them, spoke half in jest and half in earnest.

"'My Lord,' said he, 'you ought to consider whether by chance this is the thief whom you seek and whether this strange sickness from which he is suffering is not a sign that he is accursed.'

"The abbot looked at the jackdaw for a minute then spoke to his servants.

"'Climb to the place where this bird has his nest and see what is there!'

"Immediately the two servants climbed to the tree where the jackdaw nested and diligently turned over the straw and parted the twigs. There, discoloured and dirty, lay the abbot's ring. Quickly they washed and polished it, quickly they returned and gave it to the abbot, and he, placing his hand on the little jackdaw's head, stroked it gently and called for his messengers.

"Then word was sent to every parish priest that because the ring had been restored, the doors of the churches were to be opened once again and the curse lifted.

"Immediately the jackdaw, who from day to day had grown weaker, began to recover strength, to croak and caw and dance as before until at last it was restored to its first health and beauty."

Redcap sighed. He hated a story to come to an end. "Is that all?" he asked.

"That is all," said old Janet. "When we come to a happy ending there is no more to be said."

"Well I suppose he was really rather a wicked bird and deserved to be punished," said Redcap.

But old Janet shook her head. "Nobody is guilty unless he knows that he is doing wrong," she said.

At this point Jacky gave a croak, pecked Redcap's neck, flapped his wings and flew to the roof of the hut and out through the smoke hole.

Redcap looked up following his flight and saw that the sky had darkened. He began to feel a little uncomfortable, "It's late," he said. "I see a star and — and — well I oughtn't to have come, really, or stayed — but — er, I don't think it really matters, do you?"

"Nobody is guilty unless he knows he has done wrong," croaked old Janet, and her voice was as hoarse as a jackdaw's but her eyes seemed to look straight into Redcap's heart.

"Perhaps I had better go. I'll run," said he, a little shamefaced. "Goodbye and thank you."

He sped out of the door, shouting as he did so, "It's nearly dark but there's no shoe following behind."

Glancing now and then over his shoulder, he reached his father's cottage beside the smithy. He saw the light from the fire under the door, lifted the latch and crept in, but before he knew where he was he found himself lifted from his feet and turned upside down while his father's cowhide shoe was descending upon him in a series of quick, sharp whacks.

"Oo," said Redcap, "so that's what she meant."

"So that's what who meant?" said his father setting him

upright with a little shake and twisting him round so that the two of them were face to face.

"The wise woman," said Redcap, rubbing himself tenderly. "She said if I stayed out till sunset the shoe would follow behind. She said I wouldn't see it but I'd feel it."

"And she was right!" said his father. "Next time—but there's to be no next time. You mind what you're told, Redcap. When I need you in the smithy in the smithy you're to stay."

He shook his head and sighed gently, "Boy," he said, "I don't understand what's coming over you, mooning about in the woods and doing your best to avoid helping me!"

"You were asleep," answered Redcap.

"A man must rest," said his father, "and I told you to watch the fire and to stand at the door so as to wake me if you saw anyone coming. If you can't do these small things now what kind of a smith will you make when you're older?"

"I don't want to be a smith, I want to —"

"Stop that," roared his father. "You'll follow your father, your grandfather, your great-grandfather —"

"Red Eric didn't," said Redcap.

"Who told you about that ne'er-do-well?" asked his father.

"The wise woman."

"Then she showed little wisdom to mention him. He ran away from his home and has never been heard of since and much sorrow he brought to my grandfather who had fed him and clothed him and trained him as a smith. He was a bad boy and as likely as not, if he's still alive, he's a bad man."

"Mistress Janet says I look like him and I sing as he used to sing. She says he ran away to be a minstrel. I'd like to be a minstrel!"

The smith unhooked the shoe which he had hung by its fellow on a wooden peg in the wall, felt the hard smooth sole and advanced on Redcap with a threatening air, but there was a twinkle in his eye so the boy stood his ground.

"You like stories, too," he said.

"In their proper place," replied his father, "and that place

30

is not in the head or on the lips of a red-haired boy, who is going to be a blacksmith. Get to bed now and thank the saints that your father dealt lightly with you this time, tho' the good priest said only this afternoon, 'Spare the rod and spoil the child, John Smith. You must do your duty by your son.'"

"Did they whip Red Eric?" asked Redcap.

"I'm thinking not enough, or he would have behaved better," said his father. "He disgraced a good family whose eldest son has always been a smith. So you stop thinking of him. Now drink your broth and go to bed!"

He dipped a wooden bowl into the pot hanging over the fire, gave it to Redcap, and pointed to the straw mattress which lay in the far corner of the room.

"Your mother's out spinning with her gossips," he said, "and will expect you to be asleep by the time she gets back. Why!" he stared at Redcap. "Boy, where's your little wooden cross? You ought always to wear it. You haven't *lost* it?"

Redcap put his hand up to his neck.

"Jacky!" he said. "He must have flown off with it. He heard about his ancestor in the monastery and followed his example."

"Hm," said the smith, "I don't know what you're talking about, but if Jacky followed someone's example and stole your crucifix, it was a *bad* example. And following a bad example is to be avoided. Get to bed now. We'll find your cross tomorrow. And remember, if I catch you even *thinking* of a bad example, I shall follow a *good* one and do what the priest tells me."

He tumbled Redcap on to the mattress, gave him a couple of playful whacks, grinned at him broadly, then dipped the point of his knife into a honey-comb which was in an earthenware pot, and offered the boy a lick.

II

REDCAP AND THE PRIEST

In which Redcap, wondering whether animals go to heaven, is told the story of a lion, and hears more of the red-headed runaway

THE next morning Redcap woke long after sunrise. The shutter was open and the light trickled through the piece of yellow parchment across the window. It came through unevenly for a part of the parchment was thick and a part so thin that you could almost put your finger through it. Redcap knew that with the next storm of rain, if the wind blew that way, the parchment would burst and they would have to paste something across the crack.

He remembered his father nailing it there, two years ago when Blossom the cow had broken her leg, no one knew how. She had been found lying in the pasture, unable to rise, and the smith had been obliged to kill her, grumbling and shaking his head, for the loss of a cow was serious. But they had all made the best of it and had used every scrap of the dead animal that they could.

They had made yellow candles from the fat, and a whip-lash with a knotted thong at the end from the tail, and from the skin a belt for Redcap, and a leather sleeveless coat and a pair of shoes for the smith. The meat had been salted and put in a barrel, and, with a little pepper and spice added, had made excellent dinners for the family for several months. The smith and his wife had cut spoons from the horns and from some of the bones, but it was the lining of the cow's stomach which had made the parchment for the window. It had been washed and scraped and stretched, then pegged out in the sun to get dry. When it was ready the smith had nailed it across the small

oblong opening in the wall, for none of the villagers could afford
to buy glass, which was only to be seen in the church and in
the hall of the manor house belonging to my lord who owned
the village and the land.

Redcap rubbed the sleep out of his eyes and sat upright
on his straw mattress. His mother was moving about, setting
the room to rights. She had taken the board, which formed
the table, off its trestles and leant it against the wall with the
trestles in front of it. She had pushed the bench against the
oak chest where she kept the family clothing, had set the two
wooden stools on the top of it and was sweeping the flat earth
floor with a broom made of birch twigs.

"Take up your bed, Redcap," she said, "and shake it out
of doors, then come back and eat your breakfast. There's a
mug of ale and some bread and honey on the shelf. Don't
make crumbs, and wash your face and hands afterwards. The
priest'll be here this morning and I can't have you looking
sticky or the place in a mess. Stand up on the chest and whisk
off those cobwebs with my broom, there's a good boy. I'm so
stiff these days."

"What's the priest coming for?" asked Redcap.

"An egg and a chicken," said his mother dryly, "I'm late.
He should have had them yesterday, and if ever I'm a day late
he comes nosing around with a 'Good day, Mistress, God keep
you'." She sniffed and poked an untidy lock under the grey
linen coif which covered her hair. "As if it weren't enough
to pay the rent to the lord of the manor with chickens and
butter and eggs as well as with the bit of money you can make
and the work of your hands. Why poor folk like us should have
to give our tenth chicken, our tenth egg, our tenth lamb, to the
priest, I can't think. We pay him to christen us, pay him to
marry us, pay him to bury us. What more should he want?
Now, Redcap, stop playing with that broom. You've brought
down the cobwebs. I don't want the floor covered with soot
from the smoke hole."

"I suppose we *have* to have a priest in the village," said Redcap

33

a little resentfully, because he remembered the advice given to his father about sparing the rod and spoiling the child.

His mother's jaw dropped. "Why, Redcap," she said, "of course we must. Who would hear us confess our sins? Who would take Mass, or tell us the stories from the Bible? He's a good man and I'm a wicked woman to have grumbled about him. He does more for us than we rightly know, praying late at night for our sins and putting in a good word for us to the Almighty. It's our duty to feed him and pay him, so forget what I said. I'm a bad old woman, that's what I am."

"You're not," said Redcap, "you're the best and cleverest mother in the world, and when I'm grown up I'm going to buy you a scarlet gown at the fair!"

His mother laughed. "And a fine pair we'll be," she said, "me in my red dress and you with your red hair. And speaking of red hair, tonight I must give that noddle of yours a scrub or you'll be getting called 'Blackcap' instead of Redcap. And now if you've finished your breakfast go out and wash. Your father doesn't need you at the forge this morning."

"I'm going to Mistress Janet," said Redcap. "Jacky stole my crucifix and I've got to get it back."

"The villainous old robber," said his mother. "How the good Lord came to create such a thieving rascal, I can't think. Be off now, and don't be late. I hear you were in trouble last night and I don't want your father to wear out a good pair of shoes sooner than need be, so come home early."

Redcap laughed and she gave him a little push and shut the door behind him calling, "Don't forget to wash now!"

Whistling a tune the boy walked past the beehive which stood outside the door, said, "Boo, ugly-face," to the nanny goat tethered to the wicket fence surrounding the patch of garden in front of the cottage, and sauntered out of the gate.

A small stream flowed across the road a few yards from the cottage door and he stooped, dabbled his hands in the water, and sluiced a little over his face, drying it with his sleeve, then spent a few minutes filling his mouth over and over again, opening his lips on one side and seeing how far across the stream he could make the water spurt.

After a while he tired of this game, so he splashed to the other side and dawdled along the road in the direction of old Janet's cottage in the wood. It had rained during the night and he watched the mud ooze up between his toes and thought of Janet's Jacky and the crucifix, wondering how the bird had learnt to be a robber. The crows, which the village boys had to scare from the grain by clapping two sticks together, were inclined to be thieves, but most other birds seemed innocent and pretty, especially the blackbirds and thrushes which sang as though they loved the whole world.

Thinking of songs, Redcap's mind turned to Red Eric, the uncle whom he had never known, the maker of music and teller of tales, who had run away rather than stay all his life in a smithy, making horseshoes and beating out iron into plough shares, rakes, spades and hoes. Old Janet had said that his eyes were merry but wise, so if he were alive, and perhaps he was, he would surely know the answers to many a question which moved round and round in Redcap's head.

Bad people, so the priest said, would not go to heaven. What about bad animals? Red Eric might know for if he had wandered far and wide he would have found out many important things, and by this time was probably wiser than old Janet herself, and quite fifty years of age.

Jacky had stolen the crucifix but Janet had said that you were not bad unless you knew that you were doing wrong. Jacky, like the monk's tame bird, may not have known that to steal was wrong. So perhaps he was a good jackdaw and had a chance of going to heaven. But did birds and animals go to heaven? His father had told him that only human beings had souls that went to heaven. What, then, happened to animals when they died?

With his mind far away, puzzling over this question, Redcap caught his foot in a hole in the road and fell down, hitting his nose so hard against a stone that it began to bleed.

"Hey, Rednose," cried a laughing voice as he picked himself up, "mop yourself—you look like a pitcher of spilt wine! Use your hood." And the priest pulled Redcap's hood, which hung down behind his back, around to the front and began to dab his nose with it. "Wring this out once or twice in the stream," he said, "and it will soon be clean again. But why don't you look where you're going?"

"I was thinking," said Redcap, "so it wasn't my fault."

The priest smiled. "I don't know who's fault it was, since you were doing the thinking. But if the thoughts were good, maybe thinking's a good fault. What was in that red noddle of yours?"

"Animals," said Redcap.

The priest threw back his head and laughed so loudly that some sparrows perching on the branch of an elm tree flew away, chattering with surprise and alarm.

"Well!" said the priest, then he chuckled, his eyes twinkling with meriment, and the corners of his mouth twitching. "Well!"

"Why are you laughing at me?" asked Redcap indignantly. "You asked me what I was thinking about and I told you the truth."

The priest immediately became solemn. "Of course you did, Redcap," he said, "I was really laughing at my own thoughts and not at you. But tell me some more, only wipe your nose, first."

Redcap sniffed, dabbed his nose and took off his hood to remind himself that it would need to be washed.

"Mistress Janet's jackdaw stole my cross," he said, "but I don't think he knew that it's wicked to steal so I was wondering if he would go to heaven. Then I wondered what would happen to all the animals after they died. We have some goats — the nanny's *good*. She gives us the milk we drink. Then there was Blossom, our cow — what do you think, your reverence?"

"Well," said the priest, 'it's a hard question." He rubbed his chin, then scratched the back of his head gently as though he were coaxing the thoughts to come out. "I'm inclined to think that the folk who love their beasts will meet them again." He looked far away for a minute and Redcap heard him murmur to himself, "Babes and sucklings — Mary, mother of a blessed child — how can one answer their questions?"

"You needn't answer if it's too difficult," said Redcap kindly, "but I'm much older than a babe or a suckling and you know it. You christened me years ago!"

The priest seemed a little startled that what he had said under his breath had been heard, but he smiled at the boy and answered, "Yes, I christened you 'John' because of your father and they call you Redcap because of your hair and John Redcap, son of John the smith, asks the most difficult questions."

"Father says that only *souls* go to heaven," said Redcap. "What's a soul?"

"The part of you that thinks and loves and wonders and believes and leads you to do as many good things as you can," answered the priest.

Redcap wrinkled his forehead. "Doesn't the soul let bad things in?" he asked. "Nobody's good all the time. I've known things sometimes to wriggle in sideways when your soul isn't looking."

"True," said the priest, "one must always be on guard. But what's troubling you?"

"Animals," said Redcap, "do they go to heaven?"

"Well," replied the priest, "I will tell you something that was once said to me by a stranger, and I have never forgotten it. He was a big fellow, ragged, but he carried his head as though he owned the world and he had with him a little donkey and a tame bird. I rebuked him, because in my foolishness, I said that he spoke to and treated the creatures as though they had immortal souls. I shall never forget the pitying look he gave me. 'Priest,' he said, 'before ever you reach the golden gates, an old lion will have slipped in before you.'"

"What did he mean?" asked Redcap.

"It was a story he told," answered the priest.

"Do you remember it?" asked Redcap, his eyes beginning to sparkle.

"Oh, yes," answered the priest. "He had a way with him, that man. You couldn't forget what he said."

"Then you'll tell it, won't you?" said Redcap, and he caught hold of the priest's hand and pulled him to the trunk of a tree which lay by the wayside and had not yet been cut up into logs for the lord of the manor's fire. "Let's sit and you can tell it."

"Do you think I have nothing better to do than to tell stories to boys and girls?" asked the priest.

"I know you have lots to do," said Redcap. "Mass and prayers and visiting the sick and looking after your strips of land in the fields which everybody shares — Oh — and teaching some of us to read and to sing psalms."

"I'm glad you remembered that," said the priest.

Redcap grinned sheepishly. "It's not a lesson day," he said, "so there's time for the story. It's early."

The priest glanced up at the sun. "Yes," he said, "it's early and I think I have time so I'll tell you the story that the stranger told me. He called it the Soul of a Lion."

"Many hundreds of years ago, there lived a good man called Gerasimus who was abbot of a monastery not far from the River Jordan, which is in the Holy Land.

"One day, when he was walking on the banks of the river, he met a lion. The great beast was roaring with pain and hobbling on three legs with one paw dangling. The paw was swollen and bleeding, for the sharp point of a reed was deeply embedded in it. When the lion saw the old man, it limped up to him, showing him the paw and whimpering. And the old man sat down, took the paw in his hand and removed the reed, cleaning the wound and binding it with rag. Then he stroked the lion's head and said, 'Go home, now, and get well.'

"But when the lion found that he was cured, he refused to leave Gerasimus and followed him everywhere and became a

38

very gentle inmate of the monastery, eating bread and herbs soaked in water, like the monks.

"Now the monastery had a donkey whose task it was to carry jars of water from the Jordan and Gerasimus took the lion to the donkey and said, 'Lion, now that you are one of

" HE USED TO CARRY THE WATERJARS TO AND FROM THE MONASTERY "

us you must do your duty as we all do. From today, I put you in charge of our donkey. See that you take care of him.'

"One day, when the lion had left the donkey grazing and had gone a short distance away, a camel driver came along, saw the donkey and led him away, so that when the lion returned his charge was nowhere to be seen. Downcast and miserable, he went back to the monastery and stood before the old man, with head and tail hanging low.

"'Where is the donkey?' asked Gerasimus. The lion was silent.

" 'Thou has eaten him,' said the old man. The lion made no reply but looked more downcast than ever.

" 'From this day forth,' said Gerasimus, 'whatever the donkey did, thou shalt do.'

"So panniers were fastened on the lion's back and he used to carry the water jars to and from the monastery.

" A little while later the camel driver who had stolen the donkey was coming with a load of barley to sell in the Holy City, and the donkey was with him, as well as his camels. The man had crossed the River Jordan and was going along the bank when he came upon the lion, and fled in terror leaving his animals.

"When the lion saw the donkey he knew him, and running up seized the halter in his mouth and led donkey and camels back to the monastery.

"With joyful roars he took them to Gerasimus, who recognized his donkey and knew that he had mistakenly accused the lion of doing wrong.

"He stroked the great beast's head.

" 'You have done well,' he said, and the lion's delight was a joy to behold.

"For more than five years the lion never left the monastery and was nearly always at the old man's side. But when Gerasimus died and was buried by the monks the lion could not at first be found, and did not know of his master's death. And so, when he returned, he wandered everywhere looking for the old man, and would eat nothing.

"Then Sabbatius, the monk who now filled the place of Gerasimus as abbot, spoke to him and said, 'Dear lion, our old master has left us orphans and has gone to heaven. You must eat.'

"But the lion would not eat, he wandered ceaselessly looking for Gerasimus and roaring pitifully. And although the abbot and the other monks ruffled his mane and tried to comfort him, explaining that their old master had gone to God, nothing would console him.

"At last, the Abbot Sabbatius said to him, 'Come with me and I will show you where the old master lies.' And he took the lion to the grave, which was five paces from the church, and said, 'Look, our old master is buried here.' Then he knelt and said a prayer.

"And when the lion heard it and saw the tears in the abbot's eyes, he lay down beating his head upon the ground and roaring lamentably.

"He died there, on the old man's grave, and who shall say that he did not follow his master?"

The priest was silent for a moment, then he nodded his head gently.

"The stranger looked at me," he said, "and asked if I could answer the question, 'Who shall say that the lion did not follow his master?' "

"What did you say?" asked Redcap.

"I don't think I answered because I remember he went on, 'The blessed saints had many a pet animal. St. Agnes had a lamb; would she leave that behind her? And there was a saint once who preached to the birds; would he preach to something that had no soul?' He was stroking the bird on his shoulder all the time that he was speaking. Then he stood up and began to tighten the girths around the little grey ass that carried his bundles, and without looking at me, he said, 'There was a donkey who bore the blessed Lord to Jerusalem while people threw palm leaves under its feet. Because of that every donkey has a cross marked on its back to this day. And who are you to deny heaven to anything that shows the sign of the cross?' That's what he asked me, and I thought, 'Yes, who am I?' "

Redcap nodded and the old priest looked down at him.

"Has that helped you over any of your difficulties?" he asked.

The boy frowned, "Y-Yes," he said rather doubtfully, "but is it true? I mean did the lion follow the abbot?"

The priest looked grave and rubbed his chin. "That's

another of your hard questions," he said. "Of course, if seeing is believing, I might not be able to answer because I have never been to heaven. But, you know, I don't really think that to believe you need to see, at least not with the two eyes that are in your head." He paused for a minute. "There's an inner eye," he said. "Nobody but oneself is aware of it. And it's astonishing how much that eye sees."

"Where is that kind of eye?" asked Redcap.

"H'm," said the priest, "it's hard to tell. Some say in the heart, some say in the mind but I don't think it matters where it is as long as it isn't blind."

"Well," said Redcap, "if you don't have that kind of eye you must miss all sorts of things. And I wouldn't like to miss seeing all the animals in heaven with their saints."

He was silent for a minute. "I think I have that kind of eye somewhere," he said, "because now I feel almost — no quite certain that the animals go to heaven." He gave a sigh of relief. "I'm very glad. And I think the man who told you the story had a very strong inner eye."

"Yes," said the priest, "I feel sure of it. In a few words, he taught me a lot, that red-headed stranger."

Redcap jumped to his feet and began to leap up and down. "I know who he was! I'm sure I know who he was! What was his name — quick, tell me!"

"I don't think you do know him," said the priest. "I only saw him on that one occasion and it was quite a long time ago. He came with his donkey and a jackdaw and he disappeared into the woods, after he had told me the story. I think he must have given his jackdaw to old Janet because the next time I saw her, she came to her door and a jackdaw was sitting on her shoulders and in the early morning, when it was light, I descried the stranger making his way out of the village without his jackdaw. I've never seen hair so red, except your own. He had a sweet voice too, and he was singing as he went. Not a dog in the place barked at him and they generally do at strangers, especially at minstrels."

"What was he singing?" asked Redcap.

The priest thought for a moment. "The melody went something like this," he said, and hummed softly, "and there was a sort of lullaby in it and a line about Our Blessed Lady, Mary the Mother of God, but I don't remember the words although his voice was as clear as a bird's."

"I know them," said Redcap. He stood still, shut his eyes and began to sing:

> "A woman is a gladsome thing,
> They do the wash and do the wring!
> Lullay, Lullay, she doth thee sing,
> And yet she hath but care and woe.
> To unprize women it were a shame
> For a woman was thy dame
> Our Blessed Lady beareth the name . . .

and I don't know any more of it."

The priest looked at him with amazement. "Where did you learn it?" he asked. "I've never taught you that and I've never heard it except when the red-haired stranger passed through the village."

"I know who he was," said Redcap, "he was Red Eric my uncle, who ran away and joined the minstrels. And oh, I wish I could find him and I wish I could be a minstrel."

"If wishes were horses, beggars would ride," said the priest, "and you're the smith's son and the apple of his eye. Your place is at your father's side, Redcap, to carry on his trade, so let me hear no more of this minstrel nonsense. Whoever the stranger was, he had a sweet voice and a gay heart and much wisdom in his story telling, but a lad can sing well and be happy and wise without running away to the minstrels. Remember that! And now, kneel down that I may give you a blessing, for I must be about my business."

Redcap knelt and the priest put his hand on his head, "Blessed Mother," he said, "for the sake of Thy child that was born in a manger, keep this one safe, and if he strays bring him home, Amen. I have finished my prayer. Kiss your Crucifix, Redcap, my son."

"I can't," said Redcap, scrambling to his feet. "Red Eric's jackdaw stole it. I'm going to get it now. Thank you for the blessing," he cried, stopping to wave as he ran away.

But in Janet's cottage the little cross was nowhere to be found. Redcap even climbed on to the stool and scrambled up to the roof where Jacky was perching with ruffled feathers and a knowing expression in his eyes.

"The old thief! I'm sure he's hiding it," said the boy, "and I shall never find it and never have another like it."

" 'Never' never comes," said the wise woman, "and we're not at the end of the year yet. Who knows what may happen by December?"

III

CHRISTMAS IN THE VILLAGE

*In which Redcap meets the Lord of Misrule, sings the Yule-
tide song, and makes a secret plan*

DECEMBER of that year was blown in with a snowstorm
so heavy that all who ventured out of doors looked as
though they were wearing white hoods. The branches
of the trees were weighed down by layers of snow, six inches
high, and at their tips icicles hung like long fingers pointing at the
white earth. Frost glistened in the hedgerows and on the ground
the little forked imprints of birds' claws made a delicate pattern.
In front of the cottages the heavier feet of the villagers had
tramped to and fro, hardening the snow into a path which
had become so slippery that more than one person sat down
unexpectedly and found difficulty in rising to his feet again.

Redcap had no such trouble. He slid, on purpose, flinging
out his arms to keep his balance and shouting "Whoops —
whoops." For a while he forgot his longing to seek a fortune
and to find a runaway red-haired uncle whom he had never
seen. His mind was full of winter fun and he spent all his
spare moments shovelling snow off the frozen pond so that he
and the other boys could slide with sticks to guide them and
bones tied to the soles of their feet over their cloth leggings.

It was a gay winter for the children, a winter of laughter
and of chilly fingers and toes, of blue cheeks and noses red as
the embers of the smith's fire. But after an hour's play with a
wooden ball, chased the length and breadth of the pond by
curved sticks, no one was cold and everyone was hungry for a
bowl of hot soup with the fat swimming in shiny globules on
the top.

And so the December days passed merrily and busily until
Christmas Eve.

That morning the villagers had chosen the miller as the "Lord of Misrule", a make-believe King, who would reign for the twelve days and nights of the Christmas holiday. Even

THE FROZEN POND

the lord and lady of the manor had to obey his orders, and as for the villagers, he sent them here and there and everywhere on the wildest of goose chases and the maddest of pranks.

At noon he called for the boys to meet him at the edge of the wood and they went all together, keeping as close to each other as they could, for the Lord of Misrule had a blown pig's bladder as a sceptre and was known to give a playful but painful whack with it to anyone who did not obey him quickly enough.

Redcap managed to squeeze into the middle of the group for safety and went rollicking along with all the others shouting:

> Yule, Yule, Yule,
> Three puddings in a pool
> Crack nuts and cry Yule!

They all knew that the Lord of Misrule was going to bid them decorate the Yule Log and haul it to the Manor house where it would burn merrily all through Christmas Eve and Christmas Day.

And sure enough, there he was in front of the wood where the trunk of a fallen beech tree had been sawn into three parts. The thickest piece was decorated with ivy and holly and tied in several places with strong ropes so that it could be pulled, not by a sturdy ox, but by the village boys.

The Lord of Misrule looked fierce. He was crowned with a wreath of mistletoe and was jigging about with the pig's bladder. As the boys drew near, he began to march up and down saying, "Oyez, Oyez, we command of our liege lord's behalf that the peace of the village be well kept, by day and by night, and that all manner of boys, who are by nature rascals and ne'er-do-wells, shall obey their rightful master, the Lord of Misrule."

The boys shouted, "We will, we will," but Redcap, forgetting that there was safety in numbers, darted away from the others and began to hop up and down singing:

> Yule, Yule, Yule,
> Who cares for
> The Lord of Misrule!

which earned him a whack with the bladder on the side of his red pate and made him rub his ear ruefully.

"Redcap, son of John the smith," said the Lord of Misrule severely, "you shall now pay a fine for bad manners."

"Yes, milord, I'm sorry milord, as milord commands," giggled Redcap.

"You are condemned," said the Lord of Misrule solemnly, "to stand on the yule log while it is dragged to the big house and to sing the Yule Song without falling off."

The other boys laughed and cheered. It would be difficult to keep one's balance all the time although the log could only be dragged slowly.

"Milord of Misrule," they shouted, "what if he falls off? What will you do?"

"Ah," said the Lord of Misrule mysteriously, and shook his head with such a sad look in his eyes that Redcap imagined his fate would be tragic.

The others, eager to see Redcap's discomfort, harnessed themselves to the yule log and began to drag it along the slippery track while Redcap perched on the top, warily trying to keep his balance.

"Sing," ordered the Lord of Misrule, and in a slightly jerky voice Redcap began —

> Welcome be thou heavenly King
> Welcome born on this morning
> Welcome for whom we shall sing
> Welcome Yule.

He staggered but managed to right himself and continued —

> Welcome be ye that are here
> Welcome all and make good cheer
> Welcome all another year
> Welcome Yule.

Here the Lord of Misrule leant forward and nipped his calf and over went Redcap into a bed of snow.

"It wasn't fair," he shouted when he had picked himself up and shaken the snow from his shoulders, "you pinched me."

"And why shouldn't I?" laughed the Lord of Misrule. "Am I not King and the King can do no wrong. Well you've paid your fine, Redcap, now come and help pull."

So merrily the procession dragged the log to the Manor house and left it on the hearth stone in the great hall to be lighted at sunset.

The sky that night was bright with twinkling stars and with the light of a clear half moon, white as a chunk of apple with the core cut out. No one was in bed, for on Christmas Eve there was midnight Mass when everyone went to church to follow the priest in prayer.

On the altar, lighted candles glimmered and near the door, in the great stone socket, a big one burnt with a flickering flame and a black feather of smoke. It was the Christmas candle reminding everyone of the Star of Bethlehem which heralded the birth of Jesus, "the Light of Lights". Redcap had seen the village women making it by dipping peeled rushes into hot tallow, letting it harden and dipping over and over again until it was big enough.

And now when the service was done and the church door was opened, he watched the fat dripping down the sides of the candle and was so busy gazing that his mother had to pull him by the elbow.

"Come along, boy," she said, "Sir Huon and the Lady Alice are waiting to give us their greetings."

Redcap hurried after her. Outside, the lord and lady of the manor were shaking people by the hand. When it came to the smith's turn, Redcap looked at his father, sturdy and strong, with an arm hard as oak and a patch in his worn homespun doublet, and thought, "He'd be a match for Sir Huon if the two were to strip and fight as the miller fought that travelling tinker for stealing flour."

But his thoughts were interrupted by the clear voice of the Lady Alice saying, "Where is your rascal of a son? I hear the red-haired rogue tripped my boy on the ice this morning so that he measured his length and slid on his back from one end of the pond to the other!"

The smith grinned sheepishly but eyed Redcap with a look that promised a scolding.

"The lad meant no harm, milady," he said, "boys will be boys, especially on the ice."

"And why not?" asked the lady. "They may as well learn to give and to take early, or life will be difficult when they are grown men. But where *is* your boy?"

Redcap's mother gave him a push.

"Say, 'God keep you, ma'am'," she whispered, but Redcap was overcome by shyness, and could only grin, rubbing one foot against the other and tucking away a thick red lock which had escaped from under his hood.

Lady Alice smiled. "You'll be coming up to the big house for the Christmas feast, won't you, Redcap?" she said. "The priest tells me that when the cook carries in the boar's head you will lead the carol singers, now that our household minstrel is sick of a fever."

She turned to the smith's wife. "Your boy has a sweet clear voice," she said. "I heard him when the yule log was brought to the house and in the church just now. He sings like a little minstrel."

She moved away with her hand on her husband's arm and two servants walking in front, one with a lantern held high above his head and the other with a broom made of twigs sweeping away the snow.

The villagers gathered together in groups wishing each other a happy Christmas and a good dinner, but Redcap remained rooted to the spot, staring at Lady Alice. He did not see her scarlet fur-lined cloak nor her moving shadow nor the snow made pink by the light of the lantern. She had said his voice was like a minstrel's, and the word "minstrel" took him back to the runaway uncle, who was nothing more than a story to the villagers, but to Redcap, something real and alive whom, one day, he was going to seek.

He was thinking, "I must find him, I must," when a loud croak startled him and Jacky, the wise woman's ancient bird, flew from the church porch where it had been perching and alighted on his shoulder.

"Get away, thief," he said, "or I'll ask the priest to curse you, and then you'll look silly and feel worse."

Somebody chuckled at his elbow, and he turned to see the wise woman laughing at him and holding out the little wooden cross which he had lost in the autumn.

"I went to see your parents yesterday," she said, "and my sharp old eyes spied it in a corner, covered with dust."

"But — how did it get there?" asked Redcap.

"I seem to remember warning you," said the wise woman, "that a shoe would come behind you that night. When a boy's father suddenly . . ."

Redcap blushed. "I — I suppose it flew from my neck," he said. "So Jacky wasn't a thief after all." He put up his hand to stroke the bird's beak, but Jacky gave him a peck and his fingers went into his own mouth instead.

"And now who looks silly?" asked the wise woman and hobbled away. As she did so, she called softly over her shoulder, "Think twice tonight, Redcap. There's wisdom in the saying 'Look before you leap'."

Redcap was puzzled. The wise woman was always warning him about something and he never quite knew what she meant. But he had little time to think of her words, for the villagers were all moving towards their homes, and very soon he himself was lying curled up on a bundle of straw with the embers on the hearthstone glowing and his parents snoring gently on the other side of the hut.

Redcap slept quietly with his head on one outstretched arm, but after a while he began to smile and to whisper, for in his dreams he seemed to hear a red-haired singer outside, calling him by name and playing softly. He woke and raised himself on his elbow, slowly aware that the music was not in his dreams but real. Far away, yet crystal-clear came the sweet sound of a flute.

"A wandering minstrel," he whispered, and his breath came quickly. *Was* it? *Could* it be? Should he go out and see? If the flute-player had red hair, he would be sure.

Redcap sat bolt upright. He was listening intently now but when a voice began to sing he sighed as he recognized Wat, the shepherd, and remembered that the old man had found the tracks of a hungry wolf not far from the sheepfold. Doubtless he was sitting on guard, with his great gnarled club by his side, playing and singing to keep himself company.

Disappointed as he was, Redcap sat, clasping his knees, and joined in softly. He could never resist a song, and this was a carol that he loved. In the dim firelight his eyes looked like tiny candle flames as he sang:

> Terly terlow, terly terlow,
> So merrily the shepherds began to blow.
> About the field they piped full right
> Even about the middle of the night
> Adown from heaven they saw come a light
> Terly terlow!
> Of angels there came a company,
> Terly ter . . .

"Lie down," growled the smith. Like a scared puppy Redcap scrambled into the straw and was asleep almost at once.

In the morning when the stars had disappeared and the sky was pearl grey in the pale sunlight, the boy awoke.

He was still sleepy, but the murmur of voices reached his drowsy ears almost as though it were coming through his dreams. His mother was talking quietly as she blew up the fire with a small pair of bellows, and Redcap, although his eyes were shut, could feel that she was looking at him and talking to his father.

"It's Christmas Day, so whatever he does this day, you'll not scold him, will you?" she asked. "Maybe he's rough in his play, but last summer the young lord threw *him* into the pond, so . . ."

"So you think they're even now," laughed the smith. "Well, since Sir Huon and his lady did not mind, I will say nothing, but the lad needs to mend his manners."

"He pushed me first!" said Redcap indignantly, sitting up so suddenly that they both laughed. "And *he* didn't mind either. All he said was that he'd have a lump the size of an egg on the back of his head, and when we all clucked like hens to tease him, he jumped on to a bench, like this, and crowed like a cock. He said *that* showed *he* was master. I like him."

"Ay," said the smith, "he's a good lad, as like Sir Huon as two peas. And when the time comes for him to step into his father's shoes, he'll carry on the old ways and do his best — like you, my son, when you come to take my place in the smithy. You'll make a good smith, eh?"

A good smith. Redcap's face grew very still and his eyes clouded.

"She — she said I had a voice like a minstrel," he whispered.

"What's that?" roared the smith.

"Nay now, husband and son," said the woman, "surely a smith can be a singer and a singer a smith. What has come over you both? Redcap, stop looking at nothing as though you had lost your wits, and husband, take that frown off your face. Have you both forgotten what the priest said about peace on earth and goodwill towards mankind? Am I to take a broomstick to the two of you?"

She looked so like a small flustered sparrow that Redcap giggled, and as for the smith, with one stride he was across the room and with his two hands around her waist he had lifted her in the air till her head touched the roof.

"Just you try it," he laughed, "and I'll poke you through the smoke-hole."

"You be off out of here," scolded his wife, "and employ your arms to better purpose than hoisting me on to the roof. Put me down *at once*."

He set her on her feet, gave her a loud kiss on each cheek, pulled Redcap's hair and walked out into the crisp December air, restored to good humour.

When he had shut the gate and was out of earshot, Redcap's mother spoke gently.

"Come here, son," she said. "Lift up your chin and look at me — straight — that's right. Your father and I are not young. You came to us late, the only child we ever had. Your

PULLED THE HOOD OVER HIS HEAD AND STEPPED BACK TO LOOK AT HIM
(*The long tube hanging at the back of the hood is called a liripipe*)

father sets great store by you, Redcap. When he thinks of the days to come, he sees himself as an old man sitting by the smithy door while a strong son plies his trade at the forge."

She stopped and looked at him intently.

"What's in your mind, son?" she asked. "I sometimes think you're making a secret plan that you're afraid to tell us."

Redcap wriggled his shoulder away from her hand.

"Why can't I make plans?" he blurted out. "Making plans inside my head can't hurt anybody."

"If they *don't* hurt anyone, there's no harm," answered his mother. She looked at him quietly for a minute without speaking, a long steady look, then, "Be a good boy, Redcap," she said and turned away.

Redcap kicked at the hard earth floor and watched her out of the corner of his eye. How did she know that his mind was full of plans? Had she guessed anything? It could not be possible, for he himself did not know how he could do what he wanted.

"Mother . . ." he began, but he did not finish his sentence, for his mother had opened the great wooden chest where they kept the few clothes that they owned, and had pulled out a bright scarlet hood with a long liripipe to wind around a cold neck in snowy weather.

"You shall wear it when you go to the feast in the big house," she said. "I spun the wool and dyed it with fungus that the wise woman gave me and wove it when you were out."

Redcap hugged her. He had never known any but the rich and the great to wear scarlet, and he wondered what Sir Huon's son would say when he saw it.

His mother pulled the hood over his head and stepped back to look at him. "A small sprig of holly on one side, and you'll be just right," she said. "So sing like an angel, Redcap, and put minstrels out of your silly red noddle."

MINSTRELS COME TO THE MANOR HOUSE

*In which Redcap leads the Boar's Head carol, makes friends
with three strangers and hears the story of a were-wolf*

"PUT minstrels out of your silly red noddle." That was
what Redcap's mother had told him. But it was easier
said than done for that afternoon wandering minstrels
came to the manor.

Sir Huon welcomed them. His own minstrel was still lying
ill of a fever and it was unusual for a wandering troupe to
arrive at Christmas, when the roads were often almost impass-
able.

He immediately sent them up to the gallery in the great
hall where they stood playing pipe, tabor and viol, eager to
entertain Sir Huon's guests.

Below them, on a wooden dais, raised about a foot from the
floor, the lord of the manor and the Lady Alice sat at table
with their son and their daughter, the bailiff who looked after
their land, the steward who had care of everything when Sir
Huon was away, and the village priest. Before them was a
large silver salt cellar and below the salt in the main part of the
hall sat the villagers at two long boards set on trestles. At each
place was a trencher — a round slice of coarse bread used as a
plate, which soaked up the gravy from the meat and served as a
meal for the dogs when the feast was over.

Fresh rushes had been strewn on the floor and the yule log
burned merrily on the hearth stone, crackling and flaming till
it made the shadows of the guests dance on the walls.

The Lord of Misrule, at the head of the villagers' table,
cracked jokes and beláboured people with his pig's bladder.

REDCAP LED THE PROCESSION

When the minstrels were silent because of the noise he made, and their leader called "Peace, or we cannot sing," he leapt upon his stool, threatening them and shouting a verse of the "Christmas Song".

> If that he say he cannot sing,
> Some other sport then let him bring
> That it may please at this feasting
> For now is the time of Christmas!

"You make so much noise that we can do nothing," shouted one of the minstrels.

The Lord of Misrule swung his mock sceptre and went on —

> If that he say he can nought do,
> Then for my love ask him no mo,
> But to the stocks then let him go
> For now is the time of Christmas!

At this there was a tremendous roar of laughter, for nobody expected to be put in the stocks at Christmas. But it ended as quickly as it had come for the doors of the great hall were slowly being opened.

On the threshold, under a swinging lantern, stood Redcap looking small but perky. Behind him towered the cook with a huge silver platter on which lay a wild boar's head. Two red apples were thrust through its tusks and a lopsided crown of holly, bay leaves and rosemary had slipped over one of its eyes. It smelt like roast pork and was shining with so much grease that when it was carried past the fire, little yellow specks of light quivered all over it.

Some of the villagers sniffed with pleasure, others licked their lips, wiping them with the backs of their hands. Even the Lord of Misrule was silent and watched with gleaming eyes.

Redcap's eyes were gleaming too, but they were fixed on the minstrels in the gallery, and he peered up at them as though he were looking for someone. A gentle kick from the cook reminded him of his duty and he stepped forward leading the procession and singing in a clear treble:

> The Boar's head in hand bear I,
> Bedecked with bays and rosemary
> And I pray you my masters, be merry,
> Quot estis in convivio!

Behind him strode the cook bearing the great platter as high above his head as he could hold it. The other servants followed, some carrying tankards of spiced ale, others dishes of apple sauce, plates of roast hare, rabbit, pheasant, and partridge and great steaming bowls of plum porridge.

Redcap led the procession around the villagers' tables and up the the dais singing lustily —

> The Boar's head I understand
> Is chief service in this land,
> Wheresoever it may be found
> Servitur cum cantico.

He stood still, bowed to Sir Huon and to Lady Alice and stepped back for the cook to set the boar's head on a side table where the butler stood ready to carve the meats.

Then the feast began and a merry one it was that lasted from early in the afternoon until late in the evening, with mugs filled and refilled, trenchers piled high with food, arms stretched across the table to dip bread into the bowls of sauce or gravy carrying it back to mouths ringed with grease.

When the guests were not eating, they were laughing and when they were not laughing they had their mouths full and their ears cocked, listening to the music and song which came from the minstrels' gallery.

One of the servants had brought the minstrels their share of the feast and they were taking it in turns to eat the good things, one eating while the others played and sang. Redcap had stolen away from the rest of the company and was sitting up there with them.

There were three of them and by a word here and a question there, Redcap had learnt their names and had been able to piece together some of their adventures.

The leader was grandly dressed in a sleeveless coat, worn over his doublet, and scarlet trunk hose. He had once been some great lord's private musician and storyteller, but had left in anger after a fight in which his jaw had been broken. The disfigured jaw had earned for him the name "Fulk Crooked Smile" for it had made him able to smile only on one side of his face. Something in the expression of his eyes made Redcap careful not to ask too many questions lest the crooked smile, which was gay on one side and sour on the other, should lose even its one-sided merriment. But strange and forbidding as he looked, Fulk Crooked Smile could tell tales by the score and, in the telling, he himself became all the people in the story.

Then, there was Irish Nial, gentle and laughter-loving, with eyes which changed with the changing light and were now grey, now blue. He wore his black hair curling about his neck although minstrels were usually as close cropped as monks, and he carried a green cloak, "to remind him of the shamrock", he said. Years ago as a ten-year-old orphan, a merchant had found him, wandering and singing, in an Irish sea-port and had brought him to England. He had almost forgotten his native tongue, but his voice still had a soft Irish burr, his sentences a lilt that was not English and he could imitate every bird in the woods.

The third minstrel was Jack the Piper, who could play any instrument that was brought to him but was given to long moments of silence and never told a tale unless it was in verse like a poem or a song. He was short and broad with a slight limp, and he it was who pushed the hand-cart which carried what they needed for their travels.

"Have you ever seen a red-haired minstrel wandering about telling stories and singing?" asked Redcap to each in turn.

"Sure, there's yourself," laughed Nial, pulling the boy's red lock which had strayed as usual from under his hood.

60

Jack the Piper shook his head. He was a man of few words. And Crooked Smile smiled with the gay side of his mouth and answered, "Maybe I have and maybe I haven't. We three go alone lest others take the bread from our mouths. Strange minstrels are useless to us except when they teach us new tales."

He leant forward and looked over the balustrade of the gallery. "Jack Piper," he said, "the shepherd has just come in. Play and I will sing." He began . . .

> The shepherd upon a hill he sat
> His name was called joly joly Wat.

But the Lord of Misrule had espied Wat the latecomer and shaking his pig's bladder playfully, shouted, "Aha my friends, here comes one who goes star gazing like the shepherds of old. They found the heavenly King, but he finds . . . a pig's bladder," and he gave the old man a buffet.

At this there was a shout of laughter, but the old shepherd drew himself up with great dignity. "So please your worship," he said in a loud voice and bowed stiffly to the Lord of Misrule, "I was about my shepherd's business. I saw the tracks of a wolf at the edge of the greenwood, and I kept watch lest master wolf had an unlawful feast."

Sir Huon called down from his high stool on the dais, "Well done, Wat. You should have asked our help. Did you slay it?"

"My lord," said Wat, "I belaboured him with my club till he howled."

Everyone looked astonished for the bark and howl of a wolf were sounds to which all ears were so carefully tuned that they could not be missed even during a noisy feast.

"I heard no wolf's cry," said Sir Huon.

"Sir," replied the shepherd, "when I saw his black shadow slinking to the fold, I set upon him with my club to such good purpose that he howled aloud, 'For Christ's sake Wat, spare me, 'tis Christmas Day.' "

At this everyone laughed but all eyes raked the company to see whether they could discover who was absent, taking advantage of the Christmas feast to steal a sheep. Sir Huon was frowning.

"Who was this human wolf? Give his name," he said sternly, but the Lady Alice touched his arm.

"Not tonight, my lord! Not tonight," she said, "'tis the season of good will." The old shepherd looked relieved. He spread his hands and smiled a slow, wrinkled smile at Sir Huon's angry face. "There is no need for me to name him," he said, "for he'll have much ado to sit down or to walk straight for the next few weeks. A wolf's a wolf, say I, but a man should be a man."

"And what of a *were*-wolf?" called a clear voice from the gallery. And there was Fulk the minstrel, leaning over, with his smile awry and his long skinny finger pointing at the shepherd.

For a minute everyone looked uncomfortable. Grown men, women and children often heard stories about "were-wolves". They were said to be animals with human souls, who were men by day and wolves by night. They lurked in the lonely forests doing all manner of harm and seeking to devour all who came near them. Some of the villagers believed these fairy tales and crossed themselves, but the Lady Alice laughed her gay laugh, stepped down from the dais and turned to look up at Fulk Crooked Smile.

"Come down, master minstrel," she said, "the were-wolf is nothing but a story, and if you have such a tale we are eager to hear it before we go to our rest."

She clapped her hands to draw attention to her orders. "Clear the boards, men and maids," she said, "and put away the trestles. The feast is over and the minstrels will entertain us."

At these words, Redcap leapt from the floor of the gallery, where he was picking a goose bone, and ran down the stairs ahead of the minstrels. If a story was going to be told, the sooner the better and so he must help to take away the dishes as quickly as possible.

Many hands make light work, and in the twinkling of an eye, the table-boards were cleared and stacked against the wall with the trestles piled one on top of the other in a corner. In the twinkling of an eye, servants had placed cushions on the edge of the dais for my lord and my lady and their guests at the high table, while the villagers crowded together on the floor, hugging their knees or leaning against each other.

The Lord of Misrule poked the yule log with a long pointed stock and piled faggots around it till the sparks flew upwards and the hall glowed softly red.

Then, in the firelight, Fulk Crooked Smile began his story.

"Fair friends," he said, "hear now the story of Bisclavaret.

"There lived in Brittany a baron whom the King trusted and held in great friendship. He was married to a lady of much beauty to whom he gave all that she desired.

"In his castle, this lady lived graciously and in comfort, for all that she asked for she received, but she had one sorrow which troubled her greatly. For three whole days in every week her lord, Bisclavaret, was absent from her side and neither she nor anyone else in the castle knew where he went nor why.

"One day, when Bisclavaret returned to her, his lady greeted him, smiling and holding him gently by the hand.

" 'Husband, fair friend. There is something I would ask of you and yet I fear your anger.'

"Bisclavaret kissed her tenderly, 'Whatever you ask, sweet wife, is yours already,' he said.

" 'Husband,' answered the lady, 'long and weary are the days when you leave me alone. In the morning I rise, sick at heart, for fear, and in the evening I go to my bed and cannot rest, so troubled am I lest you should come to harm. Tell me, now, where do you go?'

" 'Wife,' replied Bisclavaret, 'if I tell you my secret, nothing but harm will come of it, for if you knew you might no longer love me, and then my sorrow would be too great to be borne.'

"When the lady heard this, her desire to know the secret tormented her day and night and so, again and again, she asked her husband with tears and prayers and gentle looks. And, at last, weary of her entreaties he told her.

" 'Wife,' he said, 'I become a were-wolf, feeding upon beasts and roots and living alone in the deepest part of the forest.'

"When the lady heard this she trembled and her heart beat quickly but still she begged him to answer her question.

" 'Husband,' she asked, 'do you run in the forest with the hairy coat of an animal or do you go in your own doublet and cloak?'

" 'Wife,' he answered, 'I go naked as a beast for all my body becomes the body of a wolf.'

" 'Then, fair husband, what do you do with your clothing.'

" 'Fair wife, that I will never tell you,' said Bisclavaret' 'for if I were to lose the clothes that I wear when I am a man, I should remain a were-wolf for ever.'

"Then the lady wept and wrung her hands. 'You do not trust me,' she said, 'so now I know that you do not love me.'

"And weeping she left him and weeping she went to her bed and when he came to her, she begged him with so pale a face and so many moans and tears that he could bear it no longer and told her all.

" 'Wife,' he said, 'deep in this wood there is a hidden path that leads to a ruined chapel. Near it a thorn bush hides a hollow stone. There I keep my raiment till it is time for me to return to my home.'

"When she had learnt her husband's secret, the lady was in great terror for she felt ashamed to be married to a wolf and fearful lest he should do her harm. And so, when Bisclavaret had left her, she sent a letter to a knight whom she trusted and begged him to come to her aid.

"And when this knight stood before her, in answer to her

64

" AND THERE THEY FOUND BISCLAVARET'S CLOTHING "

letter, she told him her lord's secret and together they went to the wood and discovered the hidden path, which led to the chapel and the thornbush concealing the hollow stone. And there they found and stole Bisclavaret's clothing.

"Summer became winter and winter passed to spring and Bisclavaret did not return. Many a man on many a day searched the woodland and all the country, far and near, but none could find him.

"And because she knew that he would remain a wolf for ever, the lady married the knight and they left the castle taking with them Bisclavaret's clothes.

"More than a year passed and it chanced that the King, one day, went a-hunting in the same wood. When the hounds were unleashed, they ran hither and thither and quickly picked up the scent of a wolf.

"It was Bisclavaret.

"From morn till eve they hunted him till he was weary and in great fear lest they should kill him, and seeing the King, riding close at hand, he ran to him and took his stirrup in his paws and licked the royal foot.

"And the King, amazed, began to beat off the hounds and called his courtiers. 'My lords, come to me and see a marvel. Here is a beast that has the sense of a man. He cries for mercy yet he has no words. Come, we will hunt no more. We will go home and take this creature with us.'

"Then the King brought Bisclavaret safely to his castle, and because the wolf was so gentle, he treated him as a favourite dog, loving him as a friend and permitting him to sleep in his own room. When the courtiers saw that he held the wolf so dear they too treated him kindly and there was not a man who did not make much of him.

"Hear now what happened.

"The King held a high court and called all his lords, barons and knights to a feast and among those who came was the knight who had married Bisclavaret's lady.

"Richly gowned in fur and velvet, with pages and squires

66

behind him, the knight stood in the hall, but no sooner did he draw near to the King than Bisclavaret saw him and with bared fangs and fierce cries leaped and would have done him much mischief had not the King called and scolded him. Once, twice, three times the wolf set upon the knight and was pulled away. And all men marvelled that so gentle a beast should become so fierce at the sight of one man.

" 'Truly,' they said one to another, 'this knight must have done the wolf some bitter wrong, so fiercely does the creature hate him.'

"Not long after this adventure, it happened that the King, with a company of knights and ladies, again went hunting in a forest. With them came the wolf.

"They lodged that night in a certain house visited by the lady who had once been married to Bisclavaret. Brightly dressed and with jewels in her hair and in her ears, she came into the King's presence, and smiling, was about to make a curtsey when the wolf sprang at her. So great was his fury that it was well nigh impossible to drag him away.

"From every side, lord and baron, knight and squire beat him off and drew their swords to cut him to pieces. But a certain wise man, who was the King's counsellor, prevented them and spoke in his master's ear.

" 'Sire, we know this wolf to be gentle and good. He has never harmed anyone save this lady and the knight who is her husband. This dame was once the wife of a lord whom you loved dearly and who disappeared. Strange things happen in this land of ours. Perchance the lady knows why the wolf hates her. She stands with shifting eyes, ill at ease.'

"When the King heard these words he had the knight and the lady locked in separate rooms and had them so closely questioned, hour after hour, that from fear and weariness they told the whole story.

"Then the King demanded that they should send for Bisclavaret's mantle and doublet, and when these were brought he took them into the great hall and spread them before the wolf, but he, slinking behind the King, pretended that he had not seen them.

" 'Sire,' said the old counsellor, 'you do not wisely nor well. If the wolf has the soul of a human being he will be ashamed to change from beast to man before so great a company.'

" 'I will take him to my own room,' said the King, and he carried the wolf to his most secret chamber, put the garments on the floor and shut the door fast.

"An hour or so later he returned, bringing two lords with him. Softly they entered and lo, the lost baron, whom the King had so loved, lay asleep on the bed. The King raised him in his arms and man's speech returned to Bisclavaret and he told his story.

"With great rejoicing the King restored him to his castle and gave him rich gifts, but the wife, who had betrayed him, was driven from the kingdom and she and her second lord were never seen again."

There was silence for a second or two then Redcap, who had been listening with his eyes never leaving the minstrel's face, asked earnestly and a trifle nervously, "Does — did Bisclavaret go on becoming a wolf three days of the week?"

"Wait and see," grinned Crooked Smile and his eyes looked malicious.

But Sir Huon shook his head. "Oh, no, Redcap," he said, "that was all over and it has never happened again. Have no fear. Bisclavaret was a courteous gentle lord and the creature who came after my sheep was a common thief who had a well deserved beating. He was not even a real wolf!"

He tossed a coin to the minstrels. "Sleep here by the fire, tonight," he said, "and you shall have ale and rye bread to break your fast tomorrow before you leave. God give you good night, my friends."

He and his family passed down the length of the hall and through the great door, smiling and nodding to the villagers who had begun slowly to move away, some yawning, others talking and the young jostling and making fun of each other, planning what they would do the following day.

Under cover of the crowd, Redcap slipped to the far corner of the hall and lay down with his face to the wall, pretending to be asleep. But his head was busy with his own special plan and he had much ado to keep his eyes shut and to breathe deeply when his parents found him.

"Leave him, wife, leave him," said the smith, "he's fast asleep and he's as safe here as he is with us and he'll be better fed in the morning than he will be at home."

They turned and went away.

Slowly Redcap opened his eyes. The room was dark except for the glow from the burnt yule log. At last he was alone with the minstrels. Now he could talk to them. Now he could tell them what was in his mind. He tiptoed nearer to the fire and cleared his throat gently.

Nobody answered.

Three heads covered by woollen hoods, three bodies wrapped in heavy cloaks, lay by the dying fire. On three different notes three men snored.

The minstrels were fast asleep.

V

REDCAP RUNS AWAY

*In which Redcap, afraid of the were-wolf, meets a friend and
hears the story of the good wolf of Gubbio*

REDCAP sat up, rubbed his eyes, then opened them wide.
For a second or two he had forgotten where he was, and
only remembered when one of Sir Huon's cats came rust-
ling across the rushes on the floor to rub herself against him
and purr loudly.

"Psst," said Redcap. "Stay here, Pussy, you mustn't wake
the minstrels."

The cat moved away and sat near the dais, with her eyes
fixed on a small mousehole and her tail swishing rapidly from
side to side.

Redcap peered about him.

It was almost dark in the great hall. The fire was out and the
long shutters were closed. Only at the far end of the room a
faint ray of light was creeping through the top of the door,
which seemed to be slightly open.

One or two of the serving men were still asleep on the floor,
but nowhere could Redcap see the minstrels. They must
have risen before dawn and left when they had drunk their
ale and eaten their rye bread, for where they had been lying
there was nothing but three pewter mugs.

Redcap jumped to his feet and his heart sank. He had
had no time to talk to them about Red Eric, nor to consult
them about his own secret plan, and now, unless he could
find them, he would have to wait until another troupe of
wandering minstrels or jugglers came to the village, and
several months might pass before that happened.

He kicked disconsolately at the rushes and bit his lip trying to control the tears which he knew were near because his eyes felt hot and the backs of his lids were pricking. He swallowed hard, stood still for a minute, then he made up his mind and pulling his red hood over his head, twisted the liripipe around his neck and crept softly past the sleeping men to the other side of the room.

Fortunately, the door *was* slightly open so that he need not struggle with the great bar which was used to close it, and always creaked noisily when it was pulled aside.

The door was heavy but Redcap manage to push it a bit and squeezed through the opening.

Outside, it was lighter as the sun was rising and the sky was pale like the inner side of an oyster shell. The white snow, too, made it easier to see out of doors than indoors and Redcap trotted along briskly. The minstrels were nowhere in sight but he could just make out their tracks in the snow. There were two shallow ruts made by the hand-cart which Jack Piper pushed. Redcap could see his footsteps, one a little deeper than the other because he walked with a slight limp, and he could distinguish Nial's light tread from the heavier footprints of Fulk Crooked Smile. The minstrels could not have left much earlier as the tracks were still plainly visible, although a few flakes of snow were falling.

Redcap looked around as he walked. The villagers were evidently sleeping late after last night's feast, determined to rest and to refresh themselves for more games and merriment. Even the smith was abed for there was no red glow under the door of the smithy, which meant that he had not yet risen to light the fire.

As he passed his parents' cottage, Redcap went more slowly. His feet did not seem to belong to him. They behaved as though they wanted to go in, and his heart gave a little flopping movement as though it had missed a beat.

He turned and looked at the forge. Charred pieces of wood and some twisted bits of rusting iron lay black on the snow. Every year charred wood and bits of iron would lie on the ground, every year the hammer would go clang-clang, every year people would bring horses to be shod, ploughshares to be sharpened, every year. . . .

No, he could not be a smith and live in the village all his life without ever having an adventure. His father might be angry but his mother would understand. He had thought of telling her his secret plan when she had said, "Be a good boy, Redcap," but he had said nothing. Perhaps she would guess that he had set out to find the runaway uncle who would take him through the world singing and learning new stories.

Redcap began to run. He did not want to think of the cottage. Its closed windows looked like shut eyes and it seemed a little mean to creep away like a thief when no one was looking. He pinched himself on the arm. "Silly," he said. "How could you run away if they were looking? They'd only catch you and fetch you back."

He ran faster, thinking to himself, "I must find him. I must find him. I must find him."

He was gradually leaving the cottages behind and a sudden sprint brought him to the edge of the pond. The frozen water was black in some parts and crusted with fresh frost in others. In one place under the surface there was a great star where Sir Huon's son had fallen and cracked the ice but the little puddles of water that had seeped through had frozen again, and it was clear that the ice would bear. Redcap stepped back a few paces then ran, gave a leap, and slid the length of the pond with such vigour and delight that he forgot his misgivings, scrambled up the bank and began hopping and skipping.

Before long he had passed the three open fields on the outskirts of the village and was on the King's highway.

There was still no one about and no sign of the minstrels, except their footprints. The sun was up now, a red ball glowing across the snow and making the frost and the icicles on tree and hedge sparkle. Redcap was beginning to get hungry and his legs were aching but he went on running until the village was out of sight and he knew that he could not be seen. Then he walked slowly still keeping an eye on the footprints in front of him. They went straight ahead until the highway twisted and passed along the edge of a forest. Here Redcap, occupied with his own thoughts and gazing up at the snow-laden trees, forgot to look for them and when at last he did remember, he saw that he had lost the trail.

Cross with himself for being so foolish he turned and went back, keeping his eyes on the ground. In a few minutes, looking to right and to left, he saw that the three men and their handcart had turned into the forest along a narrow path.

Redcap stood still. He had no wish to go through the forest by himself. He had heard stories of robbers and of wild beasts, and although he carried his knife in his belt, he knew that he would be no match for a fierce man or for a hungry animal. But the footprints went into the forest and trailed away as far as his eyes could see.

With his heart in his mouth and his hand on his knife, he took a few steps along the track and saw that a woodman had cut pieces of bark from the trees on each side to mark a way. Evidently people were in the habit of using this path so he went on, grasping his knife, and every now and then stopping to listen. There was no sound and the footprints were still there as far as he could see.

Walking and stopping, walking and stopping, he went deeper and deeper into the wood. Suddenly he gasped and stood still. Among the footprints and the ruts made by the cart there was something else.

Redcap bent down to look closely. Yes, he was right. The tracks of an animal mingled with those of the men — a four-footed creature with a paw which had sharp nails. Redcap's heart beat quickly. Where had the creature come from? Among the trees to right and to left of the footprints, there was nothing. Could the wild beast have dropped from a tree? Was there some *magic* at work?

Redcap looked up. A squirrel ran along a branch chattering,

73

but the footprints were too big for such a little animal. He bent down again and his heart seemed to turn over. He was sure now. The tracks were the tracks of a lone wolf — a strange mysterious creature that had suddenly come from nowhere to attack the minstrels. With a sickening feeling of terror last night's story came into his mind.

Was it a . . . ?

Before he could whisper the word, something leapt on him from behind, tore the seat of his trunk hose and grazed his skin with pointed teeth. Paws scrabbled at his back, a wet snuffling nose touched his neck.

"Get off," shouted Redcap, and slashed this way and that with his knife.

The creature was behind him, pulling at him with paws and fangs, making queer little high pitched growls, and he was half aware of a shaggy coat, sharp pointed teeth, and a long red tongue.

Screaming, "The were-wolf. The were-wolf," he fell down.

"*Rex*," shouted someone, whistling. "It's a strange thing, surely, that you run away when dinner's ready. Come here, will you?"

The creature bounded away.

Dazed and still grasping his knife, Redcap scrambled to his feet.

"Holy saints," said a laughing voice, "if it isn't the red-haired brat who sang the carol. Will you explain now, why you are here with your head in the snow and your hand on a knife?"

Still breathless, Redcap looked at Nial, who was holding a shaggy dog by the collar.

"He — he — jumped on me from behind!"

The dog seemed to grin. He was panting, with his tongue hanging out and his tail wagging.

"And wasn't he playing?" asked Nial. "Rex likes a man of his own size, he does."

"He attacked me," said Redcap with dignity.

Nial stretched out a long arm and twisted Redcap round, then addressed the dog solemnly but with dancing eyes.

"And was it yourself, my own dog, that attacked the young gentleman and exposed his hind quarters to the elements?" he asked.

Rex gave a short bark and began to jump up and down.

"Lie down, will you, now," said Nial, "while I repair the damage that you did."

A square flap had been torn from the back of Redcap's trunk-hose and was hanging down like a trap-door, but there was not a scratch on his skin, which was beginning to get rosy with cold. Nial lifted him up.

"If the young gentleman will lie across that fallen tree," said he, "my needle and thread will prevent him from being shamed before strangers."

Gently laying Redcap across the tree trunk, he began to stitch the rent with a large needle and a piece of linen thread which he took from a leather bag hanging on his belt.

"Why would you take a knife to the young dog?" he asked. "You should have been making friends, surely?"

"I — I didn't see him," answered Redcap in a muffled voice, for it was difficult to carry on a conversation from that position. "And — and before he jumped on me I was a-fraid because his tracks came suddenly out of nowhere."

"And why wouldn't they?" asked Nial. "Wasn't the creature asleep in the little handcart till a sudden jerk tumbled him out? What did you think he was?" he asked, still stitching and intent on making a neat job.

Redcap felt himself blush and was glad that Nial could not see his face.

"I — I thought he was a were-wolf," he whispered — "one of the bad ones."

Nial's needle stopped, suspended in mid air. Then he turned Redcap right side up and set him gently on the trunk, taking a seat beside him and patting his own thigh as a sign for Rex to sit down, too.

75

"Now these were-wolves," he said, "they're not things I myself would be thinking of in a forest. In a forest, that kind of thought is bad company."

"I thought of Bisclavaret," said Redcap, "and I remembered that every were-wolf isn't good like Bisclavaret. They — they live in forests and they *eat* people."

"Am I not telling you," said Nial, scratching Rex, who had rolled over on his back with his legs in the air, "a were-wolf is a *thought* and a thought like that is not good company! When I walk through the forest and think of the wild beasts, I say to myself, 'Don't be troubling yourself at all, Nial, for maybe this day you'll be meeting with the good wolf of Gubbio.'"

"Gubbio," said Redcap, scenting a story and sitting bolt upright.

"Don't tell me you've never heard of that wolf," said Nial. "Why, bless my poor soul, the wolf of Gubbio is the best thought for a forest that I know. But he began badly. He did indeed. It was like this." Redcap leant against him, feeling safe and comfortable and Nial, gazing away into the distance where the branches of the trees looked like lace against the sky, began his story.

"There was once a wolf who lived in the woods near the city of Gubbio. He had such an evil temper with him and was so savage that not a man, woman, nor child dared go into the forest by day or by night, and before long he put them in such fear of him that they could not leave the city at all.

"Now there came one day, to Gubbio, a little poor man and he said to the people, 'I will speak to this wolf,' and one and all begged him to stay safely in the city.

"'Go not, go not, you little poor man,' said they, 'for this creature will surely kill you.'

"But he paid no heed and set out with his companions and when they feared to come farther, he went alone to the place where the wolf was.

"The wolf leapt towards him with gaping jaws and sharp hungry teeth, but he had no fear at all, at all. He made the sign of the cross and he said (very quiet and clear was his voice), 'Come here, Brother Wolf. In the name of Christ, I bid you hurt neither me nor anyone else.'

"Then a strange thing happened.

"The savage wolf became as quiet as a lamb. He just lay himself down at the feet of that little poor man as though the two had been friends all their born days.

"But the little poor man shook his head at the creature. Very gentle he was but very grave.

" 'I must be scolding you, Brother Wolf,' he said, 'for you do great harm in these parts, grievous harm. Why, they tell me, hereabouts, that you kill God's creatures without asking His leave. I am ashamed of you, I am.'

"The wolf's ears went down and his tail drooped. But the little poor man went on scolding him — very kindly, mind you, but very straight.

" 'Brother Wolf,' said he, 'all the good people in this city say you are their enemy. Now I'm a man of peace, I am, and I would like you and the citizens to be friends. I must see what I can do about it.'

"The wolf looked up at him and waited for him to go on speaking. Then the little poor man began to ask him questions.

" 'Brother Wolf, have you eaten the beasts of the field?'

"The wolf whined, two little snuffling whines.

" 'Brother Wolf, have you devoured men and women and even little children?'

"The wolf put his head between his two front paws and never a word he spoke, for he was ashamed.

" 'I'm thinking,' said the little poor man, 'that you did these things because you were hungry. Now I shall ask the people of this city to feed you every day of your life. If they promise to do this, will you promise never again to hurt man or beast?'

"The wolf looked up and his eyes were very solemn when he bowed his head.

77

" 'Brother Wolf, is that a promise? Will you keep faith? I want to trust you.'

"Then the little poor man, whose name was Francis, stretched out his arm and the wolf lifted up his right paw, and put it gently into the outstretched hand.

"And so the promise was made and Francis, with the wolf trotting beside him like a pet lamb, went back to the city.

"The people flocked to meet him, a little wary they were, a trifle timid, for they could not understand what had happened, but the little poor man held up his hand to quiet them.

" 'My brothers and sisters,' he said (all mankind and every beast and bird were brothers and sisters to him), 'I have made a promise in your name. I have said that every day of his life you will feed your brother the wolf, and he, in his turn, will never again do harm to you or to any living creature. Repeat your promise, Brother Wolf.'

"Then the wolf knelt down and bowed his head and once again put his paw into the little poor man's hand."

"And did the people feed him?" asked Redcap.

"They did so," answered Nial, "and ever afterwards the wolf went in and out of their houses like a tame creature and not a soul was afraid to go into the woods around Gubbio."

He was silent for a minute then looked at Redcap. "When I'm in the forest I find that wolf a comforting thought," he said.

"But Gubbio isn't here, is it?" asked Redcap.

"I'm told it's in Italy," answered Nial, "but it might be anywhere," he went on, thoughtfully. "If you're thinking of the wolf of Gubbio now, well, he's quite close to you, isn't he? To me, that's a companionable feeling."

"Yes," said Redcap, and nodded his head.

"And talking of companions," said Nial, "friends like you and myself should have a bite of something together and maybe meet other fellows. So up with you — there's a dinner waiting for us."

Redcap jumped up eagerly.

There was a tearing, rending sound. He clasped his hands behind him, "I — I've split again," he said.

"Bejabbers!" Nial scratched the back of his head. "I'm thinking I sewed you up too tightly. Well, I can't be introducing you to my friends in that state. Come here, till I cut a bit out of your hood and make a patch."

"But my hood's scarlet and my hose brown," said Redcap with dismay.

"Red head and red tail, what's wrong with that?" asked Nial and turned him over the tree again.

VI

REDCAP AND THE MINSTRELS

*In which Redcap is put through his paces and Jack Piper tells
the tale of the Baron's Daughter and the Juggler*

IN a narrow open space in the forest, the snow had been
swept back into a heap and a fire had been lighted inside a
small circle of stones. It was burning sulkily, as the forest
wood was wet, but it had been cunningly built so that the air
could reach it, and when once the wood had dried a warm
blaze would make a cheerful glow, and the stew in a black iron
pot, hanging on a forked stick above it, would begin to simmer.
Already a pleasant smell reached Rex's nostrils and he bounded
forward ahead of Nial and Redcap.

"You have been a long time," said a voice. "Where's Nial?
Down, dog! Where's your master?"

Fulk Crooked Smile pulled Rex's ears and tickled his throat
but Jack Piper took no notice of him. He was staring with an
air of astonishment in the direction from which Rex had come.
Being a man of few words he merely pointed.

Fulk lifted his eyes and his jaw dropped. "Who in the name
of heaven . . ."

"The top of the morning to you," said Nial cheerfully. "Is
the pot boiling? The young boy and myself are all but
starving."

Both corners of Fulk's mouth turned down. "When you
went back for the dog," he said, "I didn't tell you to bring
an extra mouth to take our dinner. There's little enough
as it is."

Nial looked at him steadily.

"Rex and I will be sharing our portion with our friend,"
he said.

"How did the imp get here," snarled Fulk.

"I'm not an imp," said Redcap flushing. "Imps are of the devil and I'm wearing a cross." He pulled out his crucifix.

"Hold your peace," snapped Fulk. "Face about and go back the way you came! *At once.*"

"Now, listen," began Nial.

"Am I or am I not master here?" shouted Fulk. "When you joined me, Irish Nial, you made certain promises. One was to recognize me as master. The orders I give are to be obeyed. Boy, begone!"

Jack Piper had not spoken but he took two steps forward and put a protecting arm around Redcap.

"Wolves," he said, looking angrily at Crooked Smile.

"He faced the wolves to come here and he can face them again on the way back," said Fulk flushing.

"Will you stop putting fear into the young child's head," growled Nial.

Redcap stood his ground. Then he tossed his head, "Who's afraid of *wolves?*" he asked. 'I'll go into the forest and I'll think of the good wolf of Gubbio and I'll wait there all night, but I'll follow your tracks again in the morning. I'm Nial's friend and I'm going to be a minstrel."

His cheeks were very red but he did not take his eyes off Fulk Crooked Smile's angry face.

"Good-day t-till tomorrow," he said, and turned with a quick movement towards the forest and strode away with steps as long and as manly as he could make them.

There was a splutter of laughter behind him as Fulk, always quick to anger and quick to mirth, caught sight of the red patch on the small dignified figure.

"Good dog!" he snapped his fingers at Rex. "Fetch him."

"Will you stop giving that kind of order to my own dog," cried Nial. "Did I not patch the young lad with much trouble, and has not the creature a habit of leaping on him from behind. Arrah," he wailed, "will you look at that now."

Rex had bounded after Redcap and seized hold of his trunk

hose, and if Nial had not run after him and hit him on the nose with a twig the red patch would have been torn away.

"Down Rex. Lie down, you spalpeen," he shouted, then, "You must come back, Redcap," he said. "Fulk Crooked Smile is master and he has sent for you."

"Wolves," said Redcap with scorn, "you all think I'm afraid of wolves."

"Be easy now," said Nial, "we've lost that notion. Didn't you go like a knight without a thought of fear in your head? Then," he whispered, "let you have no fear of Fulk Crooked Smile. Speak up, man to man."

They were close to the others now and Fulk's crooked smile was gay at one side with a dimple in that cheek and a twinkle in both eyes. He put out his hand for Redcap to shake.

"Brave boy," he said, "let me welcome you to our feast. Sit down, Master Red Seat.

Furiously Redcap pulled away his hand. "How dare you," he blazed, stamping. "My name's Redcap and you know it. I won't have this patch — I'll . . ."

"Will you go easy now," laughed Nial, seizing his right arm while Jack Piper imprisoned his left, for Redcap was trying to tear off the scarlet patch. "If you take it off you'll freeze to death in this snow. And isn't it a fine decoration that no one else in the world would dream of having? And isn't it my own artistic creation? And who would make a fool of you? Am I not your friend?"

"Come, come," said Fulk, ladling a generous helping of stew into a tin pannikin. "You must excuse me for such a slip of the tongue. Every man makes mistakes, so, Redcap, sit on your red patch and put this inside you. 'Tis tasty and hot."

Redcap smiled sheepishly and squatted on the ground with his pan between his knees. The three minstrels and Rex sat around the fire in silence, each intent on his dinner. Rex gnawed a bone and Redcap drank the savoury liquid from his pannikin and drew the soft chunks of meat into his mouth with a sucking sound, while the others dipped long handled horn ladles into the cauldron or spiked out pieces of meat on sharpened sticks.

When the meal was over, Jack Piper cleaned the spoons and the cauldron in the snow and stowed them away in the little handcart where they kept their instruments, three grey woollen blankets, a mask and a few balls and knives for juggler's tricks. Redcap helped him silently, wondering what Nial was saying to Fulk for the two were in earnest conversation as they sat warming their hands at the fire.

"Redcap," said Fulk when Jack Piper and the boy joined them, "I want to ask you a few questions. Are you truthful?"

"Yes," said Redcap, then blushed, "at least," he added, "that is when I don't begin making things up by mistake." Then he blushed again, "I mean when I don't make things up on purpose," he said.

"Hm," said Fulk, "that answer sounds true enough. Tell me, do your parents know where you are?"

"No," said Redcap. "They were asleep when I left the village. They must think that I'm still up in Milord's great hall."

"Why did you come?" asked Fulk.

"I'm looking for Red Eric," answered Redcap, and all the plans with which he had been busy ever since the wise woman had told him about the runaway raced through his mind. He scooped some snow into his hand and watched it melt slowly. "He's a minstrel," he said, "and he's my great-uncle — older than father — but I'm sure his hair is still red. I shall know him by that and by a special song that he sings — I — I want to find him and go through the world."

"And what has that to do with us? He is not of our company," said Fulk.

"But you wander wherever your feet take you," said Redcap, "and maybe on your travels you'll meet him. Let me come too." He was pleading now. "I will never be in your way, *truly*, and I'll be good."

"DO YOUR PARENTS KNOW WHERE YOU ARE?"

Something echoed faintly in his mind. "Be a good boy, Redcap." Uneasily he shifted his position and leant forward staring into the fire. Suddenly he shook himself. Why shouldn't he be a good boy with the minstrels as well as in the smithy? His mother only meant — but he didn't want to think about what she meant, he wanted Fulk Crooked Smile, Nial and Jack Piper to let him follow them till he found Red Eric, even if he had to tramp to the ends of the earth.

"I can walk miles," he said. "I can push the cart for you. Please take me with you."

"To be able to walk many miles at a stretch is not enough," said Fulk, "and it is Jack Piper's task to push the handcart. He's lame and it gives him something to lean on. What else can you do."

"The Lady Alice said I could sing like a minstrel," he ventured hopefully.

"We can all sing," answered Fulk shortly. "Can you stand on your head with your legs stiff in the air?"

"I can if I'm near a tree so that I can touch the trunk with my toes and keep my balance," he said.

"Not good enough," said Fulk. "Can you turn head over heels, and somersault in cart wheels all around the fire."

"I'll show you," said Redcap, jumping up.

"You will not," cried Nial, seizing him by the belt, "for then you'll be bursting out again and not a piece of thread is left in my pouch. Sit down now."

"Keep standing," said Fulk. "My examination is not over. Can you dance?"

"I can jump, kick my legs wide apart and bring my heels together in the air. You know what I mean — the splits — I can do the splits."

"True," groaned Nial, "haven't I seen it with my own eyes and repaired the misfortune."

"What else?" asked Fulk. "Can you juggle?"

Redcap took his knife from his belt. "Lend me yours," he said to Nial.

85

"Careful now," warned Nial, and Jack Piper moved nearer to the little cart to be out of Redcap's range.

The boy's face was serious. He held one knife between his teeth and tossed the other into the air, catching it without letting it fall to the ground. Faster he threw and faster, till with a quick movement he took the other knife from his mouth and tossed that into the air, too, catching it and throwing one after another, spinning them as they flew upwards.

The minstrels clapped and he looked at them eagerly. "Milord's minstrel taught me. Will I do?" he asked.

Nial and Fulk said nothing but Jack Piper beamed on him and spoke the first sentence that Redcap had ever heard him utter.

"You have the makings of a juggler," he said.

"You have that," said Nial, "and I wouldn't be surprised at all if you were to juggle a meat bone into a horse."

"How could I?" asked Redcap.

"There's no knowing," answered Nial, "but there was a juggler who did that once. Jack Piper, here, knows all about him."

"What did he do?" asked Redcap turning eagerly to Jack Piper, and Jack, who never told a tale except in rhyme, took a long reed pipe from his belt, played a few notes and began to sing the story of the Baron's Daughter and the Juggler.

> Here beside dwelleth
> A rich baron's daughter;
> She would have no man
> That for her love had sought her
> So nice she was!
>
> She would have no man
> Was made of flesh and blood
> Unless he had a mouth of gold
> To kiss her when she would
> So dangerous she was!

Thereof heard a jolly juggler
That laid was on the green
And at this lady's words
He was right vexed, I ween
An-angered he was!

He juggled to him a well good steed
Of an old horse bone,
A saddle and a bridle both
And set himself thereon.
A juggler he was!

He pricked and pranced both
Before that lady's gate,
She thought he had been an angel
Was come for her sake.
A prancer he was!

Four and twenty knights
Led him into the hall
And as many squires
His horse to the stall
And gave him meat.

The day began to pass,
The night began to come
And wedded were the two,
The fair gentle-woman
The juggler also.

The night began to pass
The day began to spring
All the birdës of her bower
They began to sing
The cuckoo also!

"Where be ye, my merry maidens
That ye come not me to?
The pretty windows of my bower
Look that you undo,
That I may see!

My wedded lord is here
A duke or else an earl?"
But when she lookëd him upon,
He was a blear-eyed churl.
"Alas," said she.

Here Jack Piper made such a melancholy face that Redcap
was doubled up with laughter and toppled off the trunk where
he was sitting.

"Mind that patch, you," said Nial, as he picked himself
up.

"You see now what I mean?" asked Nial. "There's no knowing at all what you may be doing if you're a juggler. A good
wandering minstrel must be able to do everything — sing,
play, dance, juggle and copy every creature under the sun."

Here he put his head on one side and began to whistle like
a blackbird so beautifully that if Redcap had not been watching him, he would have looked around for the bird itself.

"Well," said he, "I can't do that but I'll learn, truly I will.
I can copy a dancing bear. I have seen them often. The
bear-wards bring them to the village and they have collars
with big rings in them and a rope goes through the ring and is
tied to a pole. When the bear-ward touches the bear with the
pole, it gets up on its hind legs and dances — like this."

He stood up, hunched his shoulders, and made little stiff
lumbering movements, breathing heavily through his nostrils
and giving every now and then a snorting growl.

"No use," said Fulk, "there are enough of these miserable
captives on the roads, without our taking an imitation one."

Redcap's face fell. Were they going to send him home after

all? He looked at Nial, who was sweeping snow over the ashes of the fire before making ready to set out again.

Nial went on with what he was doing but threw a glance over his shoulder and said, "We'll not be taking any beast but Rex and the small monkey."

"The *monkey*?" said Redcap, looking on all sides and thoroughly bewildered because this was the first mention of such an animal.

"The creature has a red head and a red tail," said Nial, still busy with the fire, and Redcap jumped on him and began to pummel him with his fists.

VII

REDCAP THE JUGGLER

In which Nial tells the fable of "Big from Afar and Nothing
near at Hand" and Redcap gives a bad performance and goes
supperless to bed

THE journey through the forest took several days, as the minstrels went at an easy pace, stopping to rest whenever they felt inclined.

They were never cold at night for they carried flints and with a little patience they could make a fire by striking sparks from them near to a handful of dead grass, which they kept for the purpose in the pouches on their belts, and blowing the kindled grass into flames. Their only difficulty was to find faggots that were not so wet with the snow that they put out the kindling, so whenever their fire was hot, they always dried some chips and put them in the handcart for the next night.

They were seldom hungry, either, for Rex often caught a rabbit, and Jack Piper had some nets and forked sticks which he set overnight in the hope of snaring a hare or weasel. Then too, each minstrel was skilful with a catapult and sometimes brought down a pheasant as it rose suddenly from the undergrowth with its raucous cry, "Acock-acock-acock".

Redcap found the new life pleasant and if he wondered about his home and his parents, he quickly put the thought away and remembered Red Eric whom he was seeking. He had little time for day-dreaming, as he had to work hard, each minstrel taking it in turn to teach him a song, a story or some juggling tricks with knives and balls. Fulk was a severe task master, making him practise whatever he had learnt for an hour or more before each meal, rewarding with a second helping if he did well and scolding him roundly or threatening dire punishment if he made mistakes.

By the time that they had left the forest, Redcap knew several stories, some different kinds of somersault, and could juggle cleverly with three knives instead of with only two. He was proud of himself for he felt that he was now one of the company and fast becoming a real minstrel who could be useful to Red Eric when they met.

"In the town that we are coming to," said Fulk, "you shall beat on the little drum, when we stand in the market place, and call, 'Fair friends, gentles all, the minstrels are here.'"

"May I do my tricks?" asked Redcap with sparkling eyes.

The crooked smile twitched with merriment then died away. "You might make mistakes," said Fulk.

"I won't," answered Redcap. "I'll begin slowly with two knives as you taught me and keep the third in my mouth till I'm ready to throw it. Then I'll do it as fast as I can."

"Woe betide you if you drop one," said Fulk, and he grinned his lop-sided grin.

"Then I may?" asked Redcap.

"We'll see," said Fulk.

He had promised nothing but he trusted Redcap to do well if he allowed him to give a performance and, in his mind's eye, he saw coins dropping into the wooden bowl which Rex had been trained to carry in his mouth.

By this time the little company had reached the city walls. The great wooden door was wide open and the snow under the archway slushy and brown from the weight of carts and of many feet passing to and fro.

"Hey, strangers," cried a voice, and a man in a short coat, made from wolf skins with the fur inside, and his ears covered with a grey hood, stopped them and demanded a toll. "No strange vehicles are allowed through without payment."

"Och," said Nial in his most wheedling voice, "this is not a vehicle, man dear, 'tis the little hand carriage of no weight at all."

"No matter, it has wheels," said the gatekeeper, "and neither the market carts nor what you are pleased to call the little hand carriage can come in without payment, so give your money or keep out."

Fulk opened the leather pouch at his belt, took out a silver penny and gave it to the man, who put it into the bag at his own waist.

"You have missed the market day," he said, "so there'll be room to spare in the square. The townsfolk like a minstrel. Go straight on and God be with you though I'll wager you are a godless set of vagabonds."

The minstrels passed through the broad archway into the town, taking a short cut to the market place by way of Leather Lane, where the glovemakers, shoemakers and all who worked in leather were busily plying their trades.

The shops were mostly two storeys high with overhanging roofs, each so close to the one opposite that they nearly touched and left only a pale ribbon of sky above. Redcap, who had never before been out of his home village, was fascinated and walked along looking from one side to another.

He gaped at the swinging shop-signs, fixed to wooden or iron rods above each door and painted with gay pictures of gloves or of shoes, to show what trade they represented. He dawdled past the shops, each of which was open-fronted with a counter across it so that people stood in the street to make their purchases while the owner was under cover inside and his craftsmen plainly seen at work beyond him.

"Come boy, hurry," said Fulk, "take your stand over there by the market cross."

Redcap saw that they had now reached a small open square clear of snow, out of which branched a number of narrow winding streets like Leather Lane. In the middle, fixed to two large boulders, was a stone cross and not far away a pillory where wrongdoers were made to stand with their heads and hands thrust through holes in a flat piece of timber. Redcap had never seen a pillory before, but he recognized the stocks, for he had often thrown mud at his own neighbours, when they had been punished and made to sit on the village green with their legs pushed through holes in a long tree trunk, cut for the purpose and fixed to the earth.

Stocks and pillory were empty now but various townspeople were strolling about and the minstrels went across the market-square to the cross.

"Drum," said Jack Piper to Redcap and took a little tabour out of the handcart.

"Walk up and down," said Fulk, "and see that you keep time."

With Rex behind him, holding the bowl in his mouth and every now and then sitting up on his hind legs to beg, Redcap marched to and fro, beating a little tattoo (drrm, drr-m, drr-drr-drr-m).

"Fair friends and gentles all, the minstrels are here," he called in a clear voice.

"Let the child lure them in," said Nial to Fulk, "and I will go to the inn and make sure that mine host can give us supper and shelter."

He strode away, nodding encouragement to Redcap, who still strutted about, enjoying himself hugely and proud as Punch that so many people were hurrying towards him. When Jack Piper began to play his flute it was not long before they were surrounded by men, women and children of all ages. Fulk signed to Redcap to hand the drum to Jack. He then stepped forward, making a low bow and sweeping his feathered cap to the ground.

"Fair friends and gentles all," he said. "A surprise, a new marvel is here this day. Allow me to bring before you Redcap the famous young juggler. He is but a child yet his skill will fill you with wonder. Who will lend him three things in every-day use? Come now, let us say three knives."

He pushed Redcap into the middle of the ring, whispering in his ear, "Take three of the same size, not too heavy," for the men in the crowd were pulling from their belts knives of different sizes and shapes.

Redcap, astonished that Fulk was really going to allow him

to do something besides beat the drum, felt a little frightened but determined to do well. He stepped towards the crowd and his face was very grave. Slowly and carefully he chose two knives, making sure that they were not too big and were of much the same weight. But when he stretched out his hand for a third, he found himself seized by the wrist and a man with narrow, cunning eyes shouted to the crowd, "Away with your knives, it takes no skill to juggle with things that are alike. My own lad can do it. Here boy, take this horse-shoe. Try that with your knives," and he flung the horse-shoe over Redcap's arm and pushed him into the middle of the circle.

Redcap dared not lift his eyes to Fulk's face. He knew that the crooked smile had disappeared and that both the corners of the mouth were turned down. Jack Piper was busy with the handcart and did not look up. If only Nial had been there, he would have saved the situation by some joke and given Redcap his own knife so that he could juggle with these as he had been taught to do.

"Begin, begin," shouted the crowd, impatient to be amused.

"If he does well — there'll be an extra penny for the minstrels," cried the man with the cunning eyes. "If not, then they lied and we'll chase them from the town."

"Yes, yes — that's fair enough," laughed the people. "Begin, boy! Begin!"

Redcap felt himself grow stiff with fright and his skin pricked.

"What a white face," giggled a young woman. "He ought to be turned back to front."

At this everyone laughed for they had all noticed the red patch and Redcap became even more embarrassed.

"Begin, rascal," shouted his enemy. "I'll warrant he's a clumsy one."

Redcap licked his lips, then put the horse-shoe into his belt and balanced the knives, points upwards on his hands as he had learnt. The crowd settled down to watch. He tossed up first one knife then another, making them spin in the air and

94

managing to catch them although his fingers were numb and his body rigid.

Scared as he was, he knew that he could manage two things easily enough. Perhaps they would not call for a feat with the horse-shoe.

The man with the cunning eyes saw that he was frightened and watching him narrowly began to make quick remarks. "You'll drop it!" "It's going to fall." "Aha, just caught it by good luck." "Whew, nearly lost it."

Redcap tried to take no notice, but he was getting confused and the faces in front of him were becoming blurred. Suddenly the man yapped like a dog, and startled, the boy dropped the knives.

"Boo-oo!" shouted the man and the crowd took up the cry so that the air was filled with booing and hissing until someone shouted, "Give the lad a chance, there's the horse-shoe yet."

"Come along, come along! The horse-shoe," shouted everyone.

Redcap felt Fulk's angry eyes piercing through his back and knew that his mouth had the evil snarling expression which he had seen the first day in the forest.

Nervously, he stooped to the ground and picked up the knives with one hand and held the horse-shoe with the other. He would try the juggling which he had practised for so long with the knives. He had never learnt to do it with two and a horse-shoe. But perhaps he could manage. Out of the corners of his eye he saw that Jack Piper had wormed his way through the crowd and was at the outer edge of it with his cart as though ready to go away. Fulk was still in the circle. Redcap could not see him but felt that he was alert and ready to spring.

He tossed up one knife then another then the horse-shoe, but in catching the latter he let the knives fall to the ground. The crowd waited in silence. He tried again and the same thing happened.

"Three times lucky," grinned Cunning Eyes and the crowd

HE TOSSED UP ONE KNIFE, THEN ANOTHER, THEN THE HORSE-SHOE

began to murmur. Once more Redcap picked up the horse-shoe and the knives, only to let them fall. He was trembling now, looking to right and to left, like a small animal at bay with the hunting dogs after it.

"What did I say?" shouted Cunning Eyes. "A famous juggler, forsooth! The little wonder, pardi! Pah! A clumsy fool, child of a liar. The minstrels think we are of so little importance that we can be put off with a poor show. They despise us!"

"Chase them," shouted the people, and began to pelt the minstrels with anything they could pick up from the street, rotting onions, apple-peelings, egg shells, decayed vegetables, all the household garbage and refuse from the market stalls that had been flung away to rot on the ground.

"Liars, rascals!" screamed the crowd. "So we're people of no importance are we?"

"If a boy of mine worked so ill . . ." began one.

"I'd put the father in the stocks for not teaching him better," cried another. "Pelt them! Chase them!"

Redcap ducked. Hardly knowing which way to turn, he ran and stumbled, picked himself up and tried to run again, but the boys in the crowd were on him, pushing and pummelling. Small girls screeched and slapped him and each other, scooping up handfuls of mud and slinging it right and left. Dogs barked, making little runs towards him and stopping to yap, while Rex, who thought the whole thing a glorious game, seized the young folks' skirts and doublets shaking them and, fortunately, keeping some of his enemies off Redcap.

Fulk did not move. He faced the angry crowd with folded arms. His crooked smile had a scornful twist, one corner turned up with an air of amused contempt, the other turned down as usual. His eye was black where some mud had splashed it. A rotten egg had hit him on the shoulder and the greenish yellow yolk was dripping in a sticky mess down his sleeve. He looked at the crowd and began to laugh, quietly with shoulders shaking.

97

Taken aback, the people stopped their shouting and pelting. "What's the jest, master minstrel?" asked one.

"Yourselves," he answered. "People are amusing when they are angry for no reason." He chuckled.

"Angry for no reason!" said Cunning Eyes. "Didn't you keep us standing here, looking at a bad show as though we were ignorant villagers?"

"Ay," said another, "didn't you treat us as though we were people of no importance who could not tell a good juggler from a bad one? We are self-respecting citizens, as anyone inside and outside the town will tell you."

"Of course, of course," cried a ringing voice on the outskirts of the crowd, "big even from afar."

With one accord the villagers turned and there was Nial, nodding pleasantly. "There's a tale about folk of your kind," he said, sitting carelessly on the big stone which supported the market cross and clasping one knee. "They say it came from across the sea in some Eastern land and the fable makers and story tellers and singers passed it on — a good tale indeed."

He crossed his legs and began to pick a thorn from one of his fingers.

The people drew nearer, interested. They seemed to have forgotten Fulk, who swiftly and silently disappeared. Even the children, who had been teasing Redcap and handling him none too gently, began to join the crowd, pushing their way to the front. Redcap followed them quietly and no one took any notice of him when he joined Nial and sat next to him, a small bedraggled figure near the tall lean one. He felt safe now that Nial had come and he sat sucking a scratch on the back of his hand.

Nial was smiling and pointing to different people in the crowd. "Of course you look big from afar — you and you and you — Why not? I'm thinking you are like those people of old."

"Tell the tale," cried a woman.

"Ay, begin," said Cunning Eyes, "if 'tis a bad tale never a minstrel shall come here again."

"Peace," shouted another. "This is a good story teller. I can see by his laughing eyes."

"True for you," grinned Nial. "Are you all ready now?"

"Yes, yes. Ready," cried the crowd.

"'Tis a grand tale, surely," said Nial, "and short, but for that none the worse at all."

Then quietly but in a clear voice that could be heard from one end of the market-square to the other, he began his story.

> Some townsmen, standing on their native shore,
> Once noticed something they'd not seen before.
> It floated on the waves. They raised a shout:
> "A warship! Hurry, call the soldiers out!"
> It floated nearer. "'Tis a boat we see."
> And nearer still. "No, 'tis a fallen tree."
> The waves then threw it gently to the shore.
> What did they find? A bit of wood — no more!
> How many, like that faggot in the sand,
> Look big from far but nothing close at hand.

He jumped to his feet. "Do you get my meaning?" he asked. "We, coming from a distance, were thinking that you were fine folk with great hearts, near at hand we find you small and mean."

Before the crowd had time to recover from their outraged astonishment, he had caught Redcap up on his shoulder and was sprinting across the square, shouting as he went, "Good day, you who are big from afar and nothing near at hand."

With a howl of rage the people were after him but Rex kept them at bay and Nial was fleet of foot. He ran down one alley to another and at last slipped into Bread Street where the bakers lived. Here, two drivers had met and the street being narrow, their carts were unable to pass. Each had refused to budge and the wheels were interlocked. Nial put Redcap down and, by pressing closely against the walls of the bakers' shops, they managed to squeeze past the carts and with a few quick steps were out of sight.

"Whew," said Nial, "that was a narrow escape!"

"Will they catch us?" asked Redcap.

"It's too late for them to be troubling," said Nial. "The sun is setting and they'll not get past the carts. If I can judge them aright, they'll be staying to hear the carters quarrel and maybe fight. Turn along here."

He put his hand on Redcap's shoulder to direct him and whistled to Rex, who came bounding towards them.

"How did the trouble arise?" he asked, and Redcap told him.

Nial rubbed his long thin nose and looked sideways at the boy's anxious face. "Hm," he said.

"Fulk is very angry with me," said Redcap. "Will he punish me?"

"Troth," said Nial, "I wouldn't know. He's master."

"But I couldn't help it," said Redcap. "I didn't know what to do. I could juggle with two knives long ago and you taught me to throw three, but I've never had a horse-shoe. I didn't know what to do."

"Then you should have made some fun," said Nial. "When they gave you the horse-shoe you should have said, 'Fair friends, I cannot use this, I am not a horse, only a poor little donkey.' That would have brought a laugh, and once people are laughing with fun in their eyes, they are kind. They are so."

"But I can't think of jokes quickly," said Redcap.

"You'll learn, surely, so let your heart rest," said Nial.

Redcap said nothing for a minute and the two walked in silence till they reached the end of the town and could see Fulk standing under the swinging sign of the "Cock and Hen", a small inn.

Redcap's steps began to drag.

"What will he do to me?" he asked uneasily.

"Am I not after telling you there's no knowing," said Nial. "Let your heart be easy, now. We are friends, you and I, and when in trouble, 'tis a grand thing, it is, to have a friend near at hand."

He slipped his arm through Redcap's and walked up to the door of the inn.

"I made time for you," he said. "I was thinking if I distracted their attention, you could slip away. And you did it with no trouble at all."

Fulk muttered his thanks but his eyes were on Redcap.

"And now," he said, seizing him with a grip of iron and shaking him roughly, "how dare you make a fool of me, eh? How dare you stand before all those people and . . ."

"I couldn't help it," wailed Redcap. "He barked like a dog and startled me — and — and — I didn't know how to throw the horse-shoe." ·

"You should have made a joke of it," growled Fulk still holding him so tightly that Redcap could feel his knuckles.

"Nial said so but, I — I — can't make jokes," protested Redcap.

"Oh, you can't?" sneered Fulk. "Then you can go without supper tonight and that's no joke. You lost us the money to pay for it and that's no joke either. In you come — quick now! And you'll stand supperless in the corner with your face to the wall while we eat, and you needn't think of jokes then for you'll be figure of fun enough."

Still gripping Redcap by the shoulder he marched him into the inn where a number of strangers were seated on benches at a trestle table, eating and drinking. There was a smell of fat and of burning wood from a big fire where a boy was turning meat on a spit, and from a pot on the table the odour of herb broth made the air heavy and thick. Redcap's heart sank and he felt pangs of hunger gnawing his inside.

"Ha," cried the innkeeper, "a good big bowl for a hungry boy, eh?"

"Not tonight, mine host," said Fulk grimly, "he hasn't earned it. He's earned something else but I'm letting him off lightly."

He kicked a stool into the corner of the room. "Get up," he said to Redcap and made him stand on it with his face to the wall, while the boy at the turnspit sniggered.

"So, so," said mine host, "discipline."

Some of the strangers looked amused.

"Hunger's a good schoolmaster," said one.

"Ay," said another. "Keep a bad boy without supper and next morning butter will not melt in his mouth."

They all laughed at this and Redcap miserably faced the wall feeling that everyone but Nial was against him.

Fulk went across the room and sat down at the table and began to drink soup, dipping a great hunk of rye bread into it, and muttering angrily to Jack Piper, who had also arrived, "We shall never be able to come here again."

Suddenly Nial rose, went over to Redcap and saying just loud enough for everyone to hear, "Will you turn your face to the wall and think over your bad behaviour," pretended to box his ears but secretly slipped into his hand a hunk of bread and a big piece of cheese.

The company paid no further attention to what they took to be a matter between father and son. Most of them had children of their own, who were in and out of trouble several times a day, and they had no doubt that Fulk had good reasons for his action.

Redcap munched his bread and cheese and felt less hungry but just as sore. He hated to be laughed at and the crowd had jeered when he had dropped the knives. The strangers at the inn had laughed, too, when Fulk had put him in the corner with his face to the wall as though he were a four year old child instead of a boy who had set out of his own accord to be a minstrel. Even the turnspit had sniggered at a boy, nearly as old as himself, being treated like a baby.

Mortified and weary, Redcap's head drooped. His legs were aching and he wanted to lie down and sleep but was afraid to do so lest Fulk should scold him before the strangers. He was so tired that the noises in the room became dim and he scarcely noticed when the innkeeper's wife and the turnspit had cleared away the table.

A long way away he heard mine host say, "In the next chamber there is a bed where four, nay five, can lie, and under it there is a small truckle bed which you can pull out. 'Twill take one. For the rest there is clean straw on the floor. God give you good night, gentles all."

Redcap heard people walking about and swayed on his stool but Fulk had not given him permission to move and although he was aware that some people had gone into the next room and others were already asleep on the floor and on the benches, he dared not lie down.

He put his arms against the wall and rested his tired head on them. He may have dozed but he did not know. It seemed much later when he felt a pair of strong arms lift him up and put him gently on the floor, stuffing some rushes under his head and covering him with a cloak. Through half closed eyes he saw by the light of the fire that the cloak was green as he fell into a fitful slumber.

VIII

SPRING SONG

*In which Redcap is homesick, Nial says a prayer at a wayside
shrine, and Fulk tells the tale of two troubadours*

I N the early morning the inn was very quiet, but Redcap
could sleep no longer and sat up watching the fire which was
burning brightly in the great stone chimney place. It
reminded him of his father's forge and he turned away restlessly
and lay on his back, staring up at the rafters. Through a small
hole in the thatch he could see a star shining dimly. Was it
the Morning Star which he always saw at dawn through the
smoke hole of his own home?

He shut his eyes tightly. He was homesick and he wanted to
go back. Why had he joined a troupe of minstrels, led by a man
like Fulk Crooked Smile, with his glowering eyes and sudden
bursts of anger and hands which gripped so tightly that the very
fingers felt like iron rods? The smith had been angry, sometimes, but only in the privacy of their own home. He had never
humbled Redcap before strangers. It was cruel of Fulk to make
people laugh at him and to hold him up to ridicule before that
turnspit, a boy scarcely older than he was. His legs still ached
from standing so long on the stool. His head and body ached
where the boys in the market square had pummelled him, but
more than anything else, his heart ached and *ached* with longing
for friendly faces that he had known all his life, and for the
safety of his own home.

Rex came up snuffling and licked his cheek. He put his arm
around the dog's neck seeking to be comforted, but he could
only whisper, "Rex, oh Rex, I want to go home."

He thought of Red Eric who had run away as a boy and had
only once returned as a grown man. Is that what he himself

was going to do? Would his mother be there still, and the wise woman? Who would be working the forge?

"I'll go back," he thought, "I'll go back before they're awake."

He stood up warily and crept stealthily over the sleeping bodies avoiding Fulk Crooked Smile who was muttering and frowning in his sleep.

At the door he bit back a cry. Someone had grabbed him by the ankle and a hoarse voice whispered, "Where are you going?" It was the turnspit, who had been sleeping across the threshold.

"It's too early to go out," he said. "I shan't be drawing the ale for breakfast till it's lighter. Lie down, boy, unless you want to perch on the stool in the corner again. Holy saints, how I laughed!"

"Open the door for me," said Redcap.

The turnspit sat with his back against it and grinned. "Where are you going?" he asked.

"Home," whispered Redcap, looking over his shoulder at Fulk and fearful lest he should wake.

"Well," said the turnspit, "you know what you're about, I suppose, but I wouldn't be in your shoes if old Sourface there catches you."

"Be quick and open the door before he wakes," pleaded Redcap.

The turnspit settled himself more comfortably against the door.

"What will you give me if I do?" he asked.

Redcap's face fell. He had neither money nor treasure and time was passing. If Fulk were to wake before he had left, there would be no chance of escape.

"Here's my little cross," he said. "It has been blessed by the priest."

"It's not silver, it's wood," scoffed the turnspit, "and I have a better one of my own. Now, I have always wanted a scarlet hood. . . ."

With a sudden movement he seized Redcap's hood by the liripipe and pulled it off his head.

"But my ears will freeze," said Redcap with consternation.

"If old Sourface catches you, he'll warm them," grinned the turnspit, "so you had better get a good start."

He pulled back the great wooden bar, lifted the latch and pushed Redcap out into the cold starlit dawn, closing the door as softly as he could behind him.

For a second or two, Redcap stood still. Should he go to the right or to the left? He could not remember how to reach the market square from the inn. Nial had run so quickly and through such a maze of winding alleys that he had not been able to see where he was being taken.

He crept about, peering this way and that, pressing back into a doorway when the nightwatchman stumped past with a guttering flame in his horn lantern and a muttered whisper, "Brr — 'tis cold, cruel cold."

In and out among the twisting streets he wandered, narrowly escaping a ducking when a housewife opened a shutter, leaned out of a window and emptied a pail of dirty water. It was slippery too, for many a woman had flung garbage into the streets overnight and anything that was wet had become frozen so that the dogs, lick as they might, could not loosen any bones, and Redcap kept sliding by accident. He walked, stepping carefully, now putting his hands under his armpits to keep them warm, now using them to cover his ears, which were growing colder every minute. He half wished that he had brought Nial's green cloak but if he was running away from the minstrels that would have been stealing and, besides, Nial was his friend and would have been cold without it.

As it grew lighter the town began to come to life. Apprentices, yawning and rubbing their eyes, opened doors and shutters and swept the entrances to their shops. They called or whistled to each other. Some peeped impishly round the doors, crept out and began to snowball their neighbours, grinning but keeping silence for fear of disturbing their masters. Before

NARROWLY ESCAPING A DUCKING

long the air was filled with flying snowballs and Redcap was hit on back, chest and face, but he stooped as he went, gathered up snow and flung balls of his own, and ran on. The apprentices took no notice of him. He might have been one of themselves and they were intent on the game.

Around a corner, he reached an open space and saw that it led to the city wall. The gatekeeper had opened the heavy door and was busy shovelling some snow into a heap with his back turned. Quick as a bird, Redcap sped past him through the archway and out into the open country.

For a few minutes he ran and then began to walk, stamping his feet to keep them warm, and frowning because it seemed to him that the great gate in the wall had looked different from the one by which they had all entered the city.

He looked back at it. Was it the same or not? He could not see well enough in the pale light so he walked on, hoping that he would find his way back to the forest and be able to follow the tracks which he and the minstrels had made and so reach his village. It would take days but if he arrived, even at midnight, the dogs would not bark for they knew him and he could go straight home and lie on his bundle of straw. His father might scold him but his mother would be glad to have him back and would say, as she had often said, "Now, husband, take that frown off your face."

Redcap tramped doggedly on, a small figure in a long empty road, with the sky faintly tinged with yellow and the few dim stars gradually fading away.

As it slowly grew lighter he stood still and looked about him carefully.

Everything was different. This was not the road by which they had come to the town. He must have left by another gate. He gazed up and down, to right and to left. Behind him some great snow-covered fields lay outside of the town walls and he was walking along a straggling piece of woodland through which the road had been cut. But this was not the forest where he had found the minstrels.

"I'm lost," he thought but he trudged on helplessly, thinking that perhaps in this unknown part of the country he might find Red Eric.

A short distance away he came to a small wayside shrine. It was a simple wooden structure put up by some pious man or woman for wanderers who might want to pray. Someone had at one time lighted a candle, for a little dab of blackened tallow lay on the ledge and above it was a crude picture of the Christ Child with a faded golden halo around His head and a wet wreath of dead flowers in front of Him. Redcap walked up to it, and stared. He had no candle to light and if he were to say a prayer, he did not know what to ask. He wanted to go home and yet he wanted to find Red Eric.

He looked earnestly at the picture and shivered a little for the wind was cold and seemed to be driving pins and needles through his ribs.

"I don't know what to say," he murmured, "I — I don't know what I want — but I'd like not to be lost."

A quick yap startled him. Something threw itself against his body and a wet tongue licked his cheek.

"Rex," he said and looked around thinking that the minstrels were on his trail and that Fulk would . . .

He could not imagine what Fulk would do but he was afraid.

"Go home, good dog," he said. But Rex continued to fawn on him giving little barks of joy.

Redcap seized him by the collar and dragged him into the ditch behind the shrine. He had heard voices and felt sure that he had recognized Fulk's ill-tempered snarling. It would be better to be lost than to be found by Crooked Smile in a rage.

He put his hand around Rex's nose and the dog scratched at him with his paw.

"Quiet Rex, lie down," he whispered.

The voices were near now and Redcap could hear, distinctly, the squeaking of Jack Piper's handcart, which needed greasing.

As they approached the shrine the boy held his breath. Fulk was speaking loudly and angrily.

"You listen to me, Irish Nial! You have given your word to follow where I go for this year at least. You shall not waste the day looking for a clumsy imp who nearly had us all in the pillory."

"If he tries to find his way home . . ." began Nial.

"Pah," said Fulk, "he'll do no such thing. He'll go wandering about looking for this Red Eric and some travelling tinker will pick him up. That will teach him a thing or two."

Nial did not answer at once. From his hiding place Redcap could see that the Irishman's eyes were scanning the ground closely, and he crouched lower, holding Rex by the collar.

"I'm thinking that you are right, maybe," said Nial, and he walked on with the others. As the minstrels passed the shrine Redcap held his breath and kept one hand around Rex's nose. Nial stood still.

"I'll catch you up, Fulk, but I'm wanting to say a bit of a prayer just here," he said, and turned aside.

The others went on and Nial stood in front of the shrine. He did not kneel but addressed the picture on the shrine, standing and talking in his ordinary voice.

"Now little Lord Jesus," he said, "there was a day, so the priests say, that you went into the temple and your parents thought you were lost. That was a grievous thing for them, it was. Yourself knows that. Well now, Lord Jesus, I've lost a boy. He is not my child at all but my friend and I'm not liking to lose my friends. It's very few I have. Have you any suggestions to make?"

There was a scuffle and a yap and Rex leapt from behind the shrine.

"Come to heel, good dog," said Nial. "I have not finished. Now little Lord Jesus," he said in a coaxing voice. "That was kind of you and the dog is my friend too. But I was asking you about a boy, I was. And you are too wise entirely to be mistaking a dog for a boy."

Quietly he stretched out his long arm and drew Redcap from behind the shrine.

"Why it's yourself," he said with an air of astonishment, "a very good morning to you. But next time would you let me know when you are starting so early and we'll go together? There is safety in numbers and two is company."

"I was running away," said Redcap.

"You wouldn't by any chance be making a habit of it?" asked Nial.

Redcap did not answer. He was feeling relieved yet anxious, comforted by Nial's presence and the friendly hand on his shoulder but troubled about the future, for Crooked Smile had turned and was facing them in the middle of the road not far ahead.

He shivered.

"Bless my poor soul," said Nial. "Am I becoming weak in the head? I was forgetting that I had a handsome knife to spare which I traded for this. You had better put it on." And he drew from under his cloak Redcap's scarlet hood.

As the boy pulled it over his red head and twisted the liripipe round his neck Nial went on speaking.

"And talking of forgetting things," he said, "did you ever notice how quickly unpleasant things pass from your mind and all? You may have seen that after a thunderstorm there is a calm time that is very consoling." His eyes wandered from Redcap's face to Fulk's and back again. "When I was a boy," he said, "I was in and out of trouble as often as not. When I was in, I was the most uncomfortable boy in Ireland. When I was out, I was forgetting what it had all been about and now it's only the grand times that I remember. If the present is ugly," he added, "it's worth while keeping your mind on the fine things that may happen for 'tis the strangest thing, it is, that one's never so happy as after one has been miserable."

He kept his hand on Redcap's shoulder, gently urging him on as the boy's steps were lagging.

"The young boy set out ahead of us," he said when they

had reached Fulk. "So now we can all go along together in good company."

Fulk made no comment. With folded arms and legs apart he stood looking at Redcap in complete silence. He never blinked and never, for one second, took his eyes off the boy's face.

Time seemed to stand still.

Something rose in Redcap's throat and he felt sick. If only he could make Fulk speak.

"I — I — I . . ." he stammered.

"Stop cackling like a goose," roared Fulk, "unless you want basting!"

His face was red and a flame flickered in his eyes.

Without another word Redcap turned and ran, slipped and fell sprawling to the ground.

The next instant, he found himself under Fulk's arm, balanced on his hip and carried struggling and kicking to Jack Piper's handcart.

Fulk jerked him to his feet, keeping hold of his belt so that he could not get away.

"Let — let — me — g-go, — I — I," babbled Redcap.

"Still cackling," shouted Fulk. "Truss the goose," and he pulled from the cart a piece of rope and tossed it to Jack Piper. Without speaking but quite gently Jack Piper tied Redcap's arms, one to each shaft of the handcart.

"Come," ordered Fulk and they all moved on with Redcap tied to the cart which Jack Piper was pushing.

Fulk walked quickly, slushing through the puddles made by the snow, which had begun to melt. Jack Piper, although he was lame, kept almost abreast of him. Redcap could feel his limping step by the way the shaft of the handcart went up and down and he had to walk as quickly as he could or Jack would have stepped on his heels. He could not see Nial, who was striding along behind them, and he tried to think of what the Irishman had said — that unpleasant things were soon forgotten if you kept your thoughts on the good things ahead. But what was ahead?

He had run away from home and he did not know where he was being taken. If he were to find Red Eric — yes — that was the thing to think about. He tried to fix his mind on this meeting, saying to himself, "I'm going to find him. I'm going to find him. I'm going to find him!"

It was warmer now. The wind had gone down and the sun was up. From the branches, icicles were dripping and drops of water fell on their heads as the minstrels walked under the trees. A robin flew low in front of them and with a flip of its wings perched on an overhanging bough, with its head on one side making a little chirping sound of friendship.

As sometimes happens on a sunny winter's day there was a hint of spring in the pale blue of the sky and in the patches of wet green moss where the snow had melted.

Nial began to whistle like a blackbird and then to sing in a voice half gay, half sad. Softly Jack Piper joined in and after a while Fulk's deep notes went booming through the woods. Scarcely aware of what he was doing and still thinking of Red Eric, Redcap hummed the tune and when the minstrels repeated the words he too lifted up his voice and sang:

> When the nightingalë sings
> The woodës waxen green
> Leaf and grass and blossom springs
> In Averil I ween. . . .

He did not notice that Jack Piper had stopped pushing the cart, that Nial was leaning against a tree with one hand on his hip, looking at him. He was singing with closed lids till he felt a hand on his wrist. His startled eyes opened and looked straight into those of Fulk Crooked Smile.

He stopped singing and shrank away but Fulk nodded to him, pleasantly.

"I had forgotten my goose was a songbird," he said, and untied the ropes which bound Redcap's arms. "There's an apple in here." He tossed the rope into the cart and pulled a small rosy apple out of a sack, rubbed it on his sleeve, and gave it to Redcap. "It's a sweet one," he said.

Redcap gaped. Crooked Smile seemed to have forgotten his anger and was speaking in a friendly voice.

"Eat, boy, it's a reward for the song. You sang well," he said. He looked as though he were going to say something else but Nial came up blustering and shook his fist close to Fulk's face. "What's this?" he said. "Are you taking the bread or rather the apple out of my own mouth? Wasn't it my song that the boy took, stealing the very words from me like the Lion Heart's troubadour in the days of old."

Redcap stopped with the apple half way to his mouth and Fulk laughed.

"If you don't know that story I'll tell it to you," he said. "So sit down and eat your apple while the others make up the fire for breakfast. You will be hungry. You had no supper."

"The bread and ch . . ." began Redcap but the rest of his sentence was cut short by Nial's pinching him and shouting at the top of his voice:

> I am so dry I cannot speak:
> I am near chokëd with my meat:
> I trow the butler be asleep
> With "How butler, how!"

"Peace with your ugly noise and make the fire," cried Fulk. "Do you think I can tell a tale while you bellow like a mad bull?"

"Your pardon, master," said Nial, and he winked with the eye nearest to Redcap, and went away to pick up sticks.

Fulk Crooked Smile shook the snow from a bough, swept clear a space under a tree and leaning against the trunk began his story.

"My lords and ladies (that is how you must begin in a great house. 'Good people, gentles all' is for the townsfolk, or you can say 'Fair friends'). In the days of old when the Lionheart was King, there lived a troubadour whose name was Arnaut Daniel of Riberac. A noble lord he was and a poet who sang of the love of fair ladies, of birds in the woods and of sweet flowers in the hedgerows.

"And because Richard the Lionheart was a troubadour himself, and his mother a fair lady who made music, to the court came singers and poets, minstrels and troubadours, all intent on winning the King's praise. It happened one Spring, when the King held tournament in Provence, that Arnaut came riding on a grey palfrey with a little foot-page leading the white ass which carried his lute and his courtly garments. Arnaut stayed at the palace for many a month, delighting all the lords and ladies with the songs that he made and the King gave him costly gifts and called for him by day and by night.

" 'Where is Arnaut Daniel?'

" 'Send for the Sieur of Riberac.'

" 'Good Arnaut, we are over-sad, sing a merry song to cheer our hearts,' or 'Good Arnaut, we are over-merry, sing some sad lay to quiet our souls.'

"And Arnaut would sing his own poems, old and new, and all would clap their hands and call for more.

"But at the court there were other singers, who listened with jealous ears and watched with envious eyes, whispering together, 'This Arnaut Daniel takes all the praise. The King never looks on us.'

"Then one who was gay with a bold heart and quick wit, went up to the King and kneeling on his knee asked, 'Have I my liege lord's permission to seek a favour?'

"And the King, made happy by Arnaut's verses, smiled and stretched out his hand with its jewelled ring, saying, 'What you ask is granted.'

"The gay troubadour rose and, with his eyes upon Arnaut, began to boast: 'There stands a troubadour who pleases my liege lord and the court with his rhymes. Yet he makes verses that I could better. Prove me, sir poet!' and he flung his embroidered glove at Arnaut's feet.

"The King leant forward with laughter in his eyes.

" 'So ho! A challenge. What says my lord Arnaut Daniel?'

"Arnaut's bow was so low that his head almost touched the ground. In silence he picked up the glove and tucked it in his girdle. In silence he looked at the gay troubadour with a slow scornful smile.

" 'Then the challenge is accepted!' cried the King. 'One poet against another. Go pages, lock them, each in his room, till the time comes for me to judge them. Go, my gay young challenger. God speed my gentle Arnaut. In two days' time, I will hear you.'

"Bowing to the King and to the Queen, to lord and to lady, Arnaut Daniel and the gay troubadour went to their rooms and the pages locked the doors and brought the keys to the Lionheart.

"Arnaut sat on a stool and looked from the long narrow window over the fair fields of Provence, but no words came to him. He paced the small room, leant against the wall, but not a note could he utter. He lay on the bed with his face on the pillow but neither line nor rhyme, note nor chord came into his head. He sat and he knelt, he lay and he walked, but his heart was empty of song.

" 'Woe is me,' he whispered, 'for I shall lose favour with the King.'

"As he spoke, the voice of the gay troubadour came to him through the wall. His rival was making a song, singing words and notes as they filled his mind.

"Arnaut listened and his heart grew heavy. The gay troubadour already made music and song, and *he* was barren of thought. He clasped his head with his hands, he covered his ears, but through the window-slit, in the great stone wall, came the lilting of the gay troubadour:

> If my love were by my side
> Tra-la-la! Tra-la-la.

"It was a good song, the air, now merry, now sad, now clear

116

and loud, now sweet and low. And as Arnaut listened the words took hold of his mind and the music stole into his heart and soon he knew every word of the gay troubadour's song, and still he could make nothing himself.

"Two days passed and the pages came with the keys and let each poet out of his chamber and led him into the presence of the King and of all the court.

"The troubadours bowed.

" 'And now,' said the Lionheart, 'who will begin?'

"Arnaut bent his knee. 'My liege lord, a boon! Grant me leave to sing first.'

" 'Leave is granted,' said the King.

"Then Arnaut, who had not thought of one line or note, took up his lute. And the air that he played was now merry, now sad, now clear and loud, now sweet and low, and he sang with his heart in his eyes.

> If my love were by my side,
> Tra-la-la! Tra-la-la.

"There was a cry of anger and the gay troubadour fell on his knees before the King.

" 'My song, he has taken my song!'

"But sweetly Arnaut sang on and when he had finished, the King turned to the gay troubadour, who was gay no longer.

" 'And you my friend, you promised a better song than Arnaut's.'

"But the gay troubadour was flaming with anger and he could neither sing nor play. All he could do was to cry aloud:

" 'My song, he has stolen my song!'

"The King, weary of hearing him, turned to Arnaut and shrugging his shoulders asked, 'What means this man?'

"Arnaut dropped again upon one knee. 'My liege,' he said, 'judge who was in fault, the gay troubadour or Arnaut Daniel. When your Royal Grace locked us in our chambers, no word, no note would come to me, think as I would. And when I sat in despair, fearful of disgrace, through the window came sweet music and the song that I sang to you. It came till I had it by heart and there was room for nothing more in my mind.'

" 'So,' said the Lionheart, and his words were cold as the blade of a sword. 'So you stole his song.'

"There was silence in the court as he stepped from his throne and moved towards the troubadours.

"He looked at Arnaut and saw a laughing penitence in his eyes and the King's lips twitched. He looked at the gay troubadour and saw bewildered rage in his eyes and the King's shoulders shook.

"He took the right hand of each troubadour and joined them.

" 'Make friends,' he said, 'for the King loves a jest.'

"And he went from the room through the great door, and as he passed along the corridor, the whole court heard his ringing laughter."

"I like the Lionheart," said Redcap.

"Yes," answered Fulk, "he had a merry heart as well as a brave one and that is to be envied. But come now, the fire's made and while the pot's boiling, you shall learn the story. Listen and say after me —

"In the days of old, when the Lionheart was King. . . ."

"In the days of old, when the Lionheart was King," repeated Redcap.

"There lived a troubadour whose name was Arnaut Daniel of Riberac."

"There lived a troubadour whose name was Arnaut Daniel of Riberac. . . ."

A PLAY IN THE VILLAGE

*In which Redcap acts the part of a simpleton, Fulk tells the tale
of Three Wives and a woman has news of Red Eric*

D A Y after day the minstrels continued their journey,
pausing by the wayside to eat or to sleep and never
failing to teach Redcap some new tale. Twelve days
had now passed since the boy had led the Boar's Head carol
in Sir Huon's Manor house, and, as he trudged along the highway with the minstrels, he thought of his father at the forge,
his mother with wool on her distaff spinning as she walked
through the village, and the old priest teaching the brighter
children to read and to spell.

He guessed that all except the wise woman would wonder
what had happened to him, but surely she would know and
would comfort his mother? She had warned him on Christmas
Eve to think before he decided what to do, saying that there
was wisdom in the proverb "Look before you leap". At the
time, he had not known what she meant, but now he was
certain that she had seen what was in his mind and was
advising him in her strange roundabout way not to be hasty.

"A penny for your thoughts," cried Nial. "Catch!" and he
threw a fir cone at Redcap's head.

The boy would have caught it had not Rex leapt and snapped
it up before him.

"A bad miss for a juggler," grinned Fulk, "and that has
put a thought into my head. You and Rex might work together
and make some fun. He can be the master-juggler and you the
simpleton. That should bring in gifts of money and of food."

"But why must I be a simpleton?" asked Redcap. "I don't
want to."

"You'll do as you're told," growled Crooked Smile, "and it won't take much learning, so we can begin now."

"But we're in the highway," objected Redcap, "and people may pass by."

"All the better," answered Fulk. "It will accustom you to being looked at and laughed at. If you had been used to people teasing you and jeering at you while you were juggling, you would not have put us all to shame."

Redcap's heart sank. He moved a step or two nearer to Nial but Fulk gave a low whistle and snapped his fingers at Rex. Immediately the dog seized him by the belt and began pulling him back to Fulk while Nial looked on, amused at Redcap's astonishment.

"You see," said Fulk, "Rex knows how to obey orders without a word. Nial has taught him. A sign is all that he needs. Stand here beside me and I'll show you something."

Redcap obeyed.

"Watch Rex," ordered Fulk, "but don't look at me."

Redcap did as he was told and for the next few minutes he was astonished to see Rex perform all manner of tricks without a word from Fulk. He walked on his hind legs, begged, lay down as though he were dead, leapt up growling, caught fir cones tossed to him by Fulk and brought them back.

"Good dog," said Nial, patting his head. "Now it's Redcap's turn."

"And I hope you will be as clever," said Fulk to Redcap.

"I'll try," said Redcap, wondering what would happen if he were as clumsy as he had been with the knives and the horseshoe. "Will you teach me the signs? You told me to look at Rex so I didn't see what you were doing."

"I shall not give you signs," said Fulk. "I shall tell you quite plainly what to do. It will be easy."

He spoke kindly but there was a strange look in his eyes, and Nial had that teasing expression which meant that one could not tell whether a thing was a joke or not.

Redcap looked from one to the other and one of Nial's

eyebrows went up. There was nothing to be learnt from *him*.

"What have I to do?" asked the boy a little anxiously.

"I shall call you 'the simpleton'," said Fulk, "and whenever I say, 'The simpleton does this' or 'the simpleton does that', you simply try to do it. Do you understand?"

"Yes," said Redcap. "But what happens if I can't do what you say?"

"It doesn't matter as long as you try," said Fulk. "The important thing is to listen for the words 'the simpleton'. Now, are you ready to practise?"

Redcap nodded. It sounded like a game and Fulk seemed to be in a good temper.

"The simpleton jumps!" said Fulk.

Redcap jumped.

"The simpleton bursts into tears," said Fulk.

Redcap rubbed his eyes with his knuckles, said, "Boo hoo," and giggled.

"Be careful!" warned Fulk. "I didn't say 'giggle', I said, 'bursts into tears'."

Redcap proceeded to sniff and wipe his nose with his sleeve, making a hiccoughing sound.

"Faith," said Nial, "'tis enough to make your heart burst inside with sorrow for the young boy's trouble."

"Quiet!" ordered Fulk. "This is a lesson. The simpleton stops blubbering, scratches his head and looks bewildered."

Redcap scratched his head and frowned.

"Good," said Fulk. "You see how easy it is. I tell Rex what to do by signs and you by words. If you do exactly what I say, the people will be delighted and all will be well."

A little puzzled but glad that nothing more was expected of him, Redcap walked between Fulk and Nial as they and Jack Piper approached the village of Brimmingford.

A little girl, herding a flock of geese on the village common, saw them coming, and thrusting her stick into the hands of her small brother told him to look after the birds, and ran as fast as her long skirt would let her, shouting, "Minstrels,

minstrels." All around the village the cry was repeated, "Minstrels! Here come the minstrels."

The ale-wife came out of the alehouse, locking the door behind her with an enormous key. The fat miller, with his doublet and apron and even his shoes white with flour, came waddling to the door of the mill crying, "Come all, here are minstrels." The woodman, the thatcher, the ditcher, the dairy-wife from the manor house, the lord's hunter and falconer, the blacksmith and his ten children, every man, woman, boy and girl in the place appeared as though by magic on the village green.

The ground was wet and soggy where the snow had melted and the big elm tree on the green dripped but nobody minded. Everyone was laughing, beckoning to tardy neighbours, calling to friends, delighted that the minstrels had arrived on the last day of the Christmas feast, for next morning was Plough Monday, when work would begin and with it all the usual round of duties.

"Fair friends," cried Fulk, "how can we pleasure you?"

Immediately everyone began to speak at once. Some called for a song, some for a story, some for juggling, others for music and a dance, until the minstrels, with Redcap following and Rex leading on his hind legs, turned and with hands over ears to shut out the noise, pretended to be leaving.

"Hey there! Whither away?" screeched the ale-wife and seized Nial by the arm only to find herself kissed on each cheek and whirled in a crazy dance around the green while the whole village laughed and cheered.

"Put me down, you and your impudence," she cried struggling. But Nial lifted her in his long arms and held her over the duck pond.

"A free drink of ale for the minstrels or a free bath in cold water for the ale-wife?" he shouted.

"Put me down, put me down," cried the ale-wife.

"But it's wet down there," laughed Nial, lowering her until she was about two feet from the surface of the pond, and, with his own grinning face a few inches from hers, he began to sing:

> Bring us in good ale, bring us in good ale
> For our blessëd Lady's sake, bring us in good ale!

while the other minstrels joined in at the tops of their voices, shaking their forefingers at the struggling ale-wife.

> Bring us in no bacon for that is passing fat
> But bring us in good ale and give us enow of that.

"Will you let go," cried the ale-wife, but Nial only lowered her nearer to the pond and the minstrels went on singing:

> Bring us in no eggs for there are many shells
> But bring us in good ale and give us nothing else,
>   And bring us in good ale.

"In with you!" laughed Nial, giving her a sudden jerk.

"Eee!" screeched the woman. "Nay, stop! Nay, stop! You shall have your ale."

And laughing, Nial set her on her feet.

"Ah, but you're a bad one," she scolded, "a rogue and no mistake. You shall all have your ale free of charge, but you shall amuse us, first."

She pushed her disordered hair back under her grey wimple and shook herself, setting her brown skirt into place. "Since the one who pays the piper calls the tune, I ask for a play," she cried.

Fulk stepped forward and bowed to her.

"And a play you shall have," he said. "Fair friends, for this entertainment, we need no masks, no strange garments, merely a dog collar and a rope!" And seizing Redcap by the arm, he put around his neck Rex's spiked collar and tied to it a length of rope from Jack Piper's handcart.

"Fair friends, good people all, we present the Juggler and the Simpleton."

Immediately at a sign from Fulk, Rex stood upon his hind

legs and walked around in a circle while the people smiled and clapped.

"Rex, the famous juggler," said Fulk, "needs to practise his art every day." Here, he threw a short stick to the dog who leapt and caught it in his mouth, brought it back, presented it to Fulk, and sat up begging. Fulk balanced the stick upright on the dog's nose, snapped his fingers, waved a cloth, whistled, but Rex remained motionless with the stick still balanced upright. Slowly and very daintily he stood up on his hind legs with the stick still on his nose and his right fore paw saluting the company. After a minute, he gave a short bark, the stick shot into the air, he caught it and brought it back to Fulk.

"The clever little beast," said the people to each other. "He knows a thing or two. Wise as a Christian he is."

"Of course," continued Fulk, "a juggler, as clever as this, requires a servant to wait on him, to fetch and to carry, and so our juggler seeks a likely lad. Let him pass among the company. He will bark once and shake his head when he wishes to say 'no'."

He made a sign, unseen by the people, to Rex and the dog ran hither and thither, sniffing at small boys' toes, seizing them by their doublets and giving, in each case, a short decisive bark until he came to Redcap, who was standing at Fulk's elbow, wondering what part in this play he was expected to act. But Rex showed no such bewilderment, he leapt up and down when he reached Redcap, giving quick little whines of delight, and suddenly seizing the rope attached to the collar, began to walk around the circle of people with Redcap forced to follow him.

Once again, the people laughed and clapped and Fulk went on with his story.

"The boy chosen by the juggler is a simpleton and when his master begins to train him he does not know what to do."

Here Rex began to shake the rope attached to Redcap's collar, growling, and Redcap, feeling his head pulled rapidly from side to side, looked so bewildered that the people shouted with laughter, calling, "Bravo, Master Juggler! That will teach him!"

Rex pulled and shook more violently than ever till Redcap, thinking that he would be strangled if this went on, seized the

REX BEGAN TO SHAKE THE ROPE ATTACHED TO REDCAP'S COLLAR

rope too, and then began a tug of war. This was fun and both pulled their hardest while the people cheered first one and then the other. But a surprise was in store for Redcap.

"Rex, the Juggler," continued Fulk, "has had enough of this and he teaches the simpleton a lesson."

In an instant, Rex let go the rope and down went Redcap on his back with his legs in the air. With short angry yaps Rex jumped to right and to left of him, preventing him from getting up by butting him in the stomach, tripping him and playfully nipping his ankles. No sooner did Redcap struggle to his knees than Rex rolled him over.

This was just the kind of rough and tumble play that delighted the crowd and when Fulk tossed a little whip to Rex and he caught it and shook it over Redcap, they laughed so loudly that the boy began to giggle until he heard an ominous note in Fulk's voice.

"The simpleton, afraid of what his master will do next, bursts into tears."

Redcap bellowed and went on roaring till Rex dropped the little whip, sat back on his haunches and barked. Surprised, Redcap took his knuckles out of his eyes and waited, still sitting on the ground.

"The servant's tears have reminded the master of water," said Fulk. "Training a simpleton is thirsty work and he wants a drink."

Rex now seized the rope on Redcap's collar, jerked the boy to his feet and began to drag him towards the pond. At the edge, he let go, and started to lap the water, turning round suddenly and looking at Redcap with his head on one side and his breath coming quickly. Fulk continued.

" 'You dirty boy,' says the juggler, 'wash that face of yours after all that blubbering.' "

Redcap did not know what to do and Fulk went on. " 'Oh, so you won't? Then I must do it for you.' "

Rex turned and began to dig at the very edge of the pond, splashing water over Redcap, who, to the delight of the crowd, kept backing and shouting, "Stop it! Don't!" while his face was spattered with dirty water.

Fulk was laughing. "But the master's back is turned," he cried, "and the simpleton runs away."

Like an arrow Redcap was off with Rex bounding after him. Round and round the pond they ran, dodging one another, while the children squealed and the grown-ups laughed. At last Rex gave a leap and caught the rope, shaking it violently from side to side.

Redcap was out of breath and he followed, while the dog pulled him once again to the edge of the pond, where the crowd was now standing, mocking the boy and cheering the dog.

Redcap knew it was a game but he was feeling tired and a little cross. The mud was caked on his face and his neck was uncomfortable. He wished Fulk would put an end to the play.

Without his knowing it, his face was beginning to look red and sulky and his lower lip stuck out.

"The simpleton sulks," said Fulk suddenly, "and the master knows that a douche of cold water is the best cure."

Before Redcap knew what was happening, he felt Rex run between his legs, and he himself was rolling to the edge of the pond.

A strong arm seized him and planted him on his feet and a voice cried, "Now, now, now. Enough is as good as a feast. I won't stand by and see a boy catch his death of cold in a pond! He's a clever one, this is, for all he's called a simpleton. Look at the dog! He knows it's gone far enough."

Rex was wagging his tail and licking Redcap's hand. Redcap turned to look at his rescuer and saw a small woman with eyes so big and brown that they looked almost like chestnuts in her thin face.

"Wife, wife," said the blacksmith shaking his head at her, "must you always go interfering! You spoilt a day's fun."

"'Tis no fun to see a lad soaked on a day like this — shame on the minstrels for allowing it!"

Fulk came up and grinned at her. "Rex is fond of the boy," he said. "The story would have ended differently, ma'am. The lad wouldn't have been ducked."

"It's only scolding women that are ducked," said the blacksmith, "so you'd best bridle your tongue, wife."

The woman laughed. "I'm mum," she said, putting her hand over her mouth but keeping one arm around Redcap's shoulders.

"There's an obedient wife for you," grinned the blacksmith. "Does everything I tell her! Did you ever know a woman do everything she's told?" he asked Fulk, winking.

"Only one," said Fulk.

"And who was that, may I ask?" cried the ale-wife.

"Give us the ale you promised and I'll tell you," said Fulk, his crooked smile lighting up one side of his face like a sudden beam of sunshine.

"Come then! Come," said the woman and the crowd moved towards the corner of the village where, as a sign that this was an alehouse, a great bunch of evergreens was tied to a pole stuck out over a doorway. The ale-wife fitted the key into the lock, and the people swarmed in, some standing against the walls, others sitting on the floor.

When the three minstrels had drunk their fill, Redcap, leaning against the blacksmith's wife, who had rubbed his face clean with her apron, sipped his ale and listened as intently as the others to Fulk's tale.

"Fair friends," said Fulk, "in days not long past there lived three merchants, each of whom had a wife at home. It befell, one day, that they were returning from the fair and one said, 'It is a noble thing for a man to have a good wife that does as he bids her all the time.'

" 'By my troth,' said one of the others. 'Mine obeys me.'

" 'Truly,' said the third, 'I think that mine is more obedient than any.'

" 'Then,' said the first, 'let us make a bargain that each of us puts his wife to the test, and let him who has the most disobedient pay for a dinner.'

"Laughing, they agreed that each one should say to his wife, 'See that you obey me in everything that I ask,' and then, to test her, each should set a basin on the floor and bid her jump into it.

"At the first merchant's house, when a basin was placed before her and she was told to jump into it, the wife asked, 'Why?' and she refused to obey until she was given a reason. Then the merchant told her angrily that she had cost him a pretty penny that day, and left the house, frowning.

"When the second merchant put the basin on the floor of his house he said, 'Wife, see that you do whatsoever I bid you.' And she smiled and asked, 'What does my lord command?' 'Leap into the basin,' said he. 'Sir, you are mad,' answered his wife, 'and I will not obey a madman.' Then her husband was enraged for she had put him to shame before the other two merchants.

"At the house of the third, a meal was ready and he invited his two companions to sit at the table, whispering, 'I will test my wife after supper and bid her leap into the basin.'

"When they were seated and the woman was about to bring in the dishes he said to her, 'Wife, whatever I bid you, let it be done.' And she, who loved him dearly, bowed her head, wondering at this command, for it was her habit to obey him.

"Now it happened that she had prepared a dish of eggs and the good man looked around and saw that she had forgotten the salt cellar and he called to her, 'Wife, I pray you, salt for the table.'

"With an air of amazement the woman looked at him, then without more ado, she leapt upon the table, kicked over the dishes, beating the board with her fists and throwing down meat and drink till all was spilt or broken.

" 'Good wife! good wife,' cried the merchant. 'What are you about? Are you mad?'

" 'Sir,' said she, 'are *you* mad that you ask me such a thing? I have done your bidding as you commanded although it was to your harm and mine. I would rather suffer harm than disobey.'

" 'Wife,' said he, amazed. 'What does this mean?'

" 'Sir,' she answered in all humbleness, 'you said, "assault the table," and knowing that "to assault" meant "to attack" or "beat" I obeyed.'

" 'Nay, nay,' he answered, 'I called for salt on the table.'

" 'By my troth,' said she, 'I thought you bade me attack the board.' Thereupon there was much mirth and laughter. And the other merchants said that there was no need to bid her leap into the basin for she obeyed enough, and it was agreed that her husband had won the dinner.

"So, as you may be sure, this woman was greatly praised."

All the men agreed that the story was a fine one and that their wives should pay heed to it, but the blacksmith's wife laughed at them saying that the woman set a bad example by throwing good food upon the floor and breaking the dishes.

"And as to that dish of eggs," she said, "there is a red-haired rascal here, whose mouth waters at the very name of it. With your leave," she added, looking at the minstrels, "I'll take the boy back with me this night. He looks cold as well as hungry. He can sleep at our place in the corner of the smithy, where 'tis warm."

She tucked Redcap's arm under hers. "He'll be ready to set out with you in the morning," she said to Fulk. "I'll feed him till his little belly's as tight as a drum. Come, boy."

Sleepily, Redcap went off with her.

"Which one is your father?" she asked, and when he did not answer, "Poor lad," she muttered, "an orphan as likely as not — dragged hither and yon, listening day and night to foolish tales."

"Don't you like stories?" asked Redcap yawning.

"Yes," said the woman, "some. But it isn't every minstrel that tells a good one. We had one here, not so long ago — in the summer it was — and he could charm the heart out of your body with his songs. Come in here, boy." She pushed open the door of the smithy. "Roll up in those sacks till I bring you something hot."

Redcap sat in the corner on a bundle of sacks and pulled one around his shoulders. The embers of the fire were still red and he felt at home and comfortable as he did in his father's forge. He pulled off his scarlet hood, which was splashed with mud from the pond, and began to rub it, trying to get out the stains, but they were still wet, so he hung it on a hook nearer the fire and sat thinking. "Father will be putting away his tools, now." "Mother will be stirring the soup . . . They're all right because they have each other and — and I'll go back soon, just as soon as I have found Red Eric."

Suddenly he sat bolt upright.

The blacksmith's wife was coming back and she was singing. Redcap caught his breath as the words came nearer.

A PLAY IN THE VILLAGE

A woman is a gladsome thing,
They do the wash and do the wring!
Lullay, lullay, she doth thee sing —

The door opened and still humming she placed a steaming bowl of pease porridge in front of Redcap. He pulled at her skirt.

"That song," he babbled, "that song. How do you know it? Who told it to you?"

"The sweet singer — the minstrel who came here in the summer," she said. "His hair was as red as your own."

X

PLOUGH MONDAY

*In which Nial tells the story of Cormac and the Wolf Cubs,
Redcap takes part in a procession, and earns his keep*

So Red Eric was in England, still singing and telling
stories and always making himself remembered. Redcap
sat with his bowl of pease porridge between his knees, his
spoon in mid-air, and his eager eyes looking into those of the
blacksmith's wife.

"I'm searching for him," he said.

"Then you'll look till the eyes drop from your head," said
she, "and your feet will walk till doomsday, for he is the kind
that comes and goes, you never know when or where. Here
today and gone tomorrow, leaving no trace but a song."

"Which way did he go?" asked Redcap.

"Maybe North, maybe South. And if not North or South
'twas East or West," said the woman, laughing. "He came like
a shadow just before sunset, juggled and told tales, then passed
round his hood for money. And because we had nothing else I
gave him soup and put a dried horse hide here in the smithy
for a bed. He bowed to me as though I were a queen on a
throne and said, 'I will sing my thanks'."

"Was that when he sang what you sang just now?" asked
Redcap, dipping the wooden spoon into the porridge and
swallowing quickly.

"Yes," she answered, "and I wanted to hear it again next day
but he'd gone when I came with a crust of bread and some
goat's milk for his breakfast. Up with the lark he was and away
before anyone saw him, and not a dog in the place barked
although he was a stranger."

"Tell me some more," begged Redcap.

"What more do I know," said she, "save that he looked merry when he talked and sad when he was silent? And when he was your age I think he would have been the spit and image of yourself. But sup your porridge now, then go to sleep. You'll be warm in here and we'll feed you in the morning."

"I want to find him," said Redcap. "I think I'll get up early and look. . . ."

"You will not," said a voice, and there was Nial in the doorway, with Rex at his heels. "I am not going to wear the shoes off my two feet hunting for you and finding you, maybe with the patch torn off and me with no thread to mend it. You'll curl up on that sack, you will so, and you'll not stir till I'm telling you 'tis time to get up, for I'm sleeping at your side this night."

The woman moved towards the door and laughed again.

"Boy," she said, "if you look for that red-haired singer, take a grown man with you and stick to the highway. There are wolves in the forest."

Nial grinned.

"He's a rare one, is Redcap, for playing with wolves. He takes second place with Cormac, he does."

"Well," said the woman, "I know nothing of Cormac but I do know that tomorrow is Plough Monday and I must be up betimes. So good night to you both."

Nodding kindly, she closed the door. Nial lay on his back with his hands behind his head, and Rex at his feet.

"Go to sleep now," he said to Redcap and he closed his eyes, but the boy moved a little closer, still sitting up.

"Nial," he said.

"I'm asleep," said Nial, "and so are you."

"Who was Cormac?" asked Redcap.

"There's no knowing," answered Nial and began to snore.

Redcap edged nearer only to find himself grabbed, rolled over on his back and covered firmly with a sack.

"One more word . . ." threatened Nial.

"Cormac," squeaked Redcap like a frightened mouse.

"And what of him?" asked Nial with a groan.

"I want to know about him," protested Redcap. "You said he played with wolves."

"Did I now?" said Nial. "Then my tongue slipped. It's a strange thing, surely, the way one's tongue behaves when one's asleep."

Redcap poked him in the ribs. He was beginning to know when Nial was teasing and when he was serious.

"I can't sleep, Nial," he said, "really and truly I can't till I know about Cormac. If you tell me I shall have another story and that'll be a surprise for Fulk."

"It's that one himself will do the surprising if you're so tired, for want of sleep, that you can't entertain the people tomorrow," answered Nial. "So if you get into trouble don't expect me to get you out of it."

"I'll sleep if you tell it," said Redcap.

"And if you don't wake betimes, tomorrow, I'll have your breakfast as well as my own," answered Nial. And he began the story.

"It was in the old days when Art, son of Conn the Hundred Fighter was the High King of Ireland, and ruling in Tara. Art was fair and comely on horseback and a keen swordsman, with a voice that all must obey. And Achta his queen had skin that was as white as snow and cheeks like the holly berries that fall upon snow, and in summer when she walked in the meadows, a serving maid walked on each side of her holding her long falling sleeves lest they touch the ground and get wet with the dew.

"Achta the queen was happy as a bright day till one night she dreamed a strange dream, and greatly troubled, she told it to the High King.

" 'Art, High King,' she whispered, 'I dreamt that one, whose face I could not see, struck my head from my body with a great sword. From my neck there grew a tree, and it had branches that spread and spread till they covered all Ireland. Art, High King, what may that mean?'

"The King looked at her gently and said, 'Some dreams are false and some are true, and I'm thinking that this is a true one that will bring you trouble and joy. The head that was struck from your body is myself and the dream foretells that I shall fall in battle, cut down by the sword of my foes.'

" 'Alas, for my sorrow,' said Achta trembling.

" 'But the dream brings joy, too,' said the High King, 'for the tree that grew from your neck and spread its branches over the whole land means that you will bear me a son who will be the glory of all Ireland.'

"Then the High Queen wept but Art took her hand and comforted her with quiet words. 'Achta, little heart,' he whispered, 'the son will be a happiness to you but take warning by the dream. If I am slain in battle, seek for Luna my friend who lives in Connacht for he has promised to care for you if trouble comes. Now sleep.'

"But Achta could not rest. By day and by night she thought of the dream and when enemies came to Tara and Art, the High King, went out to do them battle, her heart was heavy. Yet, when news was brought that the High King had been slain, she showed no surprise but secretly fled in a chariot with her serving maid to take refuge with Luna, his friend.

"Past the green hills and through the woods, they fled swiftly, while the serving maid held the reins and urged the horse to greater speed with a tasselled whip.

"They drove till the last red glow of the sun had faded away and evening darkened the woods. They drove till night closed around them and a small lonely moon shone over a green glade. It was here that the serving maid drew in her rein and loosed the horse to graze. It was here, on a bed of beech leaves and soft green moss, that Achta's son was born and she caressed him and whispered with her lips on his head, 'Sleep, little son who will one day be the glory of Ireland.'

"As night deepened Achta and her baby slept while the serving maid kept watch, but she was weary from driving the chariot and slowly her head drooped, too, and her eyelids closed.

"Not a leaf stirred, not a blade of grass whispered when into the great stillness slid a she-wolf. With swift silent movements she reached the queen's side, took the child in her mouth and slipped away like a shadow.

"At dawn, when the birds were waking, the Lord of Luna came striding through the woods, seeking Achta, for he had heard of the battle and of the High King's death and remembered his promise. As he came, with his bright sword in his hand, he heard the sound of weeping, and there in a green glade lay the High Queen in the arms of her serving woman, the two of them in deep grief.

"Then the Lord of Luna sheathed his sword and knelt upon one knee to kiss the hem of Achta's robe and she saw him through her tears.

" 'Ah Luna,' said she, sorrowfully, ''tis not yourself should be kneeling to me who was once High Queen and am now a beggar. Let you rise now, Luna, and seek my son that is stolen, the son that should be High King and the glory of all Ireland.'

"When Luna heard how the baby had vanished he sent armed men through the woods, seeking this way and that but never a glimpse did they catch of the lost child.

"In the home of the Lord of Luna, Achta grieved sorely but deep in her heart a steady flame of hope burned like a little candle.

"Time passed. The woods grew bare and the leaves made a golden carpet on the ground and still she waited for the son that was to be the glory of Ireland.

"It happened one day that a hunter left his companions and wandered alone on the hillside. As he climbed he came upon a circle of rocks where a ray of sunshine lighted the mouth of a cave. He stooped to look in and his breath came quickly.

" 'Will anyone believe me?' he muttered. 'Am I not seeing the strangest sight that not a man will have seen since the world began?'

"He stole quietly away from the cave and went down the hill to the house of the Lord of Luna.

" 'Milord of Luna,' cried he, 'let you come with me at once for I have found the High King's son.'

" ''Tis a grave thing you're telling me,' said the Lord of Luna. 'Is it true?'

" 'It is,' said the hunter. 'I have seen him and he stark naked and crawling on the floor of a cave, and a litter of wolf cubs lepping on him, batting him with their paws. Did I not see him with my two eyes, playing on all fours among them the way he might be a wolf himself.'

"When Luna climbed the hillside and looked into the cave he saw four wolf cubs and a tiny naked child cuddled together, resting from their play. He took off his blue and green cloak and spreading it on the ground, put the baby upon it. The child awoke and gave a little cry and immediately the wolf cubs awoke too, and leapt upon the cloak and lay close to the child. And because they would not move, the Lord of Luna took them as well as the baby back to Achta.

Throughout the house there was great rejoicing with music and feasting, but Achta the High Queen sat alone in her room and spoke quietly to the little wolves.

" ''Tis a grand thing you have done for the High King, little wolves, for you have been his brothers. I shall call him Cormac. Remember his name and be faithful till the time comes when a High King shall be the glory of all Ireland.' "

"And were they faithful?" asked Redcap.

"They were that," said Nial, "and all his life long Cormac never hunted a wolf. And now for the love of pity, let me have a night's rest for who knows what we'll be doing tomorrow? The dawn has a way of tickling a man's eyelids and he still sleeping like the dead."

And indeed, dawn tickled Redcap's eyelids almost as soon as he had fallen asleep, at least so he thought, for he awoke while it still seemed dark in the smithy but the laughter and the grumbling outside showed that the villagers were all up and many of them out.

"Stop it, you wretch!" screamed a laughing voice. "Ouch."

The door of the smithy burst open and in came the black-smith playfully leading his wife by the ear while she was trying to walk steadily with a wooden platter, on which there was a jug and a crusty loaf of bread.

"You be off, master smith. You've done enough damage for one day," she laughed. "Be off now and let me feed these strangers."

The blacksmith, who was a vast man, three times her size, gave her ear a tweak and grinned at Nial and at Redcap, who were sitting up, rubbing their eyes.

"She's lost her Shrove-tide cock!" he said. "On this Plough Monday I was first."

"That happened to mother once," said Redcap, "but only once. My father put his tools in a row in front of the fire before she had the pot boiling. So she paid the forfeit. But he gave her a cock at Shrove-tide, all the same. You see he hadn't been fair, he'd put his things there over night, not in the morning, so it wasn't really Plough Monday!"

"Oho," said the woman, "maybe that's what you did too? Did he come in here just before sunrise to get his hammer?"

"We wouldn't know," laughed Nial. "The heavy sleep was on us!"

The blacksmith looked sheepish and his wife's eyes twinkled.

"Plough Monday this year will make many another wife cock of the walk," she said. "The tale your leader told in the ale-house put them on their mettle. Obedience, indeed! Most of them had their pots boiling before ever the men turned in their sleep. But my big rascal played some trick, I'll be bound."

"Up at milord's house," said the blacksmith's boy, who had wandered in, "the men were first. Bet says there was a whip, a hatchet, a spade and a crossbow all laid out in a row and the water in the big pots scarcely warm. So there'll be no cocks for the maids' Shrove-tide dinner. They're cross-eyed with anger."

"More trickery, I'll be bound," said the blacksmith's wife,

"but I'll be even with my man next year. Why, ever since I can remember no woman in my family has lost a Shrove-tide cock by letting her menfolk get up earlier than she did on Plough Monday."

An old man, who had looked into the smithy, waggled a finger at her. "That'll teach ye to bestir yourself," he said. "Maybe our good forefathers thought it a wise way of getting people early to work after the Christmas feasting."

"By setting man and wife to vie with each other? For shame," laughed the blacksmith's wife, "a pretty beginning to the year, I must say. But, come now, strangers, break your fast. The boys will be drawing the plough through the village, soon, and they'll want you to sing."

She put the bread and the jug on the bench and Nial and Redcap fell to with a will, while the blacksmith gave his boy a great pair of bellows and told him to blow up the fire.

"I must be ready to work now," he said. "Twelve days' holiday puts one behindhand. Plough Monday always brings a load of this, that and t'other. So blow away my lad and ..."

But he was interrupted by loud cries, the lowing of an ox and the shrill sounds of piping.

Winding its way across the village green, came a procession led by Jack Piper playing his pipe and Fulk Crooked Smile with a ridiculous mask like a donkey's head thrumming with his fingers on a tabor and every now and then shaking his elbows, to which he had tied some jingling bells.

Behind him a number of boys with holly and mistletoe stuck in their hoods were dragging a plough to which they had harnessed themselves. They had twisted long trailing stems of ivy around the ropes and had decorated the plough with any evergreen that they could find. Shouting "Speed the plough! Speed the plough!" they were slowly making their way towards the big open fields on the outskirts of the village.

Behind them came an ox, garlanded with ivy, and gently urged along by a small boy with a long stick sharpened to a point.

"Speed the plough! Speed the plough!" shouted all the village children, hopping and skipping across the village green. As they passed the smithy Rex grew restive and ran forward, giving little whining yelps, and the boys and girls catching sight of Redcap began to point and shout, "Hiya! Hiya! The simpleton."

"Run in front of the procession and turn cartwheels," whispered Nial. "Do your best." And Redcap with Rex at his heels ran as fast as he could ahead of the procession, sprang forward on his hands and began to turn somersaults.

Head over heels he went time and time again while the children clapped and the grown-ups laughed, until at last they all reached the first great open field outside the village. Here, rosy-cheeked and breathless he stood upright and Rex, with his tongue out, sat panting beside him.

"A gift for the little tumbler," shouted someone and before Redcap's astonished eyes several apples and two or three small coins fell at his feet.

Proud that he had earned his keep he promptly stood on his head. But the old man who had teased the blacksmith's wife in the smithy seized him by the middle and set him upright.

"No, no," he said, "the fun's over, toil begins at daybreak on Plough Monday."

And, indeed, the boys were being untied from the plough and the garlands stripped from the ox's neck, while the beast itself, lowing on a discontented note, was harnessed for the task of ploughing the first furrow.

The twelve days of Christmas jollity had ended and with Plough Monday the year's work of tilling the soil had begun again.

XI

ADVENTURE IN A WOOD

In which the minstrels spend a night under the beech trees,
Redcap tries to learn the story of a damsel who lost a husband,
and Fulk falls asleep with dire results

R E D C A P was sorry to bid farewell to the friendly villagers,
but he knew that a minstrel's life was a wandering one,
and besides Red Eric had been in the neighbourhood a
few months earlier and he hoped that each journey would bring
him nearer to the lost uncle. And so, trying not to think too
much of the home from which he had run away, he trudged
along hopefully and did his best to forget that he was nearly
always hungry and that his legs often ached.

But to travel hopefully did not always mean to travel comfortably. Sometimes the going was good, but more often than
not the muddy roads were full of pitfalls, and over the bad
places the minstrels had to throw branches and stones before
Jack Piper could bring the handcart. Indeed, travelling was so

slow that Redcap began to lose all sense of time. He could only
guess how many weeks had passed since he had left home, by
counting the number of new stories or songs that he had learnt,
for Fulk insisted on his being taught something new every other
day. One day he would have a lesson and the next day he had
to repeat what he had learnt. Whether he enjoyed the lesson
or not depended upon his teacher. Nial taught easily and with
laughter, Jack Piper patiently and seldom, but Fulk was quick
tempered and Redcap's ears sometimes tingled from a sudden
cuff and he learned to stand out of reach when he knew that he
might make mistakes.

Weariness and hunger often made learning difficult, for the
minstrels did not always get a good night's rest. In the towns,
they could sleep under cover, going to an inn if they had any
money or paying for board and lodging by a tale and a song.
In a village some kind soul would give them shelter or they
would steal into the church and doze till sunrise, taking care to
be out at dawn as most priests seemed to think that wandering
minstrels were wicked godless men, who would rather sing gay
songs than say their prayers.

But it was travelling between town and village that was the
most uncomfortable, for if they were far from any human
dwelling they had to creep into some wood. Here, they would
make a fire for warmth and for cooking their food, and at night,
they would take it in turns to keep watch lest the fire should
go out or spread and cause damage. One of them always had to
be on guard, for besides the wolves, there were robbers in the
woods, who lay in wait for merchants on their way to buy and
to sell at the fairs, and a robber would as willingly steal from
a poor minstrel as from a rich trader. Fulk Crooked Smile
knew this and so he insisted on a watch being kept, saying that
whereas a fire would scare the wild beasts, it might tempt a
robber to come nearer, and what would they do if Jack Piper's
handcart were stolen?

One night, some weeks after Plough Monday, when they had
been travelling without adventure along the highway, they

crossed some small rough lanes and Fulk turned into a little wood.

"I am famished," he said. "Nial shall cook a meal and we will spend the night here."

"The manor, which those merchants spoke of, cannot be far off," said Nial, remembering that some travellers had told them of preparations that were being made for a wedding in a certain lord's house. "Why not push on?"

"I told you why not," said Fulk shortly. "I am hungry, Jack Piper walks more and more slowly every minute, and it's dark already. I am not going to risk being attacked by dogs or locked up as thieves because we come slipping in after sunset. There will be money to be made at the wedding and we must have a night's rest if we are to be ready for it."

He led the way among the beech trees, pulling aside some brambles so that Jack Piper could push the handcart.

"I am sorry," said Jack, "my lame leg is giving me trouble. I cannot go quickly."

"Think nothing of it at all," answered Nial. "Let you sit and rest now and I will be gathering firewood."

"I'll help," said Redcap.

"You come here," ordered Fulk, "and recite the story that I taught you on the road. I shall want you to tell it at the wedding."

"But Fulk . . ." began Redcap, who had had no time to repeat the tale to Nial, which he always did for fear of forgetting something. "I don't remember. . . ."

Fulk's eyes smouldered and he seized Redcap by his elbows, lifted him up, and plumped him down on a fallen tree. "Begin," he said, "and if you forget you'll keep watch with me over the fire tonight, repeating your lesson instead of taking your rest. And I do not mind how often I make you say it but perfect it shall be before the night's over."

Redcap's shoulders drooped. He liked picking up sticks with Nial, who always had something gay to tell him, but Crooked Smile was in a bad temper and he dared not make any remarks. He had no desire to sit up all night repeating the same story over and over again.

"Will you begin," growled Fulk, and Jack Piper who had sat down beside Redcap whispered without moving his lips:

"Go on son, I will help you."

"I shall tell you," said Redcap hastily, "of a rich lord's daughter who lost her marriage. She — she — she . . ."

Fulk glared and Jack Piper, still without moving his lips, whispered, "Say, 'There was a lord who had three daughters'."

"There was a lord who had three daughters," said Redcap hastily. "One was married and two were not, but a certain Knight desired to wed the second one for he knew that her father would give her land and money. He had never seen the maiden, therefore he came to visit her to discover whether she would be pleasing to him and he to her. And — and . . ."

Redcap stopped, stammered a few words, strained his ears to hear what Jack Piper was whispering and at last gave it up.

"I — I can't remember," he said edging as far away from Fulk as he could. "I'm so hungry. It — it stops me from thinking."

"It's a fine thing, surely, to eat if one's hungry," cried a gay voice, and there was Nial a few yards away with a fire burning and a pot balanced across two stones. He came up to Fulk with a bowl in his hands.

"Wet your whistle, man dear," said he, "and cease troubling the young child's head till we are all satisfied. When a man's inside or a boy's is grumbling out loud, he cannot hear himself speak and that's the truth I'm telling."

"We'll eat but I haven't finished with you, yet," said Fulk to Redcap. "You wanted to be a minstrel and a minstrel you shall be whether you like it now or not."

Nial dipped a horn spoon into the pot and put a can of rabbit soup beside Redcap on the tree trunk.

"Don't burn your tongue," he said. "Here's yours, Jack Piper. When you have finished, lie down on the blanket and I will rub that lame leg for I'm not liking the looks of you, at all."

They drank the soup silently, making it last as long as possible for they were all hungry and there was little enough of it. Redcap had a crust of barley bread which he had saved from breakfast and he dipped it in the soup and offered it to Nial who shook his head, although he was sharing his bowl of soup with Rex.

Except for the gleam from the fire which lighted up their faces and made the trunks of the beeches glow, the wood was now dark and one star could be seen in the patch of sky which showed between the tree tops. It seemed as though night had come suddenly.

"Sleep, all of you," said Fulk when the soup was finished. "I will take the first watch."

"He's forgotten," thought Redcap hopefully and slipped across to the handcart to get the blankets, giving one to Fulk, putting Nial's near to his own, and spreading another for Jack Piper who lay down with difficulty and groaned when he tried to straighten his leg.

"Be easy, now," said Nial. "I will rub you and in the morning the pain will be better. Let Rex lie close to the leg and he'll be keeping it warm."

He knelt and rubbed gently, watching to see whether Jack Piper winced, but the soothing movement of the long fingers seemed to ease the lame man, who quickly dropped off to sleep. Nial looked at him for a moment to make sure that he was no longer in pain, then rolled himself in a blanket between Jack and Redcap, lying as near to the fire as he could.

Redcap had already curled himself up in the blanket but he was not asleep. Under his half closed eyes he was watching Fulk. The crooked smile looked more awry than ever in the firelight and the long knobbly hands were clasped so tightly around his knees that the knuckles were white. He was staring at the fire.

"He's forgotten," thought Redcap again, and snuggled down comfortably, but he had mistaken his man. Fulk was not one who forgot easily, and, try as he would, Redcap could not keep his eyes shut. He felt that Fulk was staring at him, using all the power of his will to make him open them. His eyelids quivered, then opened.

"Get up and come here," said Fulk.

Slowly Redcap unrolled himself from his blanket and stood up, trailing it behind him.

"You may sit," said Fulk. "Keep that blanket round your shoulders. Now begin."

Redcap yawned and Fulk grinned. "The sooner you start the sooner it will be over," said he. "Remember, it will bring us money tomorrow."

Blinking, Redcap racked his brain, but his memory was asleep and he had completely forgotten how the story began.

Fulk looked at him sourly. "You had better wake up," he said, "for you're going to have that story by heart before you lie down again."

As though to encourage him, Rex rose, shook himself and sat beside Redcap.

"Now listen," said Fulk, "and learn as I tell you. There was once a rich lord who had three daughters. The eldest was married and the other two were unwed. But a Knight desired the second one and came to visit the rich lord that he might discover whether this damsel would be pleasing to him and he to her, for, as yet, they had not seen each other.

Redcap stifled a yawn, and Fulk went on:

"When the damsel heard of the Knight's coming, she desired to look beautiful and so she clad herself in a fair silk garment which fitted her closely. But because of the great frost, her face grew pale and blue with cold, for the garment which she wore had no warmth as it was not lined."

Redcap stretched but Fulk took no notice and continued the story.

"When the Knight, who had come to make her his bride, saw her so pale and pinched, he looked at her younger sister. This damsel was fresh and pink as a rose for she was warmly clad with a fur lined robe to keep out the cold. Therefore the

Knight chose her as a bride, saying to his friends, The, youngest shall be mine for she is the fairest and freshest and is more pleasing to me than her pale sister.' And because he chose the younger maid when he had come for the elder, people were much amazed, and especially astonished was the damsel who had expected to marry him. Her foolishness lost her her marriage."

"Her foolishness lost her her marriage," murmured Redcap sleepily.

"Begin at the beginning and go on till you come to the end," said Fulk coldly.

With much prompting and many mistakes, Redcap stumbled through the story, while Fulk lay on his back with his hands behind his head.

"Again," said Fulk, and Redcap tried again.

"Once more," said Fulk sleepily and Redcap, beginning the story again, saw that his eyes were closed.

The boy went on quietly, "And when the Knight who had come to make her his bride . . ."

Fulk was breathing deeply. Very gently Redcap stretched out his foot and touched him with the tip of his toe. He was fast asleep. So was Nial. So was Jack Piper. Rex, too, was stretched out on his side, his nostrils quivering slightly and one ear occasionally twitching.

"There's no one to guard the fire but me," thought Redcap.

This was the first time that he had ever been left to watch and he was sure that Fulk had fallen asleep by mistake but he did not want to wake him lest he should have to tell the story again.

Softly he stood up, took some sticks which Nial had collected and threw them on the fire.

Rex gave a little whimpering bark.

"Lie down," said Nial, turning in his sleep.

Something crackled but it was not in the fire. It seemed to be behind Redcap, among the trees. Rex was sitting up now, growling quietly.

"Be quiet, good dog," said Redcap. "Trust! Keep guard! Guard your master!"

Against his will Rex, who knew that "Keep Guard" was a command, obliging him to stay where he was, sat down near Nial to wait for the order "At Ease" which would release him. He gave some little snuffling whimpers and sleepily Nial flung out an arm and pulled his collar so that the dog's body was close to his own and muttered, "Lie down and stay down."

Redcap shook his finger at him and whispered severely, "Guard your master. Trust."

Resigned, Rex stayed where he was, obediently mounting guard over Nial while the other minstrels slept heavily and Redcap stole away from the fire and peered among the trees.

"I did hear something," thought Redcap. "It wasn't an animal. Animals wouldn't come so near and besides in the fire-light their eyes would gleam like green lights. I have seen them often."

He peered into the darkness, then crept forward with his hand on the hilt of the knife which he always carried in his belt.

He thought he saw something dark, a shadow that did not look like a tree, but he was now too far from the fire to see clearly.

"I know I heard something," he muttered. "I know I did." And he took a few steps forward, breathing quickly.

Suddenly there was a scuffle and something thick and stuffy was pulled over his head, preventing him from shouting, the knife was wrenched from his hand and he was lifted from the ground.

He kicked and struggled with all his might till he felt his wrists and ankles being tied and then he could do nothing. Without being able to see he knew what was happening. He was being carried through the beechwood farther and farther away from his friends.

He struggled wildly but he could not escape. His unknown enemies merely shook him and set him roughly on the ground. Then Redcap felt them push a staff through his belt, lift it to their shoulders and carry him between them, slung on it as though he were a sack of corn.

"I've been stolen," he thought. "The robbers have taken me. Rex, Rex, why didn't you help me?"

Then he remembered that he had left Rex "on guard" and when the dog had whimpered as though he had known that something was wrong, Nial had told him to "lie down and stay down".

Rex was obeying orders and Redcap was being carried away, tied hand and foot, and with a sack over his head.

XII

NO BONES

*In which Redcap is carried away by robbers, tells the story of
the changeling monk and vanishes*

INSIDE the sack, Redcap was breathing heavily. His face
and neck were wet with heat and the swinging of his body,
hanging by his belt from the pole, made him feel sick. He
had no idea of where he was being taken and he could not
guess how much time had passed since the robbers had seized
him. In his distress, he had forgotten about Nial and the other
minstrels and about Red Eric, whom he had set out to find. He
thought only of his own village, the friendly glow of the fire in
his father's forge and his own safe bed of straw in the corner of
the cottage, where he and his parents had always slept so near
to each other.

"I shall never see home again," he thought, "never, never.
What shall I do?" He was almost crying but he kept back his
tears and tried in vain to think of some way of escape.

Suddenly, his misery was interrupted by a bump and he felt
himself lying on his back on the ground while somebody pulled
the pole out of his belt and clumsy hands dragged the sack from
his head.

An ugly unshaven face, with a pair of very small brown eyes
and a black gap where the front teeth should have been, was
bending over him. Two hairy hands under his armpits placed him
upright in a sitting posture and a voice growled, "Sit quiet and
you may be given something to eat. Try to stand or shout and
you'll go back hungry into the sack."

The owner of the voice stood up and moved away. He was a
small man, shorter even than Jack Piper, and his shoulders
were so hunched that he seemed to have no neck.

Redcap, whose wrists and ankles were still tied, followed

him with his eyes and saw that he had joined two other men, who were sitting on the ground near the ashes of a dying fire. They were in a clearing in the wood and Redcap judged that it was almost morning as a grey light was filtering through the trees and the air was chilly as it always was at dawn.

The men, raggedly dressed in torn leather jerkins and long patched hose, had their backs turned, but every now and then they jerked their thumbs in Redcap's direction as though they were talking about him.

Redcap strained his ears and after a time he grew accustomed to the rough voices. One of them, who seemed to be the leader, was talking in low angry tones and the others were protesting and making excuses.

"Why did you bring the boy as well as the cart?" the leader asked. And Redcap, to his horror, saw that Jack Piper's hand-cart was standing near the fire. So they had stolen that, too. What would Fulk and Jack and Nial do without their musical instruments, their masks and their juggling gear?

"The boy was creeping with a knife to our hiding-place," protested the tall one, "and John Gaptooth and I were afraid he would shout, so we pulled the sack over his head."

"And there was a dog," said Gaptooth. "The boy had put it 'on guard' so that it didn't come with him. But we were afraid that, if he were to see us, he would release it and set it on us, so we stifled him with a sack before he could give the beast an order."

"That was well done," said the leader, "but you should have left him tied up somewhere in the wood. He couldn't have shouted with the sack over his head, and now, as soon as the minstrels wake, they'll find him gone and will send the dog to seek him. You are a pair of fools. It's as plain as a post. The dog will pick up the scent and will bring them here."

"That will take longer than you think," said the tallest of the three. "Those men were sleeping like the dead. If we set out as soon as it's light enough, it will be well nigh impossible for them to catch us."

"Humph," snorted the leader. He was now facing Redcap, who saw that he was a middle-aged man of powerful build with a healed wound on the back of his left hand and one of his eyes half closed. "Unless we want a pack of minstrels after us as well as the you-know-who" (here he winked knowingly at the others) "we had better tie up our bundles and be off. So leave the boy here and bring the little cart."

"Not so fast, man, not so fast," said John Gaptooth. "Longshanks and I saw that the lad was a spry one and thought that you could make him fetch and carry. He's nippy and with a little practice he could get away with no end of stuff quicker than any of us."

"Ay, master," said Gaptooth, "these little fellows are quick on their feet and this one's young enough to learn all the tricks of the trade. Teach him to use his eyes and fingers in a market and none of us need ever go hungry."

"Look at his bright eyes," laughed Longshanks, "they would spy what we might miss. At a fair those nimble fingers would make our fortune."

"He's quick on his feet," said Gaptooth. "On the road, while we were belabouring a merchant, he could make off with the goods."

So that was why they had taken him. They were going to train him to be a robber. Redcap grew cold with fear.

The robbers were standing up now. Longshanks was scattering handfuls of wet earth on the ashes of the fire and stamping on it while Gaptooth was stuffing some bundles under the minstrels' goods in the handcart. The leader strolled across to Redcap and began to look him up and down. Suddenly he grinned.

"Well, my little robber-to-be," he said, "how would you like to join us? A robber's life is free and easy! No singing for your supper. Steal well and you'll eat well."

He clapped a hand on Redcap's shoulder, stooped to unfasten the rope that was round his ankles, but left his hands tied.

"Stand," he roared, and Redcap scrambled to his feet.

"Do you see these?" said the Robber Chief, still gripping Redcap's shoulder and pointing to the sack and the pole which were lying on the ground. "Try to run away and back you'll go into the sack. But learn the tricks of our trade and you'll grow rich with us."

Redcap licked his dry lips and was about to speak when the Robber Chief suddenly twisted him around and saw the scarlet patch.

"Hey, you others," he cried, "look at that. Methinks that your spry lad is not so nimble as you say. He has done so much sitting that they had to put a patch in his trunk hose. If that's not the sign of a lazy boy, my name's not Squint."

"You're the man to change his habits, master," said Gaptooth. "Lazy bones are aching bones in your company, eh?" He grinned his toothless grin and rubbed himself as though he had painful memories.

The Robber Chief laughed. He had become good-humoured and he untied Redcap's wrists but kept a large hairy hand on his shoulder.

"Thank'ee lad, for showing us your sign," he said. "We'll cure you of over much sitting." He pushed his face close to Redcap's. "I am your master now," he said, "and you had better obey right smartly. It's well said that in my company lazy bones are aching bones if not broken bones."

He stretched his arm and shook his fist at Redcap, but the boy stood his ground fearlessly. He was thinking quickly.

"I have no bones," he said.

"Eh?" asked the robbers. "No bones? How so?"

"I will show you," answered Redcap.

He twisted out of the Robber Chief's grip, bent his body as Jack Piper had taught him, slowly, very slowly till his head appeared between his legs. He grinned from this position but he was saying to himself, "I must make them waste time, so much time that Nial and Rex will come and save me."

Slowly he unbent and stood upright, turned a quick somersault and lay on his back with his feet over his head, a knee on each side of it. Then he stood up, bowing low.

"No bones," he said. "They put the red patch on me to show that. Goblins have no bones. I'm a goblin, a changeling. Hee hee!" He hoped that the robbers would believe, like many of the country people, that witches sometimes left a hobgoblin in a baby's place, stealing the human baby if the mother had forgotten to hang a knife over the cradle to scare away imps and devils.

He bent over backwards, so that his head appeared between his legs again, made a hideous face and uttered a shrill cackling cry.

"Hee hee hee! They forgot the knife over the cradle and I am a changeling with no bones! Hee, hee, hee!"

Gaptooth and Longshanks looked uncomfortably at one another. Although they were robbers, they were simple men who believed many of the foolish stories that they had heard all their lives.

"He grins like a goblin," said Longshanks nervously.

"Maybe he is an imp of the Evil One," muttered Gaptooth.

But the Robber Chief threw back his head and laughed. With a quick movement he set Redcap on his feet and shook a finger at him.

"So," he said, "you think you can frighten a robber, do you?" He chuckled, still wagging his finger at Redcap. "A changeling, eh? A hobgoblin, with no bones! Whoever heard of such a thing? Shall I prove it, with this stick of mine?" He winked at Redcap, who boldly winked back, and the Robber Chief laughed again. "No goblin could have a face like yours!"

"There was never a changeling that looked as innocent as a monk," he said, throwing his stick into the handcart. "Now, we are moving — all four."

Redcap was alarmed. He was sure that, by this time, the minstrels had awoken and missed him. By hook or by crook he must give Rex time to find him. He gazed up at the Robber Chief.

"FAIR FRIENDS . . ."

"What did you say about changelings and monks?" he asked.

"I said there was never a changeling that looked like a monk," answered the robber.

"But there was," replied Redcap, "really there was. The minstrels told me!" He now saw, to his relief, that Gaptooth was sitting on the ground trying to squeeze a thorn out of his foot. "I'll tell you about it while that one's getting out the thorn," he said.

"I shall walk more quickly if I get my feet comfortable, master," said Gaptooth. "My great toe has been festering these last two days."

"Hurry then," said the Robber Chief. "Tell your tale, my young changeling," and he gave Redcap's curling red hair a friendly pull for the boy's scarlet hood had fallen off and was hanging down his back. "And if it's a bad one, you will learn a thing or two about aching bones. A changeling with no bones, forsooth!"

He guffawed again but Redcap took no notice. His quick ears had caught a distant sound which he thought was a bark, and he quickly began his story, determined to make it last as long as possible.

"Fair friends . . ." he said.

The robbers grinned.

"Gentle sirs . . ."

The Robber Chief bowed.

"Hear now my tale. It befell some two hundred years ago, that a certain monk went down to the cellar of his monastery, followed by a servant. This monk had for many years been the cellarer, whose duty it was to draw the wine from the barrels and bring it to the abbot for the holy sacrament and the altar.

"Judge of his astonishment when he found that one of the barrels which he had left full the day before was now empty and all the wine spilt upon the paving stones of the cellar.

"Groaning aloud, he scolded the servant, thinking that he had closed the peg, which men call the spigot, carelessly.

'Thou idle knave, have greater care next time,' he said, 'but say nothing of this to the abbot, or thou shalt be punished grievously.' He spoke angrily and with threats for he feared that the abbot would rebuke him and put another monk in his place as cellarer.

"After nightfall when the brethren were at rest, he returned alone to the cellar and fastened every spigot securely, carefully locking the door behind him before he, too, lay down.

"But next day, when he went into the cellar, he found another barrel empty and the wine spilt on the floor. Cut to the heart and amazed, he once again ordered his servant to breathe not a word, and that night he made each spigot doubly fast, testing them one by one.

"Anxiously, he lay down to sleep until dawn when he arose and went again to the cellar. He held his lantern high and peered at the third cask. The spigot was drawn and the wine lying in a pool on the floor.

"Stricken with terror and no longer daring to hide what had happened he went to the abbot and told his story. The good abbot called the monks together. 'Brethren,' said he, 'something evil is hiding among us. I bid you, therefore, annoint every spigot with holy water.'

"This was done and the brethren retired to their rest.

"Next morning, at dawn, the cellarer went down as usual. In some fear, he unlocked the door and looked among the winecasks.

"There, clinging to one of the spigots, was a little black creature like a boy. The cellarer seized him and — " (*here Redcap, who had been reciting the story by heart, as Fulk had taught him, invented a line of his own*) "and — and — he wriggled like a *boneless* worm!"

Redcap paused to see the effect of his words.

"The saints save us!" gasped Gaptooth, looking up from his foot.

"Go on," grinned the Robber Chief. "What next?"

"Well," said Redcap, "the — the black creature er — er —

"A LITTLE BLACK CREATURE"

the one who seemed to have no bones, was seized by the cellarer and carried before the abbot.

" 'Lo, lord,' said the cellarer, 'this little boy whom thou seest is he who has brought upon us the loss of our wine. I found him clinging to one of the spigots.'

"The abbot looked at the creature. 'The child is wondrous small,' he said. 'Let a monk's frock be made for him and let him join the schoolboys in our cloister.'

"And so, night and day, the little creature stayed in his monk's garb with the schoolboys whom the good brothers were teaching. But he learnt nothing, spoke to no one and took neither food nor drink. And whenever the others lay at rest, he would sit upon his bed, weeping and sobbing without end.

"It happened, one day, that another abbot came to stay at the monastery. As he sat with the older monks, the schoolboys passed before him, and the little child with tearful eyes stretched out his hands to him.

"The abbot saw him and said, 'This boy is strangely small. I marvel that you keep so young a child among your scholars.'

" 'My lord,' they answered, 'this boy is not what you think. He is able to do much damage and must be closely watched.'

"Then they told what had happened and the good abbot, sore afraid, groaned aloud. 'As soon as you may, cast him forth, for he is some devil or goblin in human form. He has done you no further harm because, in the holy robe of a monk, he has been obliged to pass, every day, the relics of the saints which you have in your chapel. Bring him here.'

"The boy was brought into his presence.

" 'Take off his monkish frock,' said the abbot, making the sign of the cross.

"The child was seized and stripped, and," cried Redcap leaping to his feet, "he vanished like smoke from between their hands. Like this!"

Before the robbers had time to stop him Redcap was off!

He heard them stumbling after him, cursing, and he doubled back like a hare, sprinting in and out among the trees, dodging

this way and that, now running, now crouching in the undergrowth and running again, stopping to listen, then darting off
in another direction.

He seemed to have been running for a long time and thought
that he had escaped for he could no longer hear the muttered
curses nor the stumbling footsteps. Nevertheless he dared not
stop moving and began to creep as quietly as he could through
the thickest part of the wood. A sudden cracking of sticks under-
foot startled him. A hand fell on his shoulder.

"Nial," he screamed, struggling and kicking, "Nial, save me."

"Be easy now," said a well known voice. "Isn't that just
what I'm doing?"

An arm was around him and kind merry eyes looking down at
him and Rex, dear old Rex, was jumping up and licking his
chin. Redcap was so relieved that he burst into tears, great dry
sobs that came in gulps and hiccoughs. For a minute Nial said
nothing, then, as Redcap's sobs ceased, he pulled off his own
hood and began to dry the boy's face.

"Let your heart rest, now," he said. "You are with your
friends and there is not one that would care to see you washed
away, before their eyes, with your own tears."

"I — I — was stolen and — and tied up in a sack," blubbered
Redcap.

"Were you, now?" said Nial. "And it's the wise child you
were to escape. Hey, Fulk, Jack, we are ready for a meal."

"I was stolen in the night," said Redcap, still wiping his
eyes as Nial took him to the other two. "The robbers were
going to teach me to be a thief. They said so."

"Well," said Fulk with his crooked smile as friendly as
Redcap had ever seen it, "if you took as long to learn their
tricks as you did to learn that story of the damsel who lost her
husband, they are well rid of a bad bargain. Drink a sup of this,
now, and keep quiet."

XIII

TO THE STOCKS! TO THE STOCKS!

*In which Rex follows a scent, Redcap disobeys Fulk and every-
one gets into trouble*

JOG, bump, jog, bump. . . .

Where was he? Had the robbers captured him again and slung him on their pole? Sleepily, Redcap knew that he was not on his own feet and yet he was moving. He was being carried. With a loud cry, "Let me go," he hit out in every direction.

"Ouch," said a rueful voice. "Will you destroy me entirely? Stand on your own two feet, then! Slip off, now."

And there he was, sliding down from Nial's long back, while the other two minstrels laughed at the Irishman, who was rubbing his head.

"And the next time," said Nial, "you will be kind enough to *walk in your sleep* instead of using me as your horse."

"I didn't know you were carrying me," said Redcap. "I was dreaming that I was back in the robbers' sack. I am sorry."

"Think nothing of it," said Nial handsomely. "You fell asleep while we were deciding what to do, and as we had no mind to waste time, I took you on my back. And I have walked a mile with you for small thanks."

Redcap slipped his hand through Nial's arm.

"I hit the robbers as hard as that when they were tying my hands and feet. Did it hurt?" he asked hopefully.

"Faith," laughed Nial, "you nearly took the head off my neck. A man of your size would scare the heart out of any robber."

Redcap punched him. "Well, I did frighten them," he said, and explained how he had pretended to be a hobgoblin. "And then," he continued, "I wanted to give you time to find me so I told Fulk's story of the changeling monk."

"Good boy," said Fulk. "We'll make a minstrel of you yet. A real minstrel always tells a tale to suit the moment. How did you escape?"

Redcap laughed. He felt safe now, and at his ease. "The changeling monk, 'vanished from between their hands like smoke'," said he, stretching himself to his full height and slapping his chest.

"The handcart and all our gear seem to have vanished after the same fashion," said Fulk and the crooked smile had a rueful twist. "Do you know which way those wretches were going? By his manner of dodging about, Rex seems to be following the scent of your smoke and not theirs."

Redcap frowned for a minute, trying to remember what the robbers had been talking about while he was sitting with his wrists and ankles tied. They had discussed what they would do with him, but later, they had mentioned something about a wedding at a Manor not far away.

"I think," he said, "they may be going to a wedding. Perhaps it was the same one that *we* are going to. They spoke of some cloth that they wanted to sell."

"Stolen goods, I'll warrant," said Jack Piper. "Well, Fulk, if we are to find our handcart we had best hurry. There is many a man who would be glad of our pipes and tabors at a wedding."

"But the question is which way did they go?" grumbled Fulk. "I know that the village lies to the west but they may have left the cart somewhere and just taken our things. We must trace the cart."

"Wuff," barked Rex, who was now out of sight. "Wuff, wuff."

Redcap ran in the direction of the sound and found that he was once again in the clearing to which the robbers had brought him. He saw some charred sticks and the ashes of the fire over which Longshanks had scattered wet earth and he recognized the place under the beech tree where Gaptooth had flung him and had pulled the sack off his head.

He beckoned.

"This is the place," he cried. "Fulk, Nial, Jack! Look! Here are the tracks of the handcart." And, sure enough, in the wet moss, there were the marks of two wheels and the footprints of three men.

"'Tis a fine discovery you have made, good dog," said Nial, patting Rex, "and now we have nothing to do at all but follow. How is the leg, Jack Piper?"

"The pain is not bad," answered Jack. "If I cannot keep pace with you, I'll fall behind and follow in your tracks. Maybe 'twould be wiser if we were not all together."

Fulk looked at him. "We shall not leave you alone," he growled. His tone was cold but Redcap caught a fleeting look of kindness in his eyes and said to himself, "I like Fulk. I like him deep down. He only gets angry on the top." And with this comforting thought he fell into step with Fulk and left Nial to give his arm to Jack Piper.

The tracks among the trees were not hard to follow and after walking for about half an hour the minstrels came to the edge of the wood where a rough road stretched towards a distant village.

"Rest," said Fulk shortly and Nial helped Jack Piper to lower himself slowly to the ground.

"There are dozens of footprints here," said Redcap, "and the tracks of four carts. They go to *and* from the village. We shall never find the robbers."

"Use your wits," snapped Fulk. "If the men are going to sell the cloth, they will go to the village and not away from it. We make for that village as soon as Jack Piper feels able to walk again."

Nial was using his knife to hack away some twigs from a stout stick which he had picked up. Without raising his eyes, "We shall have to prove that the cart is our own," said he, "and I'm thinking that we may have some trouble."

Fulk rounded on him furiously. "How many more difficulties are to be put in my way?" he shouted. "Keep your evil prophecies to yourself, Irish Nial. And as for you, Redcap, if you say another word without my leave, you'll be sorry!"

"Wheesht, man dear," said Nial in shocked tones, "you are speaking to one who frightened three great robbers."

Fulk burst out laughing.

PART OF THE MINSTRELS' GEAR

His sudden amusement put him back into a good humour and he sat for a moment, deep in thought, with the corners of his crooked mouth still twitching as though the joke lingered.

At last he broke the silence.

"Do you each know what was in the handcart?" he asked. "In order to prove that it belongs to us, we must be able to say what it contains."

"My pipe, a viol and bow, three catapults, four wooden balls painted red, two masks, a small tabor and a pair of polished sticks to tap it," said Jack Piper. "We have the blankets and the cooking pot here with us."

"There was a coil of rope and a sack, too," said Fulk, "and the little whip which we give to Rex when he has to threaten the simpleton. Oh — my string of bells and the donkey's head."

"There's nothing more but a horn," said Jack Piper.

"Is everyone sure of these things?" asked Fulk. "Redcap, what's in the cart?"

Redcap answered glibly, counting on his fingers.

"Let's go," he said, jumping to his feet.

"Are you master here, or am I?" asked Fulk pulling him down again. "These are my orders. Nial and Jack keep closely together and talk with the people, making friends. If you see anyone with something which you know is ours, try to find out how he came by it. But *keep friendly*. I want no trouble."

"We'll ask for none," answered Nial.

"And what shall I do?" asked Redcap.

"Keep your tongue quiet and your eyes open," replied Nial. "And if you see the three robbers, tell me. Remember, you're to stay close beside me for I'm tired of losing you."

Redcap stood up again and ran along beside Fulk, who kept his eyes on the ground, trying to follow what he thought were the ruts made by the handcart, but the road was bad and many people had passed up and down with horses and cattle so that nothing was clear.

On the outskirts of the village a group of men and women were fixing a garland of evergreens to the church porch. As the minstrels passed by, they turned to look at them and one called, "Good-day to you, strangers."

"God keep you," answered Nial, smiling. "I see fresh rushes and dried rosemary on the ground. You prepare for a wedding, surely. Or is it over?"

"Tomorrow Sir Henry's son will wed the prettiest little maid that ever set foot in a church porch," said one of the women. "Her father and her mother came horseback with as big a following of servants as ever I did see, and the bride with her damsels was carried in a litter. After hearing Mass inside this very church she'll be wed in the porch tomorrow, bless her sweet face."

"Have you strangers brought gifts from her kinsfolk?" asked another.

"We bring tales and songs," said Nial, "for we are minstrels."

165

"Then you will be right welcome in the big hall and on the green," said another, "for the whole village makes merry. 'Tis not every day that the lord of the manor's son takes a wife." She smiled broadly. "Tales of weddings will bring you listeners and gifts. Is the little fellow one of your company, the boy with the scarlet hood?"

"He's our juggler," said Fulk.

"Bless him," said the woman. "I warrant he will gather in the pennies tonight and tomorrow." She laughed. "He wastes no time," she said. "See, he has reached the green while you older ones lag behind."

Indeed Redcap, forgetting that Fulk had told him to keep close, had darted off to see what was happening on the village green, where his quick eyes had observed a crowd gradually getting larger. As he drew near he became aware that an argument had arisen and he heard angry voices, two of which seemed faintly familiar. He listened for a minute, feeling quite sure that he had heard them before.

"We did not steal it," said one.

"If you will but give us time to speak," growled another, "all will be made clear."

But a protesting voice went on, saying, "Pay no heed to the rascals. They are thieves. The cloth is mine. It has my mark on it."

"Good masters — " began the first voice, stopping abruptly to shout, "Seize the thief. There he is."

And Redcap, who had pushed his way through the crowd, found himself grabbed by a pair of hairy hands and shaken roughly while a toothless face flashed back and forth before his dizzy eyes.

"Ah, you little knave, you thieving rascal," cried Gaptooth, "you ran away (*shake, shake, shake*) when we were bringing you here (*shake, shake, shake*) to make you give back what you had stolen."

The hands held him so tightly that he winced.

"But — but," he began.

"Down on your knees and ask pardon," said Gaptooth, pushing Redcap on to his knees but still holding him in a grip of iron.

"Good friends," said Squint, "Master Gaptooth and I found the boy in the woods pushing the little cart with the stolen cloth hidden under other things. We talked with him like fathers and when he promised to be of good behaviour and restore what he had taken, we knelt with him to pray that he would be for-given, and," here he too grasped Redcap's shoulder, looked at him maliciously and added slowly, *"he vanished from between our hands like smoke."*

"For shame, the ill-conditioned little rogue," cried a man with a bundle of straw on his back, "running away with his sins heavy on him. Not even waiting to pray."

"Put the young rascal in the stocks," shouted another, shaking his fist.

"Sirs — please — sirs," stammered Redcap, completely taken aback by the lies which the robbers had told and by this time thoroughly frightened of what the people were going to do and of what Fulk would say when he found him in this trouble. "Sirs," he whispered, "I . . ."

"Peace, boy!" said an elderly man, more neatly dressed than the others and with a commanding air. "As steward of this Manor, I demand silence. Now strangers, finish your story, and cease shaking and cuffing the boy. I myself will order his punishment if need be."

Squint and Gaptooth continued to hold Redcap who was still on his knees but they stopped treating him roughly and he was able to look at the faces around him, none of which seemed friendly. He saw Squint and Gaptooth give a quick glance at the edge of the crowd, and with the corner of his own eye he caught a glimpse of Longshanks slipping away while the people's backs were turned.

Where were the minstrels and Rex? If Nial were here, he would get him out of this difficulty, somehow.

"Good master," said Squint to the steward, "when the boy

disappeared, we hunted for him high and low but could not find him. Then, because we had heard that there was a wedding here, we thought that perhaps the goods had been stolen from some merchant or pedlar, who was coming to show his wares to the groom or the bride. And so, good master, we came at once to hand over what did not belong to us."

A small man with a bandage round his head, hobbled closer with the help of two sticks.

"Sir," said he, "as I told you just now, for all I am a pedlar I am honest. Nothing in the little cart is mine save those two lengths of scarlet cloth which were stolen from me well nigh two weeks ago. Some ruffians sprang upon me from behind, pulling a sack over my head and belabouring me with clubs. They left me as a dead man in the ditch. Even now I can scarcely walk. Good master, I do not know who fell upon me, but they were more than one." He looked at Redcap, "Sir, would a child like this have the strength?"

In a flash Redcap remembered what the robbers had said in the wood. "We do not want a pack of minstrels after us as well as the 'you know whom'." This pedlar must be the "you know whom".

Once again he tried to speak but his throat was dry and Gaptooth, seeing him draw breath, turned quickly to the steward. "Gentle sir," said he, his speech whistling through his lips because of his missing teeth, "you saw how the lad struggled when I caught him. Even now, two of us have to hold him or he would be away in a trice. When we found him with the goods he confessed that he had stolen them."

"Ay, master steward," broke in Squint, "and we heard his words with much pain for the lad's father is our dearest friend."

Redcap gasped.

"Yes, yes," said Gaptooth, shaking his head, "the man's heart will break when he hears this tale."

"Sir," begged Squint, "punish the boy as you think fit, but afterwards, I pray you, hand him over to us. We will take good

care that he does not slip through our fingers and we will
deliver him to his sorrowful father."

"No," cried Redcap. "No, no!" He wanted to say that the
robbers did not know his father, that they would keep him and
force him to steal for them but the grip on his shoulder
tightened.

"The lad's afraid," said one of the people in the crowd.

"Small wonder," said another, "he knows what is in store for
him, and may it help him to mend his manners, say I."

Redcap was almost in despair. He knew that somehow or
other he must find Nial and he gave a sudden twist and broke
away but the crowd closed in on him and once again Squint
and Gaptooth forced him to his knees. Then each of them took
a bundle of the red cloth and held it before him.

"You were told to ask pardon for your misdeeds," growled
Squint. "Look at this cloth. Ha, he reddens for shame. Well
you know it, my little rascal. Confess that you stole . . ."

"And what, may I ask, is happening here?"

Fulk's tones, cold and angry as they were, brought comfort
to Redcap's heart. He looked about him hastily and saw Nial
and Jack Piper on the outskirts of the crowd.

"Why are these two knaves mishandling my boy?"

"Masters, good folk, did you hear what he said?" cried
Squint. "He called two worthy men 'knaves' and he says this
child is his son. He lies!"

"Is this child your son?" asked the steward, looking Fulk
up and down.

"No," answered Fulk.

"What did I say?" grinned Squint. "He lied!"

The people began to stare at Fulk and to mutter angrily.

"I called him 'my boy'," said Fulk, "because he is of my
company." He made a sign with his chin and Nial, with Rex
under his arm, and Jack Piper at his side, moved a few paces
forward.

"So you steal children, too, do you?" snarled Gaptooth.

"You are speaking to an honest minstrel," said Fulk. His

crooked mouth had an ugly twist as he pointed at the two robbers, "but I am speaking to a pair of thieves."

"Thieves!" screamed Squint, growing red in the face and loosening his grip on Redcap's shoulder so as to shake his fist at Fulk. "Thieves, he calls us. Did you hear him, good people?"

"Who stole that?" asked Fulk pointing to Jack Piper's handcart.

"They did," cried Redcap, finding his voice, at last, and pointing at the robbers.

"He did," shouted the robbers, seizing Redcap once again.

"That one did," cried some of the people pointing at Fulk.

"No, he!" "No, they!" "No, the boy!" The villagers were all shouting at once.

"Silence! Silence!" cried the steward, speaking twice before he could make himself heard. "I must bid you all keep silence," he said, "while this stranger answers my questions. Master minstrel, I understand that this boy is of your company."

"That is so," answered Fulk.

"This handcart?"

"It is ours."

"So-ho," grinned Gaptooth. "What did we tell you, Master Steward? These men are robbers. This miserable pedlar's cloth was found in their handcart under their minstrel's gear."

"That is true," said the steward.

"And finding a willing thief in the son of a good father, they coaxed this boy away to push their cart and to steal with them," sneered Squint.

"Ah, the villains!" "The rogues!" cried the people. "To the stocks with them!" "To the stocks!" "To the stocks!"

"Silence," shouted the steward, again. "Good people, I am not satisfied that anything has been proved against these minstrels, but, because I cannot risk having rogues at large during tomorrow's wedding, I will put them in the stocks for safe keeping."

"To the stocks!" shouted the people, beginning to pummel the minstrels, who, determined to have as little trouble as possible, defended themselves as best they could without returning the blows.

"Robbers!" "Dirty Vagabonds!" "Rogues!" yelled the people, but the steward laid about him with a stick, shouting, "Peace! Peace! I say. Will you listen to me."

Grumbling the people faced him.

"These men," he said, "are to be put in the stocks for safe keeping until tomorrow. I forbid you to mishandle them until we know that they are guilty. There is to be no mud-slinging or stone-throwing. Now take them away peaceably."

Although he was relieved that the people were forbidden to ill-treat them, Redcap's heart sank. Were they to be in the stocks all night and all next day till after the wedding? Would they have no chance of singing at the feast or of telling tales? Surely Fulk or Nial could explain.

But there was no time for explanation. Crowding around them and shouting, "To the stocks! To the stocks!" the villagers hustled Redcap and the minstrels to the other side of the green.

Fulk strode along furiously, his crooked mouth turned down at the corners, his eyes darting lightning glances of anger at Redcap, whom he considered the cause of all the trouble. Nial moved quickly and gracefully, holding Rex firmly under his arm, for the dog's teeth were bared and he was snapping at anyone who touched his master. Jack Piper limped, his body tired and his eyes anxious, knowing well that the stocks would be painful for his lame legs. Redcap tried to help the lame man but had much ado to keep on his own feet as the people jostled him, now pulling, now pushing, till they reached the stocks.

"This boy," said the man with the bundle of straw, "is too small for the stocks. He will easily wriggle his feet out of the holes. And then who knows what thievery he will be doing to our damage?"

"Tie him into his so-called master's lap," said another.

"Since the big man trained him as a robber let him bear the weight of his evil deeds."

And so, when the three minstrels had been firmly set in the stocks, Redcap was tied to Fulk so that his face was only twelve inches away from Crooked Smile's and he could not even see Nial laughing at his predicament.

But he did see something that no one else had noticed. Gaptooth and Squint had disappeared.

XIV

ENTER GREEN STRANGER

*In which Redcap and his friends are saved first by a priest and
then by a strange minstrel who tells the story of French Roland*

"THIS," growled Fulk to Redcap, who was tied into his
lap, facing him, "is your fault. You disobeyed me."
"I forgot," whispered Redcap. "Oh Fulk, will they
leave us here all night? We have done no harm."

"If any harm has been done, it's by you," said Fulk, shortly.
"Where are all the people? Can you see?"

His back was to the village green and Redcap was facing it.

"They went away," replied the boy.

"They would have no fun, at all," said Nial, "if they were
not allowed to pelt us."

Jack Piper sighed. "We shall be pelted and mocked more
than we shall like, after the wedding, for how can we prove
that we did not steal that cloth?"

"Bad luck to it," groaned Nial. "My body is aching with
cramp already, and 'tis scarcely high noon!"

"You are fortunate," snapped Fulk, "that you haven't an
unwelcome burden tied to your knees."

He stared down at Redcap, who tried to lower his eyes, but
Fulk always had the power of forcing him to look up whether
he wanted to or not, and, with trembling lip, he returned the
gaze.

"I — I — I'm too heavy for you?" he murmured apologeti-
cally.

"Ha!" jeered Fulk and his crooked smile took a scornful
twist.

"I wish I . . . " began Redcap, "oh — look!"

A tall figure, clad from top to toe in dark green with a close-
fitting hood, a short dagger in his belt and a reed pipe hanging

from a thin leather strap over one shoulder and under the other, was coming towards him, on horseback.

"What is this? What do I see?" cried a merry voice. "Fellow minstrels, men of my own brotherhood, shamed before my very eyes!"

"Faith," said Nial, "if you can pull us out of the shame without breaking our legs, the good Saints will reward you, otherwise we are likely to perish with cramps before the morning."

The newcomer laughed, leapt off his horse and threw the reins over its head.

"The stocks are locked," he said, "but as there is no one to stay my hand, I will relieve the big man of his burden," and he skilfully untied the knots which bound Redcap to Fulk, and, lifting the boy to his feet, dusted him down and turned again to the other three.

"I came to sing at a wedding," said he. "Am I likely to be put into the stocks, too? Some folk give minstrels short shrift. What has been your trouble, friends?"

His gay smile and kind voice told Redcap at once that they had found someone who would try to help them.

"It was my fault," he said, hanging his head but looking at the stranger through his eyelashes.

"The boy," said Nial, "is not one for keeping out of trouble. Would you care to listen to his tale, for ourselves have been so busy chasing him that we have not had time to understand anything at all."

"Yes," said Fulk, "and I may tell you that this is the last time we shall chase him for if we leave this village with whole skins, he will not come with us."

Redcap looked anxiously from one face to another but took courage when he saw Nial wink and the strange minstrel shake his head in mock solemnity.

"Well," said the latter, "let me hear the story. And if it is well told, maybe I will take the lad myself for I am in need of a comrade who will help me to tell good tales."

"You are welcome to him," sneered Fulk, and Nial, catching Redcap's eye, winked again.

"Tell the tale from the time that the robbers captured you until we were all put in the stocks," he said, smiling encouragement, "and have no fear at all, for I am not the man to give up my friends."

"Nor I," said Jack Piper.

Fulk made no remark and the stranger put his hand on Redcap's shoulder, turning him away from the crooked smile towards his own laughing face.

"What have you to say for yourself?" he asked.

"I know it was my fault in the end," answered Redcap, "but not at the beginning," and he told of his adventure in the wood, of how he had escaped, and how, through his own disobedience, he had been caught again. "And sir," he went on, "the robbers took our handcart and put the stolen cloth into it. I saw them."

"That," said Jack Piper, "is why we are in the stocks. The people of this village think that because the cloth was in our cart among our gear, we have stolen it."

"Hm," said the stranger, "that is unfortunate. It would be yet more unfortunate if the cloth was of the same hue as the boy's hood."

"Nay," said a voice, "'twas a shade or more darker. The cloth was dyed by my granddam, who sewed three crosses on the edge as my mark, so I know it well."

It was the pedlar. While Redcap had been telling his story, he had come hobbling towards them on his sticks.

"I ask your pardon for joining your company when you are in distress but I saw another stranger and thought that perhaps two heads were better than one. And I have a mind to help you."

"Glory be to heaven," said Nial. "Isn't he the grand man, and the people after telling him that we were thieves."

"I do not believe it," said the pedlar, sitting on the stocks. "This boy could not have given me the blows which have left me crippled. Come here, boy. Now look in my face and speak the truth. Did the big man here with the crooked smile waylay me, leaving me for dead, and make you hide my cloth in the little handcart?"

"Of course not," said Redcap indignantly. "That's Fulk. He's a very good man."

"It's a grand report you are getting, Fulk," laughed Nial, but Fulk only shrugged his shoulders.

"The boy brought us into this trouble, he may well try to pluck us out of it," he said.

"He's an honest lad," said the pedlar. "I tramp with so many who are dishonest that I know good men when I see them. I could swear, by all the saints, that my cloth was stolen by that squinting rogue and his toothless mate. I knew their voices, again, as soon as I heard them. But I think there were three who fell upon me."

"There was Longshanks," said Redcap. "He's their friend. I saw him slip away before Fulk came up to stop the other two from shaking me."

"The more fool I," said Fulk. "It's time someone shook some sense into you, for more witless behaviour than yours I never hope to see! If we meet them again I shall not prevent them from finishing what they began."

"I wonder," said the green clad stranger, softly, "whether any of us *will* see them again. Where are they now?"

"Spinning more tales for the villagers to entangle these good minstrels," said the pedlar.

"Oh no," Redcap shook his head. "They went away. I think they must be with Longshanks by now. When the people were pushing and pulling us to the stocks, I saw them hurrying away."

"That," said the stranger, "is going to help us. Now where is the handcart that you speak of?"

"We left it on the green," said Redcap, "but while that angry man was tying me into Fulk's lap, I saw the steward fetch it. He wheeled it away."

176

"For safe-keeping, I'll warrant," said the stranger. "And now if I do not get into too much trouble for untying this boy, I think I may be able to move the people's anger and coax them to call for songs which will put them into a good humour."

The pedlar shook his head.

"The task will not be easy," he said. "Listen."

From both ends of the village, people were coming towards the stocks and they sounded like a swarm of angry bees. When they saw that the boy had been released, they began to shout and to run. Redcap stiffened, trying to appear unafraid but he felt the backs of his knees shaking and the stranger linked an arm in his and looked at him, speaking in low tones:

"Now you and I will have to save the others, and we shall be a match for these angry people if neither of us shows fear and each of us speaks quietly. Did you know that you should never raise your voice in the face of anger? If you do, you are apt to grow angry, yourself. And two angry people can never bring a quarrel to an end."

He smiled down at Redcap and Nial whispered from behind, "'Tis yourselves will win the day. I am not doubting at all."

The stranger, still smiling and keeping one arm in Redcap's, waved to the people with the other.

They surged towards him, screaming, "How dare you loose the boy!" "Who told you to set the young rogue free?"

The stranger put up his hand as though to command silence and the crowd, perhaps because they were astonished at his coolness, ceased shouting and contented themselves with muttering.

"God save you, friends," said the stranger and Redcap whispered, "Ay, God save you."

"Pray for your own safety, first," shouted a man, rudely. "By whose order did you set that boy free? He is one of a company of rogues and vagabonds who deserved to be stoned. Down with the stranger! Drive him out," he shouted, facing the people.

"Ay! Down with him!" "Drive out the stranger." "Chase him from the village," screamed the crowd.

Things were beginning to look ugly when something completely unexpected happened.

"Good people," said a mild little voice. "May it please you to move aside?"

With scarcely a second's pause a path appeared in the middle of the crowd, for the mild voice, though quiet, seemed to carry a command, and the people had divided without being aware of what they were doing.

Along this path, stumbling a little, for the cord of his long black gown had come untied and was trailing along the ground, an old priest advanced with an earthenware jug in one hand and half a loaf of black bread in the other.

"May I have a quiet moment," he said, "to ask a blessing before these strangers have a meal? They are, I think, hungry."

"Father," protested the man who had stirred the crowd to anger, "these are thieving minstrels in the stocks for robbery! And you will feed them!"

"Yes," said the little priest who was hardly a head taller than Redcap. "I always remember that our Lord was kind to the thief who was crucified next to Him." And without looking at the people he gave Jack Piper, who was now stiff with pain, a drink from the jug.

'Divide the bread among them, my son," he said. The leader of the crowd obeyed with a bad grace, muttering:

"Honest folk like us called upon to feed a set of rascals who steal cloth."

"My son," said the old priest as he gave each minstrel a drink from the jug, "how should I know who has or who has not stolen this cloth?"

"At least you know that none of us has taken it!" blustered the man.

"Truly, father," cried a black-eyed woman indignantly, "you must know that each one of *us* is innocent. We could swear it by all that is sacred."

"I am so glad," said the priest, still bending over the minstrels and easing them into more comfortable positions. "Will somebody help me to lift this man so that he is less cramped?"

The leader began to grumble again and at last blurted out, "Father, you are asking us to wait upon robbers! You expect too much of us. We — we should not be asked to do things like this. We are not . . ."

"Yes?" said the priest. "You are not . . . ?"

"We are not saints, returning good for evil all the days of our life. We are not — well we are not even good men!"

"No," said the priest, mildly, "neither am I a good man and I am always a little sorry about it. But I thought you were angry because these minstrels had shown themselves to be — er — not good men."

At this the crowd began to murmur.

"They are worse rogues than we are."

"They are thieves and vagabonds."

"They are godless robbers who stole from this poor pedlar."

"They should be stoned as ne'er-do-wells."

"Ay, father," cried the leader, "they are in the stocks and Master Greysleeves, the steward, has forbidden us even to pelt them, though they well deserve it."

"Oh, indeed," said the priest softly. "Then for once I must override the steward. Stone them and pelt them, good people, as often as you like," and he bent and picked up a jagged piece of flint.

Redcap's jaw dropped and he stood rooted to the spot. The people, too, looked astonished but several of them stooped to the ground and picked up clods of earth. Their eyes gleamed and they had their arms poised ready to throw, but the old priest went on speaking, still gently as though he were talking to himself.

"Yes, yes," he murmured, musing. "Perhaps we may pelt the rogues but," here he muttered some Latin words, adding, "someone once said, 'Let him who is without sin among you, cast the first stone'." He dropped his flint, wiped the sweat from Jack Piper's face with his old gown and walked slowly away with the cord still trailing, and his bare feet stumbling when one end of it swung in front of him. The green-clad stranger watched him quietly, then turned to the villagers.

"Thank you, good people," he said, "and when I say good people, I mean it. You have sworn to the priest that *you* did not steal the cloth and since you believe that these minstrels stole it, you have shown much forbearance. You might so easily have hurt us."

"We have no desire to hurt anyone," grumbled the leader, looking a little shame-faced. "But why did you untie the boy? He might have run away and brought a gang of robbers to do us violence."

"Friends," said the stranger, "I am a minstrel and these men are of my brotherhood. I untied the boy because he and the big man to whom he was bound were in pain, and I cannot let my brothers suffer. Look at the boy," he continued, "do you, in all honesty, think that he would run away. Ask him."

Redcap took a few steps forward, away from the protecting arm of the stranger. He remembered that he must speak quietly, for the people, although they had not thrown their stones, had not yet overcome their anger.

"I will not run away," he said. "You see, I cannot leave the minstrels. They are my friends."

"Well," said a stout woman with a rosy face, "the little fellow is no coward but these grown men should be ashamed of teaching him to rob."

"They have never taught me to rob," said Redcap. "Gaptooth and Squint put the cloth into our handcart, which they had stolen."

"A likely tale, that!" sneered the leader. "If these men are so innocent, let them prove it, say I." He faced the villagers, looking quickly from one to another. "Friends, what of the *ordeal*? Let them show that they have done no wrong by passing the ordeal by heat as our ancestors did."

Redcap felt himself grow pale. He knew that in the old days, if a person was thought to have done wrong, he was made to grasp a piece of red-hot iron. His hand was then bound in a cloth, and when, after a few days, the cloth was removed and his hand had healed he was said to be innocent. If the hand did not heal he was declared guilty.

What would happen to him and to his friends? Nial and Fulk would, doubtless, know some trick or other which would save their skins. But what of himself? And what of poor Jack whose hands were already trembling so much that he could not even tilt the jug so as to quench his thirst? Although Jack was innocent, his hands would be blistered. Even when he was pricked by a thorn, the place festered. What was to be done?

Redcap looked around and saw that the people were eager to put them all to the test.

They were talking loudly, one against the other, each trying to be heard above his neighbour.

"Yes, yes! The ordeal by heat," cried one.

"Quick, friends," shouted another, "call the blacksmith to prepare the iron."

"Hurry before the priest and the steward return to take the rogues' part," urged a third.

"Nay, nay," said the rosy faced woman, who had spoken kindly of Redcap. "We must not be hasty. The steward and the priest must be here to see that justice be done."

"Hold your peace," cried a woman with scowling brow and small black eyes. "Who are you to be telling us what to do? If these men be not rogues, why should they be afraid to prove it? I call for the ordeal."

"Friends . . ." began the stranger.

"Who is this man?" asked someone.

"Ay," said the black-eyed woman. "Who may you be?"

The minstrel bowed. "I have sometimes been called 'the Green Stranger'," he said. "Some men like me. Some do not, but all are eager to hear my tales."

"The ordeal is no subject for a tale," said the black-eyed woman. "It's serious and we cannot waste time."

"I understand," said Green Stranger quietly, "but there are those here who are wise and kindly folk, and merry too. They would like my story." He pointed at random to people in the crowd. "You would, my friend, and you, sir, and you, pretty mistress."

"Let him tell it," said the girl who had been called "pretty mistress" and others, flattered to be thought wise and kindly by a man who looked wise himself, agreed.

"See that you be short, then," said the man who seemed to be the leader.

Green Stranger bowed, stepped back a few paces and sat on the top of the stocks with Fulk lying on his back on one side of him and Nial on the other. Redcap knelt by Jack Piper and gave him another sip of water, while the pedlar looked anxiously, from his one uncovered eye, across the village green, troubled that the good old priest had left and longing for the steward to appear and take control of the people, who seemed intent on punishing the minstrels.

"Fair friends," began Green Stranger, "because you have a company of minstrels before you, I will tell you the story of the minstrel and the ordeal."

The pedlar made a quick sign to him and Fulk frowned. Why could he not let the villagers forget about the ordeal and tell them something to put them in a good humour? But Green Stranger did not seem to notice. He settled himself more comfortably on the top of the stocks, crossed one knee over the other and put his reed pipe to his lips. In an instant music so delicate was wafted on the air that Redcap's heart seemed to stand still and he was afraid to draw a breath lest the magic of the moment should slip away. The people, too, fell under the spell and were charmed to silence so that when Green Stranger took his pipe from his lips, they were ready to hear his tale.

"Fair friends," he said, "in the land of France there lived not long ago a minstrel, whose name was Roland. Gay he was and full of diverting tricks which brought laughter to all who heard and saw him. But as we grow old with time so did Messire Roland and he lost favour. Yet still he repaired to all the feasts and when he came to a wedding, the women would smile and say, 'Hold out thy bowl, Roland' and he would hold it out and they would give him alms

"Now it happened one day that a silver cup was lost and the men of the household, where he was visiting, called him and said, 'Though art a thief! There is none here who would desire a silver cup for all are rich. Thou alone art poor. Therefore we know that thou hast stolen the cup.'

" 'Friends,' said Roland, 'by my troth, you accuse me falsely.'

" 'Then,' cried the others, 'thou must prove thine innocence by the ordeal of hot iron.'

" 'Yea,' said Roland, 'let the iron be heated.'

"The iron was heated and the men of the household called the minstrel, bidding him take it.

" 'Lay it here,' said Roland holding out the wooden bowl in which he was wont to receive gifts.

" 'Nay, nay, good minstrel,' said they, 'if, as thou sayest, thou art innocent, thou must needs touch the iron with thy hand.'

"To which he replied, 'Swear, likewise, that ye yourselves are innocent, and if ye desire me to believe you, touch the iron first; I will touch it after you, but not before.' "

There was a pause. Green Stranger lifted his pipe to his lips and played softly for a few minutes, then looked from one face to the other.

"Friends," he said, "I was here when you swore before the priest that you were innocent of stealing the cloth. Which of you will grasp the iron before these minstrels?"

No one answered, and silence hung like a cloud over the people.

THE BRIDEGROOM TO THE RESCUE

In which the young master is given an unusual present and Jack
Piper pays for supper by singing the story of Alfrad's Donkey

R E D C A P did not know how long the silence lasted. He
saw that Green Stranger was not smiling but looking
quietly from one face to another, while the minstrels in
the stocks lay without moving and the pedlar's mouth twitched
nervously.

It was a tense moment and Redcap, certain that no one would
come forward, was startled when a young voice called over the
heads of the people.

"By the saints, is there trouble on my wedding eve?"

Then, as though in one breath the crowd had given a sigh
of relief, everyone turned.

"God save your lordship," said the people as a young man
strode lightly among them with a quiet, "By your leave,
friends," and stood in front of the stocks.

Among the villagers in their dun coloured, grey and brown
garments, he looked like some bright flower from a foreign
garden. His yellow hood hung down behind his back and a high
grey felt hat with a jewel in front crowned a head, whose
brown hair curled about his ears. The short cape which fell
like a deep collar around his shoulders and over his chest was
cut about the hem into long strips which almost reached his
waist and showed a pale blue "cotte hardie" with long close-
fitting sleeves, like a tight jacket. Around his hips was a
jewelled girdle and his scarlet leggings ended in a pair of
black cloth shoes with long points.

He nodded to Green Stranger, raised his eyebrows when he
saw the crippled condition of the pedlar and looked at each of

the others, frowning when his eyes lighted on Jack Piper, whose lids were half closed in his white agonized face.

"Fetch the keys and release these men," he said shortly, and, with a slightly scared look on his face, the man who had led the crowd ran to obey him.

But the ill-tempered black-eyed woman, whom the people called Ann Plowman, pushed her way to the front.

"Sir," she began, "the steward put them there because . . ."

"Whatever they have done or have not done, I will hear their story from their own lips and while they are standing on their feet," said the young man. "Wipe this man's face."

The rosy cheeked woman stepped forward and knelt by Jack Piper, dipped the hem of her dress into the jug of water, which the priest had left on the ground, and moistened his forehead.

"'Tis a cruel thing to put a lame man in the stocks," she murmured, "and we have done this man harm or my name is not Meg nor my husband John the Miller. "Young master," she said aloud, "I, for one, am ashamed! This poor wretch is faint with pain and as yet there is nothing to show that he has done wrong."

"Two pieces of red cloth were stolen from the pedlar," said Ann Plowman sulkily, "and they were found in the minstrels' handcart. You have but to look inside it, young master, and you will see the cloth among their gear!"

"We did NOT steal it," cried Redcap unable to contain himself any longer.

"Ssh." Fulk frowned but Redcap refused to be silent.

"We didn't," he repeated, "I have told them so. I have told them twice. I *know* who stole it."

The young master beckoned Redcap to come nearer, then looked across the green.

"Stand aside, good people," he said. "Master Greysleeves is on his way with the keys, and, if I am not mistaken he is bringing the handcart, too, so I shall soon see for myself what is inside it. Now, boy, begin at the beginning and tell me what happened. I want your story."

Redcap was not afraid. The young man had a pleasant face and had been kind to Jack Piper, who was old and frail, so he spoke with confidence.

"The cloth was stolen by the men who stole me and the handcart. But I escaped."

"And the handcart?" asked the young man.

"I couldn't take it when I ran away," said Redcap, "they kept it and put the cloth into it to sell at your wedding and when I escaped they captured me. And then Fulk rescued me and when Fulk rescued me they put us in the stocks and when they had put us in the stocks they tied me up and when they had tied me up Green Stranger untied me and . . ."

"By your leave, by your leave," laughed the young master. "Stop, for I am a simple man, slow to understand! Master Greysleeves," he said as the steward came up, wheeling the cart, "I see you have had some trouble. Release these men and I will, then, hear what you and they have to say."

The steward bowed, unlocked the stocks and raised the upper board so that the minstrels could lift their legs from the holes; they scrambled to their feet, stretched, moving first one leg and then the other, for their cramped position had made them stiff. Nial stood up, stamped and shook his right foot, which felt as though it were being pricked by pins and needles. But when Jack Piper tried to rise he could not take his legs from the stocks until the steward and Meg the Miller's wife had raised and supported him. They managed to hoist him to his feet but, even then, he could not stand, and Green Stranger had to kneel on one knee and let the lame man use the other as a seat.

"And now, steward," said the young master, "I understand that these minstrels are accused of stealing some cloth and of hiding it among their own goods. Where is it?"

"Here, in their handcart, where it was found, young sir. We put the men in the stocks for safe keeping and while they were there I locked their handcart in the stable. I will show you."

He took off the piece of sacking which covered the handcart. The cloth was not there.

The crowd gave a little gasp and the steward's eyes nearly dropped from his head. He moved everything, putting balls, masks, musical instruments and bells, one by one, on the ground.

The cloth had disappeared.

"It's — it's gone," he said. "They couldn't have hidden it. They were in the stocks and it's gone!"

"So have the men who said that we stole it," said Fulk, shortly.

"Ay," cried Meg the Miller's wife looking to right and to left among the people. "Gone they are indeed and I'll warrant that both they and the cloth will be found together if at all."

"This boy with the red hood said that he saw them run away," added the pedlar, hobbling a step or two nearer and peering into the empty handcart.

"Did you see them with the cloth when they were running?" asked the young man.

"No," said Redcap, trying to remember what he had and had not seen. "But I never saw them put the cloth back into the cart. Before we were in the stocks they took it out of the cart and shook it in my face and tried to make me kneel and ask pardon for stealing it. Then Fulk came and I didn't see what they did with it."

"A more evil looking pair I never set eyes on," said the pedlar, and told his story, swearing by the cross which he wore around his neck that he had recognized their voices as those of the ruffians who had attacked him and left him in the ditch.

"Faith, master," said Nial, smiling at the young man, in whom he felt he had met a kindred spirit, "the little dog would speak for us if he could, for wasn't I holding his nose tightly to prevent him from biting the two rascals when they were shaking Redcap? Rex is a grand one for knowing the foul scent of men who break the King's peace. He is so!"

Rex, hearing his name, barked and sat up on his hind legs, saluting with his right paw.

The young man laughed, patted the dog's head and turned to the people.

"Master Steward," he said, "and you, my friends. I think you know that on my wedding day I desire everyone's happiness as well as my own. This poor pedlar has been robbed with violence. My lady mother will treat his ills, as she treats yours, with simples from her own herb garden. And I myself will pay for the cloth which he has lost."

The women in the crowd looked at him with shining eyes, "Ah, but he's good," they whispered.

The young man turned to the minstrels, letting his eyes rest longest on Jack Piper, whom Green Stranger was still supporting, and then spoke, once again, to the villagers.

"I think," he said, "that nothing has been proved against these minstrels. I heard some whisper of the — ordeal. Do you wish me to put them back in the stocks for judgment?"

No one spoke, but Meg Miller shook her head vigorously.

"Then perhaps you will do me a favour," the young man went on. "I ask you to grant me their freedom as a marriage gift. Do you agree?"

With one accord the people cheered, and Rex barked, wagging his tail.

There was a twinkle in the young man's eye.

"I have always known you, my people, to be generous," he said, "from those very early days when you saved me from the wrath of my father after I had stolen some of his apples."

The people laughed and one of them shouted, "Soon maybe we shall be saving your own son from *his* father's wrath!"

The young master had a boyish grin which made him look very little older than Redcap.

"You had better not try," he said. "Remember, I know all your tricks and hiding places."

He turned to the minstrels. "They have given me the best gift that I have had for many a day," he said. "My winsome

188

bride will be happy, too, for she loves a merry song and a gay tale, and so, sirs, I invite you to entertain us at the wedding feast. Master Greysleeves, my steward, will find you a lodging."

With a slight bow and a wave of the hand to the villagers the young man went across the green towards the Manor house. Redcap watched him.

"He doesn't believe that we are robbers," he said joyfully.

"Robbers, forsooth!" laughed Meg Miller. "On a wedding eve bygones should be bygones, say I. And now it's time you all had something to eat."

For the first time that day Redcap remembered that he had had nothing to eat since the bowl of soup which Nial had given him the night before, and the scrap of bread. He licked his lips, and gazed longingly at Fulk, who had always told him that minstrels must sing for their supper. He hoped that today would be an exception. Fulk looked over his head.

"We pay by a song or a tale," he said.

"Not today," replied Meg Miller. "You have paid enough as it is, and there's a lad here who's well nigh as hollow as a drum. And this poor man . . ." she put her hand on Jack Piper's shoulder, "he must rest. See, friends, he's as lame and weary as John Miller's old donkey."

"Ay," said another, "and like John Miller, the minstrels will soon have to buy a new one to fetch and carry, if they trust in *him*."

"Old donkey, is it?" laughed Nial. "I am thinking there is life in him yet. What say you, Jack Piper?"

Jack stood up, supporting himself by a hand on Green Stranger's shoulder.

"Humph," he said, "an old lifeless ass, am I? If there is not more life in me than in Alfrad's donkey, may the Lord supply the minstrel's needs for they'll miss me sorely."

"Eh?" asked Meg Miller. "Alfrad? Who may Alfrad be?"

"The nun who lost a donkey," answered Jack Piper and putting his reed pipe to his lips he began to play a number of shrill notes which sounded like, "Hee-haw! Hee-haw!"

"Clear the donkey-pasture," he said, waving his pipe in the direction of the villagers, "and let no ass bray till I have finished."

"Donkeys, are we?" laughed the leader, in a good temper at last, "Donkeys, eh? He grows impudent now that he is free! He . . .!"

But his words were stifled by Nial, who dropped Fulk's donkey-mask over his head, saying while the people clapped, "Wheesht now, he told you not to bray."

When the laughter had subsided and the villagers had seated themselves in a half circle in front of the minstrels, Jack Piper began his story, speaking as he always did, in verse.

"Good people, gentles all, hear now the story of Alfrad's donkey.

> There is a township
> (Men call it Homburg)
> There 'twas that Alfrad
> Pastured her she-ass,
> Strong was the donkey,
> Mighty and faithful.
>
> And as it wandered
> Out to the meadow,
> It spied a greedy
> Wolf that came running,
> Head down and tail turned,
> Off the ass scampered.
>
> Up the wolf hurried,
> Seized tail and bit it.
> Quickly the donkey
> Lifted its hind legs,
> With the wolf bravely,
> Long did it battle.

Then when at last it
Felt its strength failing,
Raised it a mighty
Noise of lamenting,
Calling its mistress,
So died the donkey.

And when they saw him
Wept all the sisters,
Tearing their tresses,
Beating their bosoms,
Weeping the guiltless
Death of their donkey.

Adela gentle,
Fritherun charming,
Both came together,
That they might strengthen
Sad heart of Alfrad,
Strengthen and heal it.

'Leave now thy gloomy
Wailing, O sister!
Wolf never heedeth
Thy bitter weeping.
The Lord will give thee
Another donkey'.".

Jack stopped speaking and began to play his pipe, skilfully
and softly, composing as he went along. Green Stranger listened,
put his own pipe to his lips, Nial handed Fulk the tabor, picked
up his viol which the steward had left on the ground, and with
his bow began to draw sweet sounds from it. And in their music
there was the peace of the convent on a spring morning, the
threatening sounds of the wolf and the weeping of Alfrad for
her donkey.

Redcap was watching Green Stranger. There was something about the way he moved and about his eyes, their colour and changing expression, that reminded him of someone. The minstrel turned towards him smiling slightly, and for a minute he looked so much like Redcap's father that the boy was startled.

The look was gone almost as soon as it had come and when Meg Miller cried, "Well played and well told. And now 'tis time to break your fast," he forgot all about the likeness, and only remembered how hungry he was.

XVI

THE HUMAN LADDER

*In which the minstrels go to the wedding, Green Stranger tells
the story of the Grey Palfrey, and Redcap wins a favour from
the bride*

IT was good to have slept beside Green Stranger on a heap
of straw in a hut near the mill. It was good to know that the
pedlar's wounds had been dressed by the lady of the manor
and Jack Piper's leg poulticed till it ached no longer. And it
was pleasant to have made a new friend as gay as Nial and as
full of songs and of stories as Fulk.

Redcap was standing by Green Stranger, who was with the
other minstrels at the far end of the hall, waiting for Sir Henry
to call for tales to entertain his guests.

It was a gay sight. Lighted lanterns hung from the cross
beams under the roof, for the narrow churchlike windows were
shuttered with wood, all but one through which the sunlight
gleamed in a long, fan-shaped ray. Here and there servants held
flaming torches, and slung from the rafters garlands of prim-
roses and ivy were swaying gently to and fro.

Two broad steps strewn with rosemary led to the high table
where the bridegroom sat between the bride and her mother.
Sir Henry and the bride's father were at each end with other
members of both families between them. The great silver salt
cellar, shaped like a boat, gleamed in the middle of the table
and silver mugs and pewter beakers shone at each place.
Below the dais in the main part of the hall sat the other wedding
guests at two long tables, the young men in short brightly
coloured coats with girdles over their hips and long trunk hose,
the older men in colours just as gay but in coats reaching to
their ankles, which gave them a touch of dignity.

Redcap's eyes took in every detail. The bride had a sweet pale face. At the wedding ceremony in the Church porch he had seen how kindly the old priest had looked at her as she stood with her long hair loose, down her back, and her tawny red silk dress sewn with pearls. And now she sat smiling and happy at her husband's right side and Redcap longed to do something to please her. Up till now Fulk had sung, Nial, too, and all of them including Green Stranger had played while the guests feasted. But Redcap had done nothing but look about him, nibbling candied violets, sugared rose petals, marchpane and sweet honey cakes.

He pulled Nial's sleeve. "May I juggle, now?" he asked.

Nial did not answer, but Fulk whispered sharply, "Wait till you're asked. This is no place for a child's tricks."

A child's tricks.

So Fulk looked upon him as a child and not as a juggler. Neither Nial nor Jack Piper would have said such a thing and Green Stranger had talked to him last night as though he were a fellow minstrel. Redcap gave Fulk a quick glance, half pleading, half sulky, but the crooked lips were grim and turned down at each corner.

"Whatever he says, I *will* do something," thought Redcap. "Even if it makes him angry, I will."

But his defiant thoughts were interrupted by Sir Henry, who was now on his feet addressing the company.

"Good friends," he said, "now that the feast is over these minstrels, who have come to us at my son's bidding will tell us a tale, merry or sad, foolish or wise. Come, choose."

At this one of the wedding guests cried, "Sir, we have but lately had a narrow escape from rascally thieves, let us have the tale of a robber."

"Nay," cried the young master, "such a story will frighten my wife. Since this is her wedding day I call for a fair romance about a bride."

"Humph," said Sir Henry, "I have no fondness for thieves and these good minstrels have proved their honesty. As for brides, some say they are more trouble than they are worth. I will leave my son and my sweet-faced new daughter to prove it. Nay, minstrels let a horse be your hero for he is a man's best friend."

Then there was a clamour in the hall, some crying, "Give us the robber," others, "Nay, a bride, a bride," and Sir Henry, "Tush! A horse, I say, let it be about a horse."

Nial and Fulk laughed, shrugging their shoulders. Jack Piper looked bewildered, but Green Stranger bowed. "My lords and ladies, you have asked for a robber, a bride and a horse. I will give you all three in a fair tale called 'The Grey Palfrey'."

He set one foot on a bench at the end of the hall, leant his elbow on his knee, and with Nial softly playing his viol, began the story.

"You must know that there dwelt in Champagne a valiant knight whose name was Messire Guillaume. Courteous and chivalrous he was, and very fair to see whether armed or on horseback.

"Now this knight, who was poor, loved a damsel right beauteous to behold. She was the daughter of a rich lord and many a man sought her in marriage, but as yet her father had deemed no one worthy of her and had turned all her suitors away. Nevertheless Messire Guillaume would go to see her in secret, riding through the forest which separated their dwellings, by a path that none knew save himself and his grey palfrey.

"At last Messire Guillaume, desiring above all things to wed the maiden, made so bold as to visit her father.

" 'Sir,' said he, 'I am come to your house to ask a boon. May God let you grant it.'

"And the old man answered, 'What may it be?'

"Then said Messire Guillaume, 'Sir, if it be your will, I would ask of you your daughter.'

"Without pause the old lord replied, 'My daughter is young and fair and of noble birth. She is my only child and when I die all my land and my riches will be hers. Think you that I am so witless as to give her to a poor knight when a prince or a count or perhaps a King may well be her husband? Begone.'

"Then the knight in much sorrow made his way to his own house. But when next he met the damsel on the secret pathway in the wood, she bade him be of good cheer.

"THE KNIGHT, IN MUCH SORROW, MADE HIS WAY TO HIS OWN HOUSE"

" 'Fair friend,' she said, 'I have thought long about this matter and now, I pray you, do as I say. You have an uncle, whom my father knows and trusts. He is a man of much wealth, go to him and tell him of our plight. If he loves you let him visit my father and say, "In return for your daughter my nephew shall have three hundred pounds of my land." Because my father thinks highly of your uncle he will surely agree. Then, when we are wedded, you will return to your uncle all the land and money that he has promised. This, I believe, is our only hope.'

"Speedily Messire Guillaume took leave of the damsel and rode on his grey palfrey to the house of his uncle and told him of his plight.

" 'Nephew,' said the uncle, 'be of good cheer for I will contrive the wedding.'

"Rejoicing greatly Messire Guillaume went on his way, and the uncle, taking six wealthy knights with him, rode to the house of the rich old lord and was made welcome with feasting and with merriment.

"When the minstrels had played and the wine was drunk, he called the old lord aside and said to him, 'Sir, you have a fair daughter whom I would fain make my wife. I ask you to give her to me in marriage.'

"The old lord, delighted that one so rich and so well-born desired his daughter, gave his consent and preparations were made for the wedding. But the damsel, who had given her heart to Messire Guillaume, sat joyless, weeping bitterly.

"Now, it happened that there were not enough horses for the wedding procession and the old lord sent a squire to Messire Guillaume to borrow the grey palfrey, for no horse in the land was gentler nor more beautiful. In this way Messire Guillaume had tidings of the wedding and knew that his uncle had betrayed him.

"The night before the wedding, there was feasting and merriment and when, at midnight, the moon rose bright and clear the guests, confused by the wine which they had drunk, thought that the day had dawned. Sleepily they mounted their horses and rode, nodding in their saddles, through the forest towards the distant Church.

"The damsel, in her bridal garments, was lifted to the back

of Messire Guillaume's grey palfrey and an aged knight had charge of her. Heavy was her heart, and tears fell from her eyes while the old knight, riding beside her, dozed with his head nodding. The others rode ahead and, before long, the sleeping knight and the bride were alone.

"Now the grey palfrey, who had ofttimes carried Messire Guillaume through the forest, and always by the secret pathway, finding that the damsel rode with a slack rein and that the sleeping knight did not guide him, turned aside and ambled gently along the path to which he was used.

"The weeping damsel, unaware of what was happening, saw nothing until the grey palfrey pawed the ground and neighed on the bridge across the deep moat around Messire Guillaume's house.

"The watch on guard, sounding his horn at daybreak, heard the clatter of the palfrey's hooves upon the bridge and called aloud, 'Who rides at this hour?'

"And the damsel answered, 'Surely, the most unhappy lady that ever was born. In God's name let me in until it is light, for I am lost.'

"Then the watch put his eyes to an opening in the postern gate, saw the grey palfrey and knew it for his master's. And he ran to Messire Guillaume, who lay joyless upon his bed, and called to him, saying,

" 'Sir, your grey palfrey has returned and with him a lady in a mantle richly furred and a gown of scarlet. Heavy hearted, she is, and yet I have never seen a maid more fair and winsome.'

"Hearing these words, Messire Guillaume sprang to his feet and came to the door, and when he saw the damsel he took her by the hand and led her into his house, speaking to her words of gentleness.

"That morning he called his chaplain, and right joyfully married the damsel whom he had loved for so long.

"And since the deed was done, her father must needs agree, and Messire Guillaume's uncle, the old man of the twisted moustaches who had stolen the bride, took what comfort he might."

"Well told! Well told!" cried the wedding guests, and Sir Henry tossed Green Stranger one of the small gold rings that he wore on his little finger.

"Neatly contrived, master minstrel," said he. "I never guessed that the robber would be one who would steal a bride nor the horse a friend who would rescue her."

"I'll warrant that Messire Guillaume had as joyous and as loving a wedding as my own," said the young master, "yet without merriment and not according to custom."

"True," said Sir Henry, "but since we speak of merriment and of custom, let our own feast end in the usual manner. Rise, friends."

At this all the guests at the high table and those below the salt rose to their feet. The bridegroom bowed to his father and then to the bride. Smiling, he took her hand and while the minstrels played on pipe, tabor and viol, and the servants held the torches high above their heads, he led her down the centre of the room.

The jewels in her ears and around her neck sparkled and a ray of sunshine, coming through one of the long narrow windows, sent quivering pin-points of light across her face and Redcap, watching, thought that she looked like one of those faerie beings about whom the wise woman had so often told him.

Down the long hall and back walked bride and bridegroom, stopping before a doorway decked with wild violets, white and mauve, which led to the bridal chamber.

Immediately, all the young men among the guests began to press around them and cry, "The garter! The garter!"

"Nay, friends, not so close!" laughed the bridegroom, pretending to draw his dagger, while the bride half laughing, half confused, turned her back and appeared to be making a deep curtsey to the door. Quickly, she slipped her small jewelled hand under her skirt, rose, twirled around and with eyes sparkling and cheeks blushing, waved above her head her garter of coloured ribbons, cunningly plaited and twisted, with the long ends hanging loose.

The young men gathered about her, trying to snatch it.

"Who comes too close shall be pricked by my dagger's point," threatened the bridegroom. "Throw, sweet lady, and he who catches shall wear your favour for the rest of the year."

"Throw! Throw!" cried the young men, jostling each other. Even the minstrels stood on tiptoe at the back of the crowd and Green Stranger hoisted Redcap to his shoulder crying, "Lady, here is a gallant minstrel for your favour."

Seeing Redcap above the heads of the others the bride smiled at him and tossed the garter as hard and as high as she could.

Everyone leapt into the air, arms outstretched, to catch the ends of the ribbons and tear them apart so that each might have a share in the lady's good graces.

"Who has it?" shouted Sir Henry.

"Who has your favour, child?" cried the bride's father.

"Good gallants," ordered the bridegroom, "stand aside that those who have caught the ribbons may come forward and kiss the bride."

The wedding guests stood aside, each looking in front, behind to right and to left. But no one came forward.

The garter had disappeared.

There was a moment's silence. The bride looked frightened and plucked at the young master's sleeve. "Milord," she whispered tremulously, "this is surely a sign of ill luck."

But Green Stranger, standing by Nial at the back of the hall, called in a ringing voice, "By my faith, the lady looks no lower than heaven! She has bestowed her favour upon an angel."

His green-clad arm pointed to the rafters, and there, around the neck of a small gilded angel, carved upon one of the cross beams, hung the bride's garter.

"After it!" cried the young men. "Fetch a ladder."

"Nay, nay," shouted Sir Henry, "is there any among you worthy or innocent enough to touch an angel?"

"None, milord, but a cherub," laughed the Green Stranger and he leapt nimbly on to the table and knelt upon one knee. Immediately, Nial followed, stepped lightly on his knee and up to his shoulders, where he sat, stiff and straight. Then as Redcap leapt upon Green Stranger's knee, Nial swung the boy up to his own shoulders.

"Ready," he whispered and slowly Green Stranger rose to his feet, till he towered like a giant on the table.

"The wingless cherub, with the flaming halo will bring down the garter," he cried, glancing up at Redcap who was astride Nial's shoulders and, indeed, in the flickering light of the torches, the boy's glowing red hair looked like a fiery halo.

There was a hum of excitement among the people whose eyes were on Redcap while the ribbons of the garter moved and floated in the warm smoke from the torches, and were still out of his reach.

"Careful!" said Fulk frowning. His whisper was loud enough for Redcap to hear, but he sent it upwards scarcely moving his lips and the wedding guests, talking excitedly together, caught no sound.

"Careful!" said Fulk again as Redcap rose wobbling to his feet and stood upright on Nial's shoulders. "Steady yourself and keep your balance with your arms as you have been taught. Look up and not down and play no tricks."

The human ladder was steady now as a wooden one, and slowly Green Stranger moved until he was directly below the gilded angel.

Redcap was unafraid. When he had practised different kinds of somersault and acrobatic feats with Nial and Fulk they had shown him how to stand on their shoulders, and, if he slipped, how to turn in the air and land on his feet, unhurt.

He felt the firm pressure of Nial's fingers around his ankles as he stretched towards the rafters, flicked the garter off the angel's head, caught the ribbons and twisted them around his wrist.

The wedding guests cheered.

But Redcap was not satisfied. He knew that every eye was

turned upon him and he was seized with a desire to show how clever he was. Fulk had told a tale, Nial and Jack Piper had sung and played, Green Stranger had delighted everyone with his story of the Grey Palfrey but Redcap, alone, had been asked to do nothing. He had been treated as though he were a child instead of a budding minstrel. Even Green Stranger had laughingly called him a cherub which is nothing more than a child angel. And, in any case, cherubs, he knew, were singers in heaven, and he had not even been asked to sing.

Well, he would show them.

He felt Nial's fingers slacken, shook them off his right ankle and proceeded to stand on one leg, waving the other in the air.

The people gasped.

"No!" cried the bride and hid her face.

"Will you be careful now," whispered Nial. "Stand on your two feet."

Redcap brought his right leg back to Nial's shoulder. "I can stand alone," he said under his breath, "take your hands off my ankles."

And Nial feeling that his balance was perfect withdrew his hold for a second.

In that second Redcap was standing upside down, with his own hands grasping Nial's shoulders and his legs in the air.

And now, contrary to all instructions, he looked down. He could not help himself, since his legs were in the air and his head where his feet should have been. His gaze met a sea of upturned faces which seemed to hover in the smoke and one pair of eyes, smouldering with anger. Fulk glared up at Redcap and the boy's legs, hitherto straight as needles, began to wave like a couple of feathers in a breeze.

Nial gripped his wrists.

"Have no fear at all," he whispered, "you are safe. Jump wide, Fulk will catch you."

But the thought of Fulk catching him was too much for Redcap and he lost his balance.

THE HUMAN LADDER WAS STEADY NOW

The bride screamed. The guests shouted. And the next thing Redcap knew was that Fulk was pulling him out of an immense basin of apple sauce and bumping him into a sitting posture on the table while Nial was picking himself up from the floor with a bleeding nose and one eye half closed, where Redcap's heels had struck him.

Green Stranger, however, was unhurt and unabashed. He sat on the edge of the table swinging his legs and singing, to gusts of laughter from the onlookers,

> A little human cherub
> He climbed up to the sky
> For to fetch a garter
> That was flung too high!
> A-down derry, derry-down!

> His halo it was scarlet,
> But angels wear them gold!
> He's but a saucy varlet
> Who tried to be too bold!
> A-down derry, derry-down!

At the words "saucy varlet" he took a towel from one of the servants, who had poured water over the guests' hands after the feast, and began to wash Redcap's sticky face.

"May it please you, gentles all, to permit the winner of the garter to claim his reward?" he asked, carefully wiping the boy's mouth.

"Nay!" laughed one of the guests, "Only roast pig is served with apple sauce. 'Tis the boy who is the griskin not the lady."

The guests laughed, for a griskin is a pigling, and Redcap certainly looked pink and sticky, but his air of embarrassment and the half frightened way in which he kept glancing at Fulk's angry face, won the bride's pity.

"If he will not claim his reward," she cried, "I will come and give it to him," and she ran to the table and held out her hand for Redcap to kiss.

"Manners," hissed Fulk in his ear.

Hastily the boy scrambled up, shyly he knelt on one knee and put his lips to the outstretched hand.

The bride raised him to his feet, and fixed the ribboned garter to his hood with a silver pin from her own hair.

"For this year, you are my chosen knight," she said, and with Jack Piper beating a triumphant tattoo on his tabor and Green Stranger drawing sweet notes from his pipe, she led Redcap to the door of the hall and waved him a smiling good night.

XVII

REDCAP AND THE GRISKIN

*In which Green Stranger teaches Redcap the story of Willy
Gris and Fulk gets a pleasant surprise*

NEXT morning, before the other minstrels had left their
various resting places in the village, Redcap sat in the
shed next to the mill, where Meg had made beds of
straw for him and for Green Stranger. He was almost naked
with a flour sack around his shoulders and he sat with his arms
hugging his knees and his chin resting on them waiting for his
doublet and trunk hose. He remembered vaguely that Meg
had come in, early in the morning, saying, "Pull off the lad's
clothes and I will clean away the apple stains. By the look of
him he hasn't had a mother's care for months," and he awoke
later feeling the straw prick and tickle his ribs.

He was glad that Green Stranger had asked him to share a
lodging after the wedding, for Nial had stayed with Jack Piper
to poultice the lame leg, during the night, with herbs from the
lady's garden. And after his mishap at the marriage feast,
Redcap did not fancy a night alone with Fulk. Besides, there
was something about Green Stranger which reminded him of
his own people and of the wise woman. He seemed to cast
a spell over the villagers, too, as though there were magic in
his voice.

Until long after dark, Meg and the miller had kept him
singing and telling stories. At first, Redcap, sleepy as he was,
had sat listening, entranced, but the excitement of the last few
days had tired him, and after a while, he could not keep his
eyes open. How he came to be in the shed, he did not know.
He must have staggered there, too sleepy to have any recollec-
tion of what he had done. He only remembered that voices,
music and laughter had drifted in and out of his dreams, strange

dreams, in which he kept catching a glimpse of Red Eric but never seeing his face.

Once, in his sleep, he thought that he heard Red Eric's song, "A woman is a gladsome thing", and awoke at the words, "And yet she hath but care and woe." He sat up, thinking that the runaway uncle was found but he saw only Green Stranger in the doorway and heard Meg Miller saying, "Thank you, Master Minstrel. God send you good rest." Then, not really awake, he had fallen back on the straw and was sound asleep again before Green Stranger had shut the door and had lain down beside him.

He wondered now what this new day was going to bring. Perhaps Red Eric would arrive to take part in the marriage festivities, which would last for some days. Wandering pedlars, merchants and parties of wedding guests would have spread the news, and surely no minstrel could resist turning an honest penny at anything so gay as a wedding?

But was he near enough to have heard about it? Redcap sighed. It was summer, now, and he had been searching since Christmas, and although Nial had been like a father and an elder brother to him, he was missing his own people. And in spite of Nial's oft repeated, "never fear, we will find the lost uncle, yet," he was discouraged.

"Get up and put on your clothes."

Green Stranger pushed open the door and tossed his garments to Redcap. The sunshine poured into the shed so that the straw gleamed like a heap of gold on the brown earthen floor and Redcap blinked at the sudden brilliance.

"I slept a long time," he said, pulling on his trunk hose and noticing that the stains had been rubbed away.

"You did," laughed Green Stranger. "I pulled you and poked you and tumbled you over when I stripped off your clothes, but you slept as soundly as a griskin in apple sauce and looked as pink as one, too."

Redcap did not appreciate this reference to his adventure at the wedding, but he said nothing.

"You squeal like a griskin, too," said Green Stranger, passing him the scarlet hood to which the bride's garter was still fixed with the pin.

"I never do," said Redcap indignantly.

"No?" Green Stranger raised his eyebrows. "Perhaps you call it grunting? You made some very strange sounds in your sleep last night, something between a squeal, a grunt and a mutter. I thought I heard the words, 'I must find him, I must! I must!' Or was it 'mast'? Beech-mast and acorns are what pigs usually seek in the woods."

He looked down at Redcap as though he were making a polite inquiry, just as the boy's father looked when he was pretending to be serious but was laughing, inside. His lips were solemn but his eyes twinkled. The eyes, too, were the same colour as the smith's, grey with bushy eyebrows which made the sockets look very deep and the eyes, themselves, like pools in a forest.

This faint resemblance to his father made Redcap feel homesick, and he wanted to tell Green Stranger how he had run away and whom he was muttering about in his sleep.

"I am trying to find . . ." he began.

But Green Stranger interrupted.

"There's little one can find in one's sleep save rest," he said; "and now if you have rested long enough, you may like to hear some good tidings."

The boy pricked up his ears. Had Green Stranger news of Red Eric? But no, it must be something else, for Redcap had never yet told him about the lost uncle.

"Meg Miller tells me that the villagers have offered a prize for the best story," said Green Stranger. "It is to be a fat griskin and as I am sure that the winner will share a meal of roast pig with his fellow minstrels, whether we win or not we shall all be in luck."

"Well!' snorted Redcap indignantly, "If I were to win a little pig, I wouldn't *eat* him!"

"What else can a minstrel do with a pig?" laughed Green Stranger.

"Keep him as a pet and teach him tricks," said Redcap. "Green Stranger?"

"Yes?"

"I wish I could tell the best story and win the pig. It might put Fulk into a good temper."

Green Stranger stroked his chin, "The big man with the crooked smile is a good minstrel," he said. "I think he's worth pleasing."

Redcap sighed, "He's very difficult to please. That's why I would like to win the pig."

"I see. Then, if that's what you want to do, I think I can help you," said Green Stranger. "I know a story about a boy and a pig. It is so apt a tale that whoever tells it will win the prize."

"But," objected Redcap, "it won't please Fulk if you win it and then give it to me. I shall have to juggle well or tell a good tale or sing and win it for myself."

"And that," said Green Stranger, "is what you are going to do. I shall give you the story, not the pig, and you will tell it to the people and if you tell it well, you'll win the prize, so listen."

He stood, leaning against the wall, his green-clad figure dappled with flecks of sunlight, his face as he told his story, now gay, now grim and suspicious, now wise and gentle.

"There," said he when he had finished, "that is the tale that you will tell and the big man with the crooked smile will forget about your unfortunate mistake at the wedding feast. Come, we will go."

"Now?" gasped Redcap. "But you've only told the story once. I can't tell it your way till I've learnt it by heart."

"Tell it in your own way," said Green Stranger, "each of us puts his own magic into words. You cannot capture mine nor I yours."

"But I shall fumble with the words," said Redcap, "and then the people will laugh at me. Green Stranger, if they laugh at me, I shall tell it worse than ever!"

Green Stranger put both his hands on Redcap's shoulders and looked straight down at him.

"That," said he quietly, "will only happen if you think of Redcap and not of pleasing the people. Are you ready? It's time that we went. If the big man with the crooked smile has to come and fetch you I fear that his temper may wear so thin that there'll be no patching it."

"He's coming," said Redcap, looking through the open door.

Green Stranger linked an arm through his, and together they went to meet Fulk. At first Crooked Smile took no notice of Redcap but addressed his companion.

"The people are ready," he said. "They are calling for the Green Stranger. You have cast such a spell over them that I can scarcely hold their attention. Nial with one eye bruised and a nose so swollen that he can't sing, is fooling to keep them good humoured." He turned to Redcap. "But for your witless antics, he would have gained the prize, for Nial had a winning merry face till last night."

Redcap looked distressed. He had no idea that he had kicked Nial so hard that his face had changed, but Green Stranger relieved his mind.

"The swelling will be gone by tomorrow," he said, "and since Redcap did the damage, he had better try to repair it by telling a good tale in Nial's place."

"He had better keep quiet," said Fulk, frowning. "He's so cocksure of himself that he never knows when to stop. I'm weary of his putting us to shame. Do you hear me?" he went on, placing a heavy hand on Redcap's shoulder. "Unless someone calls for you, you are not to open your lips, and even then you are to wait for my permission."

Redcap nodded but looked wistful. There seemed to be no way of pleasing Fulk now, and he stood at the back of the crowd and disconsolately watched Green Stranger edge his way to the front. He saw the little pig which was to be the prize. It had a collar of plaited straw around its neck and Meg Miller was holding it by a thin rope attached to the collar.

"Come, minstrels," she cried, "a witty tale wins a curly tail. What say you, Ann Plowman?"

The black-eyed woman who had threatened the minstrels with the ordeal by heat, when they were in the stocks, looked about her sourly. "Good tales, forsooth," she sneered, "I would send the rascals packing! Not a wink of sleep did I get last night for the singing and the chattering."

"Hold your peace, wife," grumbled the ploughman, "and let us be merry."

"Ay, smile for once, Ann Plowman," cried Meg. "Give your scolding tongue a holiday."

The woman's black eyes flashed but she contented herself with muttering something which was lost in the people's cries of, "A tale!" "A song," "Nay, give us a tune."

And then the fun began. Stories, songs, fables, riddles, games and juggler's tricks, there seemed to be no end to what the minstrels could do. As fast as one story ended, the people called for another.

At last Meg Miller shouted breathlessly, "Enough, good friends. Let us decide who shall have the griskin. Hold up your hands for the Green Stranger."

Up went a number of hands, which the ploughman counted. "Now for the lame piper!"

"Now, for young Swollen Nose with the black eye."

"Now for the big man with the crooked smile."

"By my troth," said the ploughman, and scratched his head, "you had better roast the griskin for their dinner, Mistress Meg, and give one and all a share, for each man has won the same number of hands."

The people and the minstrels laughed, but Green Stranger stepped forward. "Friends," said he, "there is still one minstrel who has not been heard."

Nial stood tiptoe and looked over the heads of the people.

"Will you look at him now?" he cried. "The big fellow skulking in the scarlet hood. The fellow who nearly sent me to heaven, with a kick that broke my nose and put out one of my eyes, so that the good saints didn't take me for a man at all, and sent me packing. Come out of that, will you?" he said doubling his fists and pretending to fight.

When the people saw Redcap, half smiling, half shy, in the background, one and all began to shout, "The little minstrel! Give him a turn. The little minstrel!"

And Redcap was pushed into the circle. He glanced at Fulk knowing that he should have asked his permission, but Fulk stared back without moving a muscle of his face. He looked at Nial, who tried to wink but, with one eye already half closed, this had such an absurd effect that Redcap burst out laughing and could only point at him feebly and stutter, "He c-can't wink. He c-can't. He—He—hasn't enough eye."

Whereupon all the villagers looked at Nial and laughed, too. But Green Stranger wagged his finger at Redcap and said, "Good people, the boy who laughs at his own misdeeds should be punished. I order him to make amends by telling a story about that pig! And teaching a lesson from it, too!"

"Nay, now," said kind-hearted Meg, "what child could teach a lesson from a pig!"

"Let the little minstrel tell what he likes," said the plough-man. "After all, it was he who won the bride's garter."

But Redcap, pushing back his hood, and pinning the garter to his shoulder, grinned at Green Stranger and bowed to the people.

"Good friends," said he, "I will do as the Green Stranger says."

Fulk's lips were a thin slanting line in his unmoving face. Nial's expression was surprised and he scratched the back of his head. But Redcap looked only at Green Stranger, whose eyes were sending him messages of encouragement.

He cleared his throat, put his hands behind his back and began to tell his tale, timidly at first, but with growing confidence, choosing words which he thought a minstrel would use.

"Fair friends," said Redcap, "hear now the story of Will o' the Griskin.

"Not long ago, there lived in Norfolk a simple countryman who had many children. Above all the others he loved one little boy whose name was William. For this child he set aside a pigling, and therefore the boy's playfellows called him 'Will o' the Griskin', or Willy Gris. When the pig was sold the father put the money to good use so that every year it gained a little more and all was kept for William, so that when he grew to manhood he could provide for himself without burdening his parents.

"It happened that when he had passed his childhood, the boy, following his father's bidding, hastened to France, there to earn his living, and in his purse he had nothing but the money gained by the sale of the griskin.

"For many years he worked well and wisely, and married a woman of wealth who brought him a large house and servants. As time passed, because he was diligent and careful in all that he did, he was often called to meetings of importance by the King and his great men.

"As he grew in riches so did he grow in favour and all men, great and small, held him in love and in honour.

"Now this good man, fearful lest his future should lead him to forget how poor and humble he had once been, caused a fair chamber to be built in his house and painted as he willed. This room he kept under lock and key and would let no one enter, not even his wife. Yet whenever he came home from the courts of the great he would neglect all other business and go alone to the painted chamber, staying there as long as he willed and returning to his family, thoughtful and quiet.

"As time passed he did this so often that all men were curious to know what was in the secret chamber and they took counsel, one with another, each saying to the other 'Go, ask him.'

"At last, weary of their complaints, he called them together, turned the key in the door and made them enter.

"There, upon the wall a pigling was painted, with a little boy holding it on a string and above their heads was written,

> 'Willy Gris, Willy Gris
> Think what you was
> And what you is.' "

Redcap, lost in his story, was startled at the outburst of clapping.

"Bless his heart," cried Meg Miller, "there's none can deny him the griskin."

Even black-eyed Ann Plowman grudgingly put up her hand in Redcap's favour, muttering, "Since someone must have it, give it to the boy who doesn't keep one awake o' nights."

"Take the rope, lad. The griskin is yours," said Meg, and Redcap looking up to thank her, became aware of Fulk beaming at him over her head, his mouth twisting upwards at one corner, his eyes alight with pleasure.

Crooked Smile was in a good humour, at last.

XVIII

WAIT FOR ME!

*In which Redcap is told of a cure for lost courage but forgets
about it in a bitter disappointment*

A DAY or two after he had won the prize, Redcap, with the
griskin at the end of a rope pattering after him, strolled
into the courtyard of Lord Henry's Manor house.

He had asked Fulk if he might lead the pigling into the
wood which stretched along one side of a lane beyond the
village. Fulk had taken very little notice, calling over his
shoulder, "Yes, yes. But be back in time to sing for the priest
in the church. He has asked for you." And he had turned
away to continue a teasing argument with Ann Plowman, who
was angrily bidding him and the other good-for-nothings leave
the village before she had them in the stocks again for disturbing the peace.

Her voice was shrill, and Redcap was glad to get out of
earshot to the peaceful sounds in the courtyard, which was full
of haunting melody, and he thought how Jack Piper would have
listened, head on one side, and turned all that he heard into
music. Indeed, there was music in the courtyard now, the soft
scraping of saws at work in the carpenter's shop, the clang of
the hammer in the smithy and the swish-swish of the milk
slowly turning to butter in the dairy churns.

The hunting dogs, too, were lying in their kennels. Redcap
could distinguish their voices. There were the lymers, heavy,
smooth-haired, black and tan hounds, who were taken out
early in the morning to find the scent of a hart. Their deep
bass notes mingled with the higher cries of the greyhounds, who
were used to chase the smaller animals.

Redcap stood still for a moment, picking out all the different
noises, his senses keenly aware.

Under the eaves of the house, where Lord Henry's dovecote stretched below the entire length of the roof, pigeons were cooing. Like a sudden whisper of the wind they flew to the ground with a whirr of grey wings. Horses stamped in the stable, their hooves making a ringing sound. A colt whinnied, the stable cat purred, rubbing herself against Redcap's legs, and everywhere there was a faint bitter sweet smell from the ale which was being made in the brewhouse.

"Whither away?" cried a voice.

It was milord's falconer, who had charge of the sparrow hawks and falcons used for bringing down wild fowl when lord and lady went out hawking. He was now coming towards the mews where the birds were kept.

"I'm going to the wood," said Redcap. "Fulk says that a griskin, who can only eat milky sops, is too young to travel with us, so I'm going to try him with beech-mast and acorns. What's in that dish?"

"Neither beechnuts nor acorns," replied the falconer. "One of our hawks is huddled miserably on her perch. She seems to have lost her courage and I am going to give her some medicine. Milord will not have a cowardly bird in his mews, and this one looks as though she would never dare attack."

"Is it a good medicine?" asked Redcap. "Does it really give courage?"

"My father used it when he was falconer to Lord Henry, and his father before him."

"What is it made of?" asked Redcap, wondering whether it might be useful for himself or for the griskin. He knew that he often felt discouraged after a long journey with no glimpse of Red Eric, and he thought that the pigling might suffer from the same ailment if it had to walk too far, for in spite of what Fulk had said, he was determined to take the little creature with him.

"How do you make it?" he asked again.

"You take oil of Spain and mix it with wine and with the yolk of an egg and add a little beef. You give five morsels to your hawk and set her in the sun. Then in the evening you feed her with an old hot dove. You do this at least three times. And back comes her courage."

"May I watch you while you give it to her?" asked Redcap.

He wanted to see what a hawk was like when her courage was returning. Besides, a visit to the mews was even more

A VISIT TO THE MEWS

interesting than a peep into the kennels. He liked to look at the birds, each fastened with a long slender chain or cord to a wooden perch, some with little black hoods hiding their eyes and heads and leaving only their curved beaks uncovered, others unhooded, preening themselves. He liked the strange sharp smell of the mews, the shallow covering of sawdust on the floor and the row of stout leather gloves hanging from pegs on the wall — plain gloves for the bird's attendants, not the kind, with embroidered and jewelled gauntlets, which ladies and

gentlemen wore, when they carried their falcons on their wrists
to the chase.

He edged himself closer to the door, but the falconer put his
arm across it.

"The birds must be kept clean and quiet," he said, "and
your pig will cause too much disturbance, so be off to the
woods, lad, and go about your business while I mind mine.
Here's something to eat on the way."

He handed Redcap an apple and stood waiting for him to
go, and the boy, knowing when immediate obedience was
expected, with a backward glance of longing made his way to a
small wooden door in the wall.

This wall surrounded the Manor house, garden and courtyard and outside it there was a wide deep moat, filled with
muddy water and with patches of weed and reeds. A plank
had been flung across the moat to make a bridge, for this was
a short cut from the Manor house to a lane, which by twists
and turns gradually found its way to the high road. Opposite
the plank, on one side of the lane, was a wood, and it was here
that Redcap meant to teach the griskin to eat beech-mast and
acorns, to prove to Fulk that it was no longer a suckling.

"Come along," he said munching his apple. "Follow your
master." And he set out across the plank with one hand behind
him, holding the griskin's rope.

Half way across the pig stood still.

"Come along," said Redcap, giving the rope a slight pull.

The griskin pattered along for a few paces, then stopped
again.

Redcap turned. The pig's tiny narrow eyes, fringed by a
few coarse lashes, were blinking first at the water then at Redcap.
Its pink body and small curly tail looked very young, and
Redcap, thankful that Fulk was not there to see what slow
progress they were making, decided to carry it across the
plank.

"Now remember," he said, "I shall not carry you again. If
you want to be a performing pig, you must learn to keep up."

He stooped, but before he knew what had happened he stepped on the apple core which he had dropped and down he came on his red patch and found himself sitting astride the plank, with both hands tightly grasping the edges.

He picked himself up quickly. "Come on," he said.

Then his heart turned over. The griskin was no longer on the plank. It was in the moat.

Redcap stared down at it. It seemed to be trying to swim, for its front trotters were moving quickly, criss-crossing each other under its chin as though it were attempting to paddle water, and it made little gasping squeals.

Clearly it was losing courage, and as there was no hawk-medicine at hand, something had to be done at once.

Redcap knelt, put first one leg and then the other over the side, then slowly lowered himself till he was clinging by his hands to the plank. He looked down, saw that the water was still some distance from his feet, and knew that he would have to drop.

He let go.

The water covered him, making a gurgling sound in his ears, and he came up blowing bubbles and wiping mud out of his eyes. Thrashing about with his legs, he was relieved to find that he could stand, as his feet were touching something hard like a large boulder and from this position the muddy water was no higher than his chest.

He looked around quickly. The griskin, struggling feebly, was almost under water but luckily near enough to be grasped. Redcap seized it and with difficulty, for it was heavy, hoisted it to his shoulder where it hung like a pink rag from which muddy water dripped "plop, plop" into the moat.

Redcap felt about with one foot. He was certainly on a boulder and not on the bottom of the moat, so he dared not walk across to the farther bank, which, in any case, was too steep to climb. He looked up at the plank. It was out of reach and he could not jump and scramble up with the griskin on his shoulder.

"Plop, plop," dripped the mud from the griskin's snout.

"Help, help," shouted Redcap at the top of his voice.

Silence.

"Plop, plop."

"Help, help."

But there was no answer. The muddy water did not move except when a falling drop made a widening ring. The lane was quiet as though asleep in the sun. Not a bird sang. The clouds in the sky were motionless. Redcap looked across at the wood. The trees were still, not a branch moved, not a leaf fluttered, and yet, among all the living things around him, they alone seemed aware and listening. And this comforted Redcap.

Time dragged.

The sun beating down on his scarlet hood was hot but the water, soaking through his clothes, made him shiver, and the arm which held the griskin on his shoulder was beginning to ache.

If only someone would come. He looked up and down the lane, listening, but it was empty. Once he thought he heard a faint "clop-clop" as though a horseman were riding towards him from the village. He could see nothing because the lane took a sudden turn and was lost to view, and although he strained his ears to listen, he could not be sure of the sound. He shifted his weight from one foot to the other, tried to hold the griskin, which was on his right shoulder, with the left instead of with the right arm, but this was no better.

"He-e-e-elp," he shouted.

A voice cried, "Hillo, ho-ho!"

Horse-hooves trotted round the bend in the lane and Green Stranger, with his saddle bags bulging and a pack on his back, pulled up at the edge of the moat.

"But Will o' the Griskin had the pig on the end of a string and not on his shoulder," he said grinning down at Redcap. "How came you into that mess?"

"The griskin fell in," said Redcap, completely confident that he was now safe.

"The griskin fell in and you went in after him and now I have to come in after you?"

"If you would be so kind," said Redcap politely.

"I shall do nothing of the sort," answered Green Stranger, "for I'm just off on my travels and intend to keep clean and dry."

Redcap smiled up at him. He knew quite well that he was not going to be left there, for Green Stranger had dismounted.

He crossed the road, tied his horse to a tree, then strode back to the moat.

"Now," said he, sitting on the plank and swinging his legs, "before I rescue the pair of you I have a piece of unwelcome news to tell."

"Yes?" said Redcap.

"The big man with the crooked smile is not pleased," continued Green Stranger. "He said that you had been away too long and that if I saw you I was to send you back with a flea in your ear! Doubtless the griskin on your shoulder is covered with fleas so perhaps that part of the bargain has been kept."

He scrambled to his knees, stretched out his arm, plucked the pig off Redcap's shoulder, then stood up and carried it to the edge of the wood.

"Rescue, number one," said he as he returned. "Now what about you? Have you enough courage to face Crooked Smile? Or shall I leave you here among the eels?"

For answer Redcap stood tiptoe and stretched out his arms, and Green Stranger, kneeling on the plank, swung him to dry land.

Redcap heaved a sigh of relief.

"You know," he said seriously, "it doesn't matter as much as I thought about courage. There is a medicine for it."

"A medicine?"

"The falconer told me of something that he gives to a hawk that has lost her courage. I dare say it would do for a person."

Green Stranger shook his head and keeping one hand on

Redcap's shoulder guided him along the plank till he stood in the lane.

"No," he said, "if a man or a child loses courage no medicine will help him to find it again."

"Then what can he do?" asked Redcap.

"He must find something inside himself."

"Well, what?"

"I think it would be a sort of strength that is hidden very deep down and he has to make it come up, till he brings back his heart and his courage. Not so easy to do but always possible."

"It's a pity that the medicine only works in a hawk," said Redcap.

"Yes," agreed Green Stranger, untieing his horse. "It would be very useful to all of us. But tell me, why are you here with the pig?"

"Fulk says he mayn't come with us because he's a suckling, so I was going to teach him to eat what full-grown pigs like."

"I think," said Green Stranger, "that he is not old enough. The journey will do him harm. He is suffering a little now."

Redcap looked at the griskin and then at Green Stranger.

"I wonder if you have courage enough to leave your little friend behind," asked Green Stranger.

For a minute Redcap did not answer, then he swallowed something which seemed to stick in his throat.

"Yes," he said huskily.

Green Stranger shook hands with him.

"I am glad to hear that," he said. "If you had not agreed I should have been disappointed, and I hate to carry away a disappointment from a place where I have enjoyed myself."

Redcap's face fell. So he was going to lose Green Stranger as well as the griskin.

"Are you really going?" he asked.

"Yes."

"Can't you come with us? I mean with Nial and Jack and Fulk and me?"

"No, your friends have promised to stay for a few days longer, but I am saying goodbye!"

"Where are you going?" asked Redcap, thinking that he would ask him to look out for Red Eric.

Green Stranger vaulted to the saddle, shook the reins and laughed. "Where am I going? To the far ends of the earth."

He cantered away, then leaning forward galloped till his laughter grew fainter and fainter. At a turn in the road he pulled off his hood and waved "Goodbye".

And in the sunlight Redcap saw that his hair was as red as his own.

He dropped the rope tied to the griskin's collar and ran, calling aloud, "Red Eric. Wait for me. Red Eric! Red Eric!" but the red-haired minstrel had turned the corner.

Redcap put wings to his feet and ran as he had never run before. He reached the corner, but the road stretched ahead of him, empty.

"Wait for me. Red Eric. Red Eric," he screamed, his heart pounding, his breath coming so quickly that he seemed to be choking.

He ran again, on and on till he came to the next turn. Here, before the road reached the highway, it split into two grassy tracks, and Green Stranger was nowhere to be seen. Which way had he gone? Straight ahead or to the right or to the left.

Redcap ran on, came back, turned right, then left. He ran till he could run no farther and fell by the roadside.

Miserably he dragged himself upright and sat with his head in his hands, whispering brokenly, "He has gone to the far ends of the earth and no one knows where they are."

"The far ends of the earth, the far ends of the earth." Over and over again the words were beating a maddening rhythm in his head.

At last he seemed to remember where he was and he stood up, swaying a little for he was dizzy and his head felt too light for the weight of his feet. Slowly he turned back, his body trembling, his breath coming in quick gasps. He had a burning pain behind his eyes and his hands were cold as ice.

"The others are waiting," he thought. "I must go back. And the griskin's in the road." But even this did not seem important and his legs carried him along without his knowing why.

He seemed to have been walking for hours before he came upon the griskin, lying like a small pink baby on a patch of green by the roadside.

"Come," said Redcap, picking up the rope.

The pigling, too young to grunt, made a sharp squealing sound and wriggled its snout in a way which had made Redcap laugh a few hours earlier, but now he did not even notice.

With dragging footsteps he walked along the dusty road, so slowly that the griskin, trotting beside him, had no difficulty in keeping pace. At the plank bridge the little creature stopped and squealed. Redcap, hardly knowing what he was doing, picked it up and carried it to the other side of the moat, half aware that the animal was afraid of the water in which it had almost drowned.

At the other side of the moat, Redcap went through the door in the wall, crossed the courtyard of the Manor house and made his way into the village. He passed a few people busy about their usual tasks but he did not see them. He walked as though he were blind.

Near the village green Fulk, Nial and Jack were seated on the wall surrounding the well. The old priest was with them. He was looking towards the sunset, shading his eyes from the glory in the sky and peering across the green. He seemed relieved when he saw Redcap and turned with a smile to Fulk, pointing at the figure moving so wearily towards them.

Redcap did not see him. Neither did he see Fulk jump up impatiently and advance with quick strides towards him.

"Where have you been?" said the minstrel angrily. "Am I to spend every evening seeking you high and low? Answer."

Redcap neither moved, nor spoke. He stared straight ahead and his hands shook.

"Answer!" thundered Fulk, then saw the boy's white face and was appalled. "Redcap," he said, "boy, you must not be so *afraid* of me. Come, sit here." He lifted the cold hand and rubbed it against his cheek. "Did I frighten you?" he asked.

"No," answered Redcap tonelessly.

"Why are you wet and covered with mud? Has someone hurt you?"

"No."

"You fell?" said the priest.

Redcap did not seem to hear and Nial put a hand under his chin and tilted his head.

"Are you not going to say anything to us, at all?" he asked. "Listen, Redcap, I am talking to you. Will you pay heed, now!"

Redcap heaved a long deep sigh which seemed to come from the very depths of his being and Nial looked at him with anxiety.

"Can you tell me what happened to you?" he asked gently.

As though he were reciting something from memory that he had learnt and did not understand Redcap closed his eyes and said, "The griskin — fell into the — moat, and I went in — after him. He was — drowning."

"Well, well," said Jack Piper in a soothing voice, "it's over now. The piglet is safe and we must take you somewhere to get dry. You will come to no harm, neither will the griskin."

"That is not troubling him," said Nial.

Redcap swallowed and went on in dry jerky sentences.

"The griskin — must be given — back. It is — too young."

"Oh," said Fulk, "so that is the trouble? But you knew that before!"

"The little pig will be happier at home than on the road," said Jack.

"Yes," said Redcap, "I — am — taking — him to the lady who — gave — him — to — me." He turned and walked away very slowly and stiffly.

Fulk looked at Nial, raising his eyebrows, "Would you have

thought he would be so distressed about losing the pig? I warned him that he wouldn't be able to keep it."

"It's not that," said Nial. "I think he has lost something bigger."

"Someone *must* have frightened him. Do you think he saw the robbers again?" asked Jack Piper, watching Redcap with troubled eyes.

"It's not that," answered Nial. "I know fear when I see it. The heart has gone out of him."

"Father," said Fulk to the priest, "please help us. The sooner the child has some rest, the better. If he could have a sup of hot wine to put an end to his shivering and send him to sleep. . . ."

"I will bring you some," said the priest. "Take him back to Meg Miller and cover him with all your blankets."

"Redcap," called Fulk, striding after the boy.

"Be easy with him," said Nial. "Some little world of his own has fallen to pieces, and I'm doubting if any one of us can put it together again."

He turned and walked away with the priest, thinking that Fulk's quick orders would be better for Redcap, this time, than his own gentle attempts at persuasion.

"He would quietly put me away if I were kind to him, now," he muttered. "But what has taken the heart from the child?"

XIX

GO IN PEACE

*In which Fulk tells the story of Benno's frog, a scold is ducked
in the pond and Redcap learns the meaning of "Go in peace"*

REDCAP was ill. For three days he lay on the straw in Meg Miller's cottage, covered with the minstrels' blankets, and coughed continuously. Meg poulticed his chest with hot herbs and Nial came in and sat with him, telling him stories, but Redcap turned his face to the wall and said nothing.

Once Jack Piper brought him a bowl containing hot wine mixed with oil and a beaten egg, bidding him drink it and sit out in the sun, but Redcap only turned his back and said crossly, "I'm not a hawk that has lost its courage."

Jack, amazed at this reply, put his hand on the boy's forehead to see if he was feverish. "Is his mind wandering?" he asked Meg.

"No," snapped Redcap before the woman could answer. "I have all my wits. And I'm not a hawk to be given medicine for courage. And — and — whatever people say about that strength that's hidden inside you, you can't call it up if it isn't there. I won't drink courage-medicine. Go away."

"Go to sleep, boy," said Meg and took the bowl from Jack and covered Redcap with a blanket.

She went out with Jack and Redcap heard her say, "He is still a sick boy, but I would rather see him getting ill-tempered than lying too still. I think he'll be well in a day or two."

Gradually he did get better although he still coughed and his heart was heavy with disappointment, so heavy that he could not speak of Red Eric even to Nial.

He began to take short walks and to play with the griskin which he knew he must leave behind when the minstrels took to the road again. Sometimes he watched the villagers shooting with their long bows for practice, sometimes he strolled into the courtyard of the Manor house to visit kennels, stables and mews.

He was pale now and thin and he seemed to have grown taller, for his sleeves were too short and his bare feet stuck out of his hose.

One morning he sat in the hut, idly wondering what to do, when a footstep on the threshold startled him and Nial came in.

"Fulk and Jack are packing the handcart," he said. "Are you ready?"

"Where are we going?" asked Redcap, listlessly.

Nial stretched. "Oh," he said yawning, "to the far ends of the earth, I suppose."

In an instant Redcap flew at him, butting him with his head, striking him with his fists, hitting him blindly wherever he could. At the words "the far ends of the earth" all his pent-up grief for Red Eric seemed to break from him in a great wave of fury.

"I hate you," he cried. "You never do anything but tease. How dare you mock me? How dare you? How dare you?"

Furiously he struck to right and to left but, after a first look of astonishment, Nial never moved. Redcap seized his hand, put his teeth to the thumb but caught Nial's eye and was afraid to bite.

He backed sulkily, his eyes smouldering, his lower lip quivering. Nial held out his hand.

"Would you care to finish what you began?" he asked quietly.

"No," screamed Redcap. "I never want to touch your hand again. I shall never speak to you again. You're not my friend. Go away." He stamped. "Go away, I say."

"I am never one for staying where I am not wanted," said Nial and went out, closing the door softly.

Redcap stamped around the room muttering, "Foul beast! Foul beast!" He knocked over a stool and left it with its three legs sticking up in the air. He kicked at the wall, saying, "I hate you! I hate you!" But Nial was not there to hear him and he was beginning to feel miserable instead of angry. "He need not have said it," he thought. "He need not have yawned when he talked of 'the far ends of the earth'. He might have known. . . ."

But how should.Nial have known when he had not told him? Nobody knew what had happened on the day when the griskin had nearly drowned.

Redcap stood still looking at the closed door through which Nial had gone. He had lost Red Eric, whom he had set out to find, and he had driven Nial, whom he loved, away.

Tears began to gather under his lids. He dried them with his sleeve but they overflowed, trickled down his cheeks and dropped from his chin. He picked up his scarlet hood, which was lying on a bench, and mopped his eyes but he was crying in earnest now and, do what he would, the tears continued to pour down his face.

The click of the latch startled him and he looked up to see Fulk in the doorway.

"We're waiting," said he. "Blow your nose and wipe your face. You look like a drowned badger. What's the matter?"

"I think," said Redcap meekly, "I think I would like to go home."

"Think again," said Fulk shortly.

Redcap's voice quavered. "I want to do nothing b-but go home."

"You are being foolish," said Fulk. "You know quite well that you're too far away. Put on your hood and come before we all outstay our welcome and before you make me lose my temper. Step out gaily, now, like a minstrel and stop snivelling."

He took Redcap firmly by the arm and walked so quickly that the boy could scarcely keep up with him without running.

"We may have some trouble," he said as he strode along, "and you are to keep beside me and do as I tell you. That ill-tempered ploughman's wife with the black eyes threatened Jack Piper and me with the stocks again. The people have been good to us but I mistrust that woman and I mean to leave as soon as we are able."

Redcap looked across the green. A small group of men and women had gathered not far from the duck-pond where Nial, standing beside Jack Piper and the handcart, was amusing them with a song. They seemed gay enough but under the elm tree something was happening and it looked unpleasant. The black-eyed woman, whom Fulk distrusted, was struggling with two men, each of whom held her by the arm.

"Come peaceably, now; come peaceably, mistress," they urged. "'Tis by order of the steward. And the sooner you come, the sooner 'twill be over."

"Get you gone," screeched the woman and her arms swung around like the sails of a windmill, but the two men caught and held them while a third bound them to her sides with a rope. Scarlet with rage she faced her neighbours, whom Fulk and Redcap had now joined.

"So you will have me punished, will you?" she stormed. "Falling on innocent folk when it's these rascally minstrels who are to blame. It's their lies that have brought me to this."

"Nay now, mistress," said one of the men. "You were brought up for trial at the manor court together with Mark Fisher who stole a pike from the lord's pond and Ned Whiteface who took his neighbour's nag. There were good men who spoke for them, but never one who stood by you. Your own husband spoke against you."

"And he shall hear from me again. Calling me a scold! You wait, Tom Plowman," she cried, shaking her fist in the direction of her own cottage. "You wait! You lying numskull!"

Fulk laughed. "Mistress," he said, "your own words speak against you."

"Ho, indeed," screamed the woman, "and what of you minstrels who escaped the stocks by a trick? Singers, forsooth. Frogs, say I, who make the night hideous with noise! Get you gone with your croaking! Keeping honest folk from their sleep."

Fulk went up to her. "So," said he, "you do not like the croaking of frogs?"

"None of your impudence," shouted the woman, growing redder than ever. "If your evil tongues wag at me I will have you and your vagabonds stoned."

"Pay no heed to her, master minstrel," cried the miller, who was standing beside his wife Meg. "She is nothing but a common scold who will soon get what she deserves."

"And that hour is not far distant," said another, "and when it comes I warrant she will know more about the croaking of frogs than she does now for she will be down in the pond among them."

The villagers laughed aloud, and even Redcap, whose eyes were still red, smiled half-heartedly. He had once seen a scold ducked in his own village pond and he remembered how she had gulped and spluttered.

The woman tossed her head angrily at the laughing people.

"And you mend your manners too," she said, "miscalling me as always. Who gave these beggarly minstrels the right to sing after dark, breaking my sleep? Croaking like frogs they were and taking no notice when I bade them keep quiet." She sniffed, glaring at Fulk. "Waking honest folk! Disturbing their prayers."

"'Tis a grand thing, surely, when a lady prays in her sleep!" said Nial and the villagers laughed again.

"What say you to that, mistress?" asked the miller.

The woman glowered. "If they come outside my door again, I'll say what I said before," she screamed and her voice was hoarse with rage.

Fulk pulled off his cap and swept her such a low bow that his bedraggled pheasant's feather picked up still more dust.

"The lady should know the story of St. Benno and the frog," he said. At this the villagers leant forward with so sudden a movement of interest that they looked almost as though they were taking part in some sort of drill.

"Tell it," cried Meg Miller, "but be speedy, master minstrel, for when the bell rings, Master Greysleeves will be here and the scold will be ducked before we go to our daily tasks."

"Ay, be speedy, be speedy," cried everyone and Jack Piper beat on his little drum for silence.

Fulk took a step back into the middle of the circle and the angry woman stared at him with eyes hard as flint.

"There was a saint," said he speaking quietly and looking steadily at the woman's scowling face. "His name was Benno and the old books say that he would pray in the fields and by the rivers when he walked for exercise, and it was his habit, every day, to stand for a while by a certain marsh and collect his thoughts so that he might turn them to holy matters.

"It happened one evening that a frog was croaking in the water. 'K-k-k-kek, k-k-k-kek.' And because it was so talkative Benno was disturbed and could not give his mind to his prayers, so he shook his finger at it.

" 'Frog,' said he, 'be a Seraphian.' And straightway the creature ceased croaking, for in Seraphus (a place, my friends, which I have never set eyes on) the frogs are dumb.

"All was quiet now and the saint went on his way, murmuring a prayer, but he had not gone far when the words of the prophet Daniel came into his mind, and he found himself, instead of praying, saying aloud what Daniel had said: 'O ye whales, and all that move in the waters, bless ye the Lord.'

"Forthwith, he went back to the pond and beckoned to the frog, which was sitting mournfully and silent upon a wet stone. 'Frog,' said he, 'the prophet bade all that move in the waters bless the Lord. Perchance your singing is more agreeable to God than my own prayer. Forget what I said to you and continue to praise God in the way that you always do.'

"No sooner had he spoken than the pond came to life. Up from the waters, among the reeds, in the slime and on the wet stones, frogs appeared and the air was filled with their joyful croaking.

"So mistress," said Fulk, "if we disturbed your prayers by what you were pleased to call our croaking, perchance we were praising God in a manner more agreeable than yours. We bid you take example from St. Benno."

Once again, he swept her a bow but the woman could not answer. "You — you . . ." she began. Her breast was heaving, two blue veins stuck out on her forehead and a little pulse seemed to be beating in her throat.

"May the evil one fly away with you," she screamed at last and Redcap, who had never seen such anger, was frightened and moved closer to Nial, but his heart sank for he saw that Nial did not even look at him.

At this moment the church bell began to ring and the steward appeared in the porch followed by the priest and two men carrying a roughly made stool fixed between a pair of shafts.

When they reached the green they stood still and Master Greysleeves the steward addressed the angry woman.

"Ann, wife of Ned Plowman," he said, "at the manor court, held yesterday, you were condemned to the ducking stool as a common scold. None spoke for you but many against you."

"They lied," said Ann.

"I think not," said the steward. "Last night, although you knew that your unbridled tongue had brought judgment against you, I myself heard you reviling these minstrels who are our guests."

"You lie, you foul mouthed, evil speaking . . ."

"Daughter," said the priest, "be silent for your own lips condemn you."

"Do your duty," said the steward with a nod to the two men who had brought the stool.

Quickly and skilfully they tied Ann into it almost before she had time to struggle, then, standing between the shafts, one in front and one behind, they lifted the stool and carried it to the edge of the pond. The villagers followed, silent and expectant, till one called, "Make friends with the frogs, Ann," which brought a gust of laughter.

A long plank fixed in the middle to the stump of a tree stood by the water's edge. To one end of this the ducking-stool was strapped and the plank, working on a swivel, was turned until the ducking-stool and its unfortunate occupant were over the surface of the pond. Then, as though they were playing see-saw, three men sat on the empty end of the plank, which stretched across dry land. The steward gave a sign, up in the air they went, and down, splash, into the water went Ann. The people cheered.

Down came the men and up in the air above the pond came Ann, sneezing and coughing. She tried to shout something but down went the ducking-stool and the muddy water was over her head.

Up and down she went, in and out of the water, gurgling, spluttering, sneezing and coughing. Her hair hung in muddy wet streaks over her face. She was drenched to the skin.

"Have you had enough?" cried the men on the other side of the plank.

She cursed them and down she went into the water again.

Up, down. Up, down.

"Nial," said Redcap, "she'll choke."

Nial paid no attention to him and the ducking-stool continued to move up into the air and down into the water.

"Ann Plowman, have you anything more to say?" asked the steward.

Ann shook her head feebly and the men at the other end of the plank twisted the swivel, brought her to dry land and unfastened the ropes. With downcast eyes, she stepped off the ducking-stool, wrung out her skirt and walked away, subdued, dripping and silent.

"Teach the frogs to croak as quietly as you do now, Ann!" shouted one of the village women, but the priest shook his head at her and said quietly, "Judge not that ye be not judged."

No one spoke, now, until Master Greysleeves glanced up at the sun with one eye closed and said, "Be off to work, all of you, we have wasted enough time."

"Off to work?" said Fulk. "Then we will away, too, for the

UP AND DOWN SHE WENT

life of an idle vagabond is a busy one. Fare you well, friends, and many thanks for much kindness."

"God keep you, good minstrels," cried the people and hurried away to their daily tasks.

"We thank you for many a happy hour," said the steward, and he gave each minstrel as well as Redcap a silver coin.

The priest came up and shook hands with them.

"Your blessing, father," said Nial and each of them knelt before him as he murmured a prayer.

When he had finished, they all made the sign of the cross, rose to their feet and walked away towards the Manor house so as to take the short cut across the moat.

The priest stood watching them for a moment, then he called, "Redcap."

The boy came running back.

"Yes?" he said. "Yes, father? You called me."

"Did you hear my blessing?" asked the priest. "I said 'Go in peace'."

"Mm?" said Redcap, puzzled, for he had often heard these words.

"You may be going a long way," said the priest. "Remember that you go in peace."

"How can I?" asked Redcap, suddenly distressed. "I quarrelled with Nial and — and he won't speak to me, now."

"Run along," said the priest.

And Redcap, glad to relieve his feelings by moving as quickly as he could, dashed away and caught up his companions. They were talking together. Fulk turned for a second to see where Redcap was and Jack Piper smiled but Nial never even glanced at him, so Redcap walked behind, snapping his fingers at Rex to coax the dog away from his master. But Rex sensed that something was amiss and trotted faithfully at Nial's heels with his tail between his legs as though he himself were in disgrace.

Across the plank over the moat they walked single file, Fulk leading, Jack Piper following with the cart, Nial humming behind him and Redcap in the rear. At one place the boy pretended to stumble and called, "Nial," but Nial walked ahead without turning and Rex, standing half way between the two of them, looked first at one, then at the other, and decided to join his master.

Once across the plank, they were out of the village and moving along the dusty lane. They did not walk quickly and Redcap, tired of lagging at their heels, ran ahead to pick some buttercups glowing here and there in the grass at the roadside. He stuck them in his belt and as the three minstrels passed him, he called huskily, "Nial."

"Shall I give you a hand with the cart, Jack?" asked Nial without looking at Redcap.

"It's light enough," said Jack, "and I'm feeling strong after the good food we have eaten and the lady's herb poultice on my leg."

"Nial," whispered Redcap.

"Shall we sing, Fulk?" asked Nial, taking no notice of him. "I'm thinking it's a long while since we tried 'Summer is i-coming in' and the time is ripe for it." He began to carol blithely,

> Summer is i-coming in
> Loud sing cuckoo!
> Groweth seed and bloweth mead
> And springeth the wood now.
>> Sing cuckoo now, sing cuckoo
>> Sing cuckoo, sing cuckoo now.

"Nial," said Redcap, but the Irishman did not seem to hear and went on humming, "Sing cuckoo now, sing cuckoo!"

Redcap was growing desperate. He plucked at Nial's sleeve.

"Nial," he pleaded, "I am sorry. I-I'm trying to beg your pardon."

Nial stood still and the other minstrels went on.

"Yes?" said Nial.

"I'm sorry," whispered Redcap, looking at the ground and rubbing the dust off one foot with the other.

"When I am talking with a man, I like to see his face and hear his voice," said Nial frostily.

Redcap cleared his throat. With an effort he looked up and said, "I beg your pardon. I never meant any of those things that I said."

"'Tis a bad thing," said Nial, "not to mean what you say, for that leads to a misunderstanding. Have I your meaning correctly, that you are sorry when you say you are sorry?"

Redcap nodded and Nial put out his hand.

"Please will you be my friend again," asked Redcap.

Nial looked down at him seriously. "Did you think I had stopped?" he asked.

A load seemed to be slipping from Redcap's mind. For a minute or two he did not speak, then he looked at Nial and said with difficulty, "Nial, Green Stranger was Red Eric."

"I wondered," said Nial.

"He told me that he was going to the far ends of the earth."

"Oh," said Nial, a light seeming to dawn on him.

Redcap choked back a sob and went on bravely.

"Nobody knows where the earth ends," he said, "and I thought you were being cruel to me and — and — mocking when I was — when I was . . ."

"When you were unhappy," said Nial, finishing the sentence for him. "I am sorry you thought that of me. And as for the ends of the earth maybe we shall meet Red Eric somewhere on the way, for there's no knowing at all where a minstrel will find himself."

Redcap shook his head disconsolately. "He's gone," he said, "and I shall never find him, now."

"A very long word is 'never'," answered Nial. "I'm thinking that 'hope' is a shorter and better one for there's a promise in it." He looked away into the distance where the shadows of the summer clouds were skimming across the fields. "All his life a man sees clouds and shadows of clouds," he said, "but once he loses hope of finding the sunshine, he's not a man at all."

"What is he?" asked Redcap staring at Nial.

"A thing without a heart," replied the minstrel. "Just something that's alive yet destroyed entirely. So now you and I take the long road again, and around every corner we are saying to ourselves, 'Ha, Red Eric may be there.' We hope to find him at a fair and if not at a fair at a monastery gate drinking a bowl of soup with other beggars. And if not at the monastery gates, making his way with some pilgrims to a shrine and if not with the pilgrims, at a wedding, in the city, and if not there, in a castle or a church or a . . ."

"There is no end to where he may be," said Redcap.

"No end at all till our hopes are fulfilled." Nial smiled down at the upturned face.

"So now we go on looking," said Redcap cheerfully.

"Yes," said Nial, "but maybe you had better pay some attention to looking up the road, just now."

Redcap turned his head.

Standing a short distance away, in his usual attitude, with legs apart and arms folded, was Fulk, waiting, impatience printed on every line of his body.

"Whew!" said Nial.

Redcap chuckled. "He's angry with me as usual," he said happily. "Coming Fulk! Coming!" he cried and ran, hopping and skipping, up the road.

For the first time, since Red Eric had disappeared, he was himself again.

Nial followed, whistling like a blackbird.

O DEAR, WHAT CAN THE MATTER BE?

*In which the minstrels go to the fair and.Redcap, meeting
a gang of ragamuffins, comes to grief*

TIME passed.

Summer drifted towards autumn with red squirrels
leaping from tree to tree collecting acorns and beechnuts
for their winter hoards and the moss in the woods smelling
earthy and wet. Blackberries were nearly over, the hazel nuts
getting ripe and sweet, and in the hedges there were scarlet hips
and haws, but nowhere was there a trace of Red Eric.

To Redcap time seemed to move more slowly, now, because
he had not quite recovered from his illness and coughing made
him tired. But he was happy, for Nial had said that the missing

uncle might well be found at a fair, and, this morning, to a fair they were bound.

Redcap knew that it would be held for the serious purpose of trade and that English and foreign merchants would be there, buying, selling and placing orders. But there was always the "fun of the fair" where bear-wards brought their dancing bears, jugglers performed tricks and minstrels told tales or sang songs. And it was at these sideshows that he hoped to find a "green stranger", so he trudged along cheerfully, looking on all sides and taking in every detail.

Never had he seen so many people going in the same direction.

A woman on horseback ambled along with a large lamb across the front of her saddle. Men came driving cattle and pigs, and girls had flocks of geese, for at this season beef and mutton were salted and kept in vats for the winter and all but the poor ate goose and poultry when they wanted fresh meat.

Redcap eagerly scanned the crowd, stepping aside as a cavalcade of merchants in pointed hats and coats of sober shades trotted past him, their bridles jingling, their voices rising and falling as they made rapid bargains one with another. But Red Eric, he knew, would not ride with such a company.

A carrier with his cart full of casks and leather bottles of wine, cracked a long whip, and a line of pack horses, loaded with wool, stopped every now and then to crop grass at the roadside, heedless of the shouts of their driver. Some people walked, others were in covered carts or litters, borne between shafts, to which a horse was harnessed in front and behind. But Red Eric was not among them.

There were pedlars with packs on their backs, filled with ribands, packets of needles and the trinkets that young women liked to buy. There were herbalists, describing the wonders performed by their pills and powders. There were beggars, travelling tinkers and cut purses whose eyes darted here, there and everywhere in the hope of snipping a leather bag from an unguarded belt. But Red Eric was not to be seen.

"Nial?" said Redcap, watching the moving crowd. "If Red Eric comes, where will he lodge? I don't see where so many people can sleep."

"I'm thinking that most people will sleep out of doors," answered Nial. "The inns will have beds only for merchants and mine host will make a pretty penny. Some of the citizens may take in their friends and the monastery has a guest house. But a wandering minstrel must shift for himself."

"Shall *we* make a pretty penny, too?" asked Redcap.

"That remains to be seen," said Nial. "It's to be hoped that we make more than they take from us at the entrance. We shall have to pay a big toll for Jack Piper because he has a handcart."

"How else do you think the good monks grow fat?" asked Fulk dryly. "The monastery has the right to hold this fair outside the city. Every merchant, cart, litter, waggon and pack horse pays a toll. Every stall holder, too, has to give ground rent. Even a poor minstrel is taxed. And it all goes to the monks who live in that monastery." He jerked his thumb over his shoulder at the high stone wall which they were passing.

But Redcap was not looking at the monastery. He was watching the crowd.

"I think we shall make much more money than our toll," he said. "There are crowds of people. If you all sing and tell stories and Rex goes around on his hind legs and I do my somersaults . . ."

Fulk stood still in the middle of the road.

"I would like to remind you," he said, "that I am master of this troupe and it is I who order what is to be done."

"But I wasn't giving orders," said Redcap.

"I am glad to hear it and since we are talking about orders, I will now tell you what *you* are NOT to do. Today you are to do no juggling or somersaulting."

Redcap's eyes grew wide with surprise and distress.

"You have been ill," said Fulk more kindly, "and each time

you practise we have to stop because you cough, so until I have put you through your paces with a *perfect* result, there is to be no performance. There will be many other minstrels and jugglers at this fair and I cannot have you stumbling because you catch your breath or . . ."

"But Fulk . . ."

"I have given my orders. For the next few days you are to sit still and rest while *we* do the work. Afterwards you may help Rex collect the money."

Redcap was perturbed. He was still proud of what the minstrels had taught him and liked "showing off" before appreciative grown-ups and envious boys and girls.

"But Fulk, I'm well again. I can perform every . . ."

"The only performance you are asked to give is obedience. And since your best trick is the disappearing act, there's to be no wandering off by yourself. Remember. *You stay by me, all the time, day and night.*"

Nial knew what was in Redcap's mind.

"In the evening I shall be seeking Red Eric, myself," he said kindly.

"And if you find him," answered Fulk, lightly cuffing Redcap, who was looking sulky, "say that we shall be glad to hand over his surly nephew, who has been nothing but a burden ever since he joined us. *Take that look off your face,*" he roared.

At this shout Redcap lost his temper. Since his illness he had grown cross very easily and now for the first time in his life he rounded on Fulk.

"If I'm a burden, I don't see why you wouldn't let me go home when I said I would," he blazed, his face scarlet with anger.

Fulk looked at him with eyes as cold as steel.

"I shall do what I like," muttered Redcap. "Rex can collect your old money by himself."

He had spoken this last sentence under his breath but Fulk's ears were sharp. Without making any remark he stretched up to the branch of an elm tree growing outside the Monastery and broke off a stick.

This looked serious and Redcap, swaggering so as not to appear frightened, eyed him warily.

"Best legs forward," said Jack Piper suddenly, "we shall be late," and he pushed his cart between Redcap and Fulk and began to sing lustily,

> The bear-ward with his dancing bear
> The carrier with his cart and mare
> The pack horse, bringing wool to wear —
> They're all a-coming to the fair!
> With a heigh ho, hey.

Some of the people stopped, a little crowd gathered around the minstrels and Jack Piper, still with his cart between Fulk and Redcap, went on singing:

> The money-changers will be there
> The merchants, too, bowed down with care,
> Forget ye not the minstrels' share.
> They're all a-coming to the fair!
> With a heigh ho, hey.

"And right welcome a minstrel will be. A man cannot spend all his time buying and selling," cried a pleasant voice.

And there was Master Greysleeves, riding a pot-bellied nag, on his way to order the year's supply of salt, spices and sugar for Lord Henry's household.

He threw a coin to Jack Piper, nodded to Nial and poked Redcap in the ribs with his whip.

"Be on your best behaviour," he said, "for I see that the Master Minstrel has a stick, and by the look in his eyes he is not going to spare even the winner of a garter or a griskin."

He winked at Fulk and rode on, little knowing how near to the mark he had been, and some of the people, recognizing a bride's garter in Redcap's hood began to chaff him, saying, "Who's your sovereign lady, young red patch?"

This caused much laughter and drew sympathetic attention to the minstrels, which was satisfactory, and so, since the people were obviously amused at and interested in Redcap, Fulk could hardly carry out his intention. But he did not throw away the stick. Instead, he put it with elaborate care into his belt and the expression on Redcap's face brought a new outburst of laughter from the people, who thought that master and boy were playing for their benefit.

Crowd and minstrels moved on.

They were near the outskirts of the town now and the fair with its covered booths and open stalls lay spread before them, a triangular city in miniature, bounded on one side by the town wall, on another by the long wall around the monastery grounds, and on the third by a rough barricade where monks stood at intervals, receiving the tolls.

At the main entrance, a fat man in grey hose and a belted brown woollen tunic with wide sleeves was standing near a trumpeter. At a blast from the trumpet, he stepped forward.

"Oyez," he cried, "Oyez, be it proclaimed on the King our sovereign lord's behalf that every person having recourse to the fair, keep the peace and that no man make any affray by which the same peace may be broke, on pain of imprisonment or the pillory or grievous fine to be made as Mayor and Aldermen deem fitting."

He stepped back. "Tarara", went the trumpet. The fair was open and the crowd surged forward.

"Up, Rex!" whistled Jack Piper and the dog jumped into the handcart.

"Keep your hand on my belt, Redcap," said Nial. "Then you'll not get lost." But Fulk had pushed Jack and his cart ahead of him and was holding Redcap firmly by the arm.

"Anyone who loses himself today," he said, "knows what to expect when he's found."

"Master dear," said Nial. "I never was more fearful in my life. A man like myself is apt to get mislaid. If you could

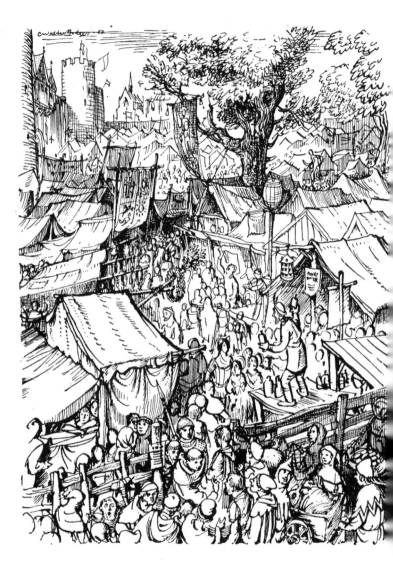

A CITY IN MINIATURE

coax the young boy to steal that stick from your belt, now, I would feel easier in my mind, I would."

'I am not joking," said Fulk stiffly.

"Well now, who would have thought it?" sighed Nial and took Redcap's other arm as they pushed their way through the chattering crowd.

Now, indeed, the fair looked more than ever like a city on market day. Booths, stalls and warehouses were set closely together in lines resembling narrow streets, and wooden notice boards, pointing north, south, east and west directed anyone who could read to "Wine Street", "Spicery Corner", "Wool Lane", "Silken Way", "Pitch and Timber Alley". In one or two places a sign representing a large coin carried the words "Foreign Money Changed Here", and groups of thin-lipped quick-eyed men from Lombardy were seated at wooden tables stacked with small bags of gold and silver

Broken English and foreign languages mingled with cries of "Penny a bunch", "Hot pies", "New brooms for sale", and Redcap heard the voices of Venetian spice merchants, French vendors of wine, Northern timber sellers from overseas and wool dealers from the Cotswolds, all eagerly taking orders.

But the minstrels' business was not at the counter, and Jack Piper, carefully pushing his handcart with a polite, "By your leave, my masters," wound his way to a small open space near the city wall where a man with ninepins was offering passers-by "Balls for hire! See how many you can knock down. Come, come, come! Hire a ball and hit a pin!"

"Out, Rex," cried Jack Piper.

The dog leapt from the cart and sat up on his hind legs. A wooden bowl was put in front of him, Jack beat on his drum and Fulk and Nial began to sing.

It was astonishing how quickly a crowd gathered, but everyone was not buying and selling, and for many of the towns-folk fairtime was a holiday. They laughed and clapped and Redcap, sitting somewhat dismally on the handcart, longed to join in the singing but was afraid that he might cough and this, he knew, would annoy Fulk, who was already frowning at him.

He jumped to his feet. The people, in carefree mood, were tossing coins into the circle and Crooked Smile's frown was a sign that he should collect the money. He picked up the wooden bowl, soon filled it and poured the coins into a leather bag which he stuffed inside his jerkin for safety, then returned to his place.

Never had the minstrels been so popular and Redcap, feeling neglected and forlorn, was soon hidden by the growing numbers who surrounded them.

He kicked his heels against the sides of the handcart and thought how mean it was of Fulk to prevent him from sharing all this praise and applause.

"I could have done every trick that I've learned," he thought, "and the people would have clapped more than ever and thrown me pennies. He *needn't* be mean to me. Nial says I help him."

"Psst, boy!"

The sound made him look up.

A ragged urchin, some two or three years older than he was, stood in front of him and the expression on his face was one of extreme curiosity and some contempt.

"Psst! You, in the red hood! Who are you?"

"I am one of the minstrels," said Redcap loftily. "I am the chief juggler and tumbler." He leant back, swinging his legs.

"Likely tale!" said the urchin and suddenly put two fingers into his mouth and gave so shrill a whistle that Redcap nearly jumped out of his skin.

He turned quickly to see if the minstrels had heard. But they were still singing, hidden from him by the crowd, and when he looked back again the urchin had been joined by half a dozen equally ragged friends.

"Says he's a minstrel," said the first, indicating Redcap with his thumb.

"Pah," said another and spat over his shoulder. "If he's a minstrel, why isn't he singing?"

"Says he's their juggler and tumbler," sneered the first.

"Then why isn't he juggling or tumbling?"

"Because he's piping his eye," grinned a third. "I saw him. He's no minstrel. A whimpering babe-in-arms, he is! Rock his cradle!"

They made a combined dash for the handcart.

Redcap slipped off quickly and doubling his fists squared up to them. They backed, grinning, luring him away from the crowd to a more open space.

"Showing fight, eh?" cried the first urchin and his freckled face scowled. "Stand aside, all, I'll show him," and he rolled back his ragged sleeves and spat on his hands. "Juggler, eh?"

"Yes," shouted Redcap with blazing eyes.

"Tumbler, eh?"

"Yes," said Redcap, taking a step or two nearer, his breath coming quickly. "I can do every kind of somersault. *You* can't! I can do trick tumbling!"

"Then tumble," shouted his enemy and struck him a blow which sent Redcap on to his back.

"One, two . . ." counted the delighted urchins, and Redcap scrambled to his feet and closed with his assailant, while the minstrels, ignorant of the fray, continued to sing blithely.

Redcap hit wildly in every direction as his enemy pranced around him, now feinting, now planting a shrewd blow. Redcap, being smaller, could never strike higher than the other boy's chest, but he himself took blows on each side of the head, on fists, arms and ribs, and soon he began to feel weak.

His lip was swollen and his nose bleeding, but still he returned to the charge while the excited urchins danced about shouting for their champion and booing Redcap.

He felt his right eye closing, began to cough and received a violent punch which sent him reeling to the ground. Instantly his enemy was on him and they rolled over and over, locked in each other's arms.

The freckled boy tore at Redcap's jerkin, which burst open. Out flew the leather bag and the pennies rolled in all directions.

"After them," shrieked the boys, scattering and scooping up the money.

Redcap's enemy jumped to his feet. "You dare take them all!" he cried. "I am your captain. Stop!"

He stooped to pick up a penny and Redcap leapt on him from behind, twining his arms around his neck, and his legs around his body.

"Get off," shouted the boy, battering Redcap's legs and trying to twist his wrists.

"Not till you say I'm a minstrel," gasped Redcap. "Say I'm a juggler. Say I'm a tumbler!" and he pummelled the freckled boy on the head.

"Get off, will you!" yelled the boy, and with a sudden heave dislodged Redcap, seized him and flung him bodily into the middle of the crowd, scattering the people to right and to left.

"A fight! A fight!" they cried. "Stop them!"

But there was no need.

Slippery as an eel, the freckled boy had slunk away. His companions, too, had vanished, just as the guardian of the fair with two stalwart men on each side of him appeared on the scene and pushed his way among the startled people.

"What is all this?"

Somebody thrust Redcap into the middle of the circle and he stood there, bleeding from the nose, one eye closed, his mouth out of shape and his knuckles bleeding.

The three minstrels gasped and Fulk, scarlet with anger, stepped forward.

But the guardian of the fair waved him back and addressed Redcap.

"Have you been fighting?"

"Yes," said Redcap, "but I didn't have time to finish."

"He would have been cat's meat if he had finished," laughed a man in the crowd. "Look at him."

"Silence," said the fair-guardian. "Who is this boy?"

Out of his one eye Redcap could see that Fulk was too angry to speak. Nial spread his hands.

"Boys will always be fighting now and then," he said.

"I didn't ask for information about all boys," said the fair-guardian. "I asked who is *this* boy?"

Jack Piper limped up and put his hand on Redcap's shoulder. 'The lad travels with me," he said.

The fair-guardian turned on him, severely.

"If the boy is of your company it's you who should keep him out of mischief. At the opening of the fair you were all given public notice that anyone guilty of disorderly conduct would be imprisoned or fined. You have no doubt collected money by your minstrelsy, so you will now follow me to the fair court and pay whatever fine the Mayor and Aldermen decide. Come.'

The two stalwart men stepped up to Jack Piper and stood on each side of him.

"But — but, Sir Guardian," babbled Redcap in dismay. 'I had all the money and — and — it fell out of my pouch in the fight and the boys took it. There is only this penny."

He opened his fist and showed a penny which had lodged between his belt and the sheath of his knife.

The guardian looked at the outstretched palm, then at Redcap's miserable face.

"You have put your father, or maybe he is your master, into a sorry state," he said, "but before he is taken away for punishment, I will give you a chance of helping him."

Here some of the onlookers cheered and he put up his hand for silence.

"How did this — er — affray begin?"

"I told some boys that I was a juggler and a tumbler," said Redcap, "and they wouldn't believe me. So we fought. I *am* a tumbler."

Fiercely he said it and fiercely he thought that all this was Fulk's fault. If he had been allowed to show what he could do, he would have been praised by the onlookers instead of battered, black and blue, by a silly unbelieving boy.

"Why did you not prove it instead of fighting?" asked the guardian.

"I wasn't asked," muttered Redcap.

"Then you may prove it now," said the guardian, "and if you do well, I may pardon the man who is responsible for you because you seem to have been fighting on his behalf, wishing to prove him a good master."

This was scarcely true, for Redcap had wanted to prove himself a good tumbler and had not given a thought to Jack Piper or to either of the others.

"Clear a space," said the guardian. "This boy is going to prove that he speaks the truth."

Nial raised his eyebrows at Fulk, who shrugged his shoulders irritably, but Redcap did not see them. He had sprung lightly on to his hands and was walking on them within the circle of people. True, his legs wobbled a little when he passed Fulk, but he gave a good performance and the people clapped.

Encouraged, he stood up, made a bow as he had been taught, said, "I will now show you the tumbler's tricks," and turned a series of rapid cartwheels.

Once on his feet again, he looked about him. Things were going well and he steadily kept his back to Fulk. Suddenly he became aware of seven faces, seven smiles of studied innocence and fourteen malicious eyes. The freckled urchin and his six friends had returned, wriggled their way through the crowd and were sitting in front as though they had never seen a fight and were interested in nothing but somersaults.

"A tumbler's somersaults . . ." began Redcap.

The boys leant forward and smiled politely.

"I will show how they are done," said Redcap, glaring malevolently at his enemies and thinking, "*Now* they shall see."

He braced himself, leapt forward, but slipped.

"Stumbler, not tumbler," said the freckled boy in a loud whisper.

The crowd laughed.

Redcap, determined to win more applause, stifled a fit of coughing and began again with the same result.

"Did he say bungler or tumbler," asked the freckled boy.

The crowd laughed again and Redcap, feeling dry about the mouth, stood up. His nose was bleeding afresh and there was a crimson splash in the middle of his face.

"Is he standing with his front or his back towards us?" asked the freckled boy innocently.

At this reference to the red blotch on his face and the scarlet patch on the seat of his hose, the entire crowd burst into great guffaws of laughter.

The freckled boy jumped to his feet. "Tumbler, tumbler!" he jeered and in a flash Redcap sent him sprawling.

A hand fell on his shoulder. Blindly he wrenched himself free, kicked his captor's shins and fled.

"Stop that boy!" shouted the fair-guardian, struggling to his feet, for Redcap's kick had tripped him. "Stop him!"

But Redcap was out of sight. Worming his way among the stalls, he had reached the boundary of the fair-ground and was running like a hare along the highway.

By the great elm tree, he was suddenly and violently sick.

XXI

FOR THE GLORY OF GOD?

In which a monk who does some strange sums tells the story of Our Lady's Tumbler and Redcap hears distressing news about Jack Piper

"WE never like the step to be dirty," said a plaintive voice, "so please throw this shovelful of earth over that mess and clear it away. The ditch will do."

A very fat monk in a black garment with a cowl over his head was standing at the top of some steps in a narrow wooden doorway.

"Thank you," he said when Redcap, still looking green and shaky, had obeyed. "And now, if you will follow me, I will take you into the brothers' washroom."

His eyes passed rapidly over Redcap's face.

"You are a horrible sight," he said.

"I was fighting," said Redcap, feeling that he ought to apologize for looking so dishevelled.

"It is quite unnecessary to explain by word of mouth since your appearance speaks for itself," said the monk. "One black eye, plus one bloody nose, plus one cut lip, plus two grazed knuckles, multiplied by one queazy stomach. Total, one boy who has been fighting. The sum is simple. Come in."

Redcap followed him through the doorway into the monastery grounds, where a narrow path, bounded on each side by a thick lavender hedge, led through a herb garden.

"Turn to the right, through that archway," directed the monk, "and you will see the monastery buildings. That door — over there — leads to the brothers' dormitory and next to it is the washroom. Sluice water over your face and hands but don't blow your nose on the towel. It's against the rules."

Around the stone floor of the washroom was a broad shallow gutter leading to a hole into which the dirty water passed when the monks had washed. In front of this gutter stood a row of wooden pails.

"Wash yourself in that one. Then throw the water into the drain and I will take you to the hospital-room for Brother Pierre to dress your cuts and bruises."

Redcap bathed his eye and dabbed his cut lip carefully. Both felt sore and his head ached, but the cold water seemed to clear his mind and he had a momentary pang when he thought of Fulk's remarks about disappearing and what might happen when he was found.

"I am sometimes called Brother Pudding Face," said the fat monk suddenly and handed Redcap a worn and rather dirty towel. "Now your face — but why fight?"

"They wouldn't believe what I said."

"That is a very usual human failing," said the monk. "What made you sick?"

"Turning somersaults after the fight, and running when the people laughed at me and . . ." Redcap coughed, then when he had recovered blurted out, "They mocked me. I hate them. I — I only wanted to show that I *could* do tumbler's tricks."

"I see," said the monk, leading the way out of the washroom. "A different sum this time. One somersault, plus two tumbler's tricks, plus much loud clapping: total one clever boy? Is that correct?"

"Well . . . You see. . . ."

"No," replied the monk. "I have given the wrong answer. Let us try again. One somersault plus two tumbler's tricks, plus much loud clapping: total one boastful boy. Take away the pride which goes before the fall and you get . . . ? What is the answer?"

Redcap did not speak.

"Is it one ashamed boy?"

"But I wanted them to know that I *could* do it well."

"Some people have such strange reasons for doing things," said the fat monk. "Now these brothers here . . . peep in with the eye that the fight spared."

They had reached the scriptorium, a low cool room where three monks were busy with reed pens copying manuscripts on to sheets of vellum. At a bench near the long high window, a young monk was pounding and mixing gum with warm water in a stone mortar, every now and then adding soot from an earthenware jar, to make a good black ink. Another had before him a sheet of old parchment covered with lists and figures which he was scraping out with pumice stone and a sharp knife, so that the parchment could be used again.

But it was behind a brother who was painting that the fat monk stopped. He was illuminating the border of a book with a gold, green and blue pattern of vine leaves on one of which rested a minute vermilion ladybird. And the smile on his face was one of pure delight.

Redcap peered over his shoulder and he looked up for a minute, without noticing the boy, then bent again over his work and on the page, handled so tenderly, appeared a butterfly with pale wings as delicate as gossamer.

The fat monk drew Redcap away, breathing loudly in his effort to be quiet.

"Do you know why he is doing that?" he asked as he led the boy through a stone corridor towards the hospital where the sick monks were nursed.

"For the library," said Redcap without hesitation.

The fat monk laughed. His sides shook and his eyes disappeared. "He has another reason, too," he said chuckling. "I will tell you about it in a minute but now we must put a plaster on that cut and a bandage over your eye. Brother Pierre, I have brought you a patient."

He opened a door and walked into a small room leading into the hospital. A thin monk with the sleeves of his heavy robe tied back and a linen apron bound around his waist was bandaging a lame man's foot.

"Tiens, voilà! It is finished. Have a care, mon frère, how you walk. Peace be with you."

"And with you, peace," said the lame monk and hobbled away on two sticks.

Brother Pierre turned to the fat monk.

"A new patient, you say? Mais, quel horreur! What have you done to yourself, mon petit?"

"I fought," said Redcap.

"A young knight, hein? Sit here while I put a salve on that lip and bathe your eye. It is well that you are come, for the cut above the eye, it is not clean, and without attention it would fester and give you pain. You will sit very still. Yes?"

"Ouch."

"Pardon, mon fils! I regret that I hurt you. It will soon be over. So! Now again. So. Ça va mieux? That feels better? Yes?"

"Thank you."

Brother Pierre dabbed and swabbed gently and skilfully, put a dressing over the eye and a firm bandage to keep it in place, then stood back and surveyed Redcap.

"The knuckles will heal quickly," he said, "and the lip is already less swollen. You feel better, hein?"

"Yes, thank you, but I'm hot," and Redcap pulled at the collar of his jerkin.

Brother Pierre touched the boy's neck with the back of his hand, then felt his forehead.

"He has a little fever. Let him rest on that pallet for an hour and I think he will be better. I go now to tend the sick. Au revoir, mon enfant, lie down and sleep a little."

"Go in peace," said the fat monk and closed the door after him. "Now, boy. Lie down there and shut your eyes. I will sit with you."

Redcap stretched himself out on the straw mattress but he did not shut his eyes. He looked at the fat monk and smiled.

"The jest?" asked the monk. "You are trying not to laugh?"

Redcap chuckled. He was thinking that the monk's fat face

257

was like the stone one carved in a pillar which he had seen when they walked past the church, but he did not like to say so.

"It is my face," said his companion, reading his thoughts. "Two eyes like damsons in a lump of dough, plus one nose like a slice of lemon peel, plus one pursed mouth like a glazed cherry: total a fat monk or a pudding face. I know the sum!"

He laughed and his eyes disappeared again. This reminded Redcap of something.

"Why did you laugh when I said that the monks were making books for the library?" he asked. "I couldn't see that it was funny, and you laughed at me."

"I have discovered," said the monk, "that you do not like being laughed at. Life is more comfortable if one gets used to it."

"I know," said Redcap, "but I never do like it. Do you?"

"I delight in it," said the monk. "It's like spice in a pudding. The other person's laughter is the spice and I am — the — pudding."

He chuckled till his sides shook and Redcap laughed too.

"Ha!" said the monk, wiping his eyes and pointing at Redcap. "You are laughing at me. Good boy, I do enjoy it. But you asked me something? Yes, yes of course. You said the monks in the scriptorium were making books for the library." He paused. "That was the truth but not the whole truth."

"What else do they do it for?" asked Redcap.

"For the glory of God," answered the fat monk. "Now, if that had been your reason for turning those somersaults. . . ."

Redcap sat up and stared. He was, in fact, rather shocked.

"One can't turn a somersault for God. That would be very — *queer*."

"Not at all," said the monk, pursing up his lips so that they really did look like a glazed cherry. "It has been done. Lie down again and shut your eyes while I tell you about it. I always find that I can *see* a story if I listen with closed eyes."

He put a pillow, stuffed with hay, under Redcap's head,

pulled the bench on which he had been sitting nearer to the straw pallet, and leaning forward lightly closed the boy's eyes with his forefinger.

"It is the story of Our Lady's Tumbler," he said.

"In France there lived, not long ago, a minstrel, who had journeyed to many places and had lived so wild a life that, weary of the world, he gave up all that he had and became a monk.

"But when this tumbler, who was so graceful and fair to look upon, became a monk, he could neither read nor recite an Our Father or a Hail Mary. He knew only how to leap and to spring, to tumble and to turn somersaults.

"Because of this he was sorely grieved, for everywhere he saw the monks and the novices serving God. There were priests at the altars and deacons at the gospels. Acolytes rang the bell for the services. One monk recited a verse, another a lesson. Each in his own work laboured for the glory of God.

" 'Alas,' said he, 'never shall I be of service here for I know nothing. Why did I become a monk when I cannot even pray as others do? If it is discovered that all I do here is to eat my bread, I shall be turned away.'

"And he wept bitterly and prayed, 'Holy Mother Mary beseech your Heavenly Father, of His Grace to guide me that I may be able to serve Him and you.'

"Lamenting thus in his heart he wandered mournfully about the church until he came to the crypt and there he crouched beside an altar where there was an image of Our Lady, the Holy Mary.

"He felt safely hidden, but when he heard the bell ring for Mass he leapt to his feet, trembling and crying aloud, 'Woe is me, each monk is praying and saying the responses and here I live like a tethered ox, neither speaking a prayer nor chanting. How shall I serve God?'

"He fell silent for a moment, then with a sigh lifted up his hands to the altar saying, 'Mother of God, I can do only what

259

I have learnt. Others do service by prayer but I, after my own manner, will do service by tumbling.'

"Then quietly he stripped off his monkish habit, leaving only a close-fitting tunic, and turning to the image, said, humbly, 'Lady, I commend to your keeping my body and my soul, despise not the manner of my service.'

"Swiftly and with deep earnestness, he began to turn somersaults, now high, now low, now backwards, now forwards, and between each tumbler's trick, he fell on his knees before the image and said, 'Lady, the others serve and I serve, too.'

"And he turned the somersault of Metz and the somersault of Champagne, the Roman somersault and the somersaults of Spain, of Brittany and of Lorraine. Then he leapt from his feet to his hands, walking upon them and twirling his legs.

" 'Lady,' he said, 'I do this for your sake and for love of God, in no wise for myself. In the Church they are singing but I am come here to divert you.'

"As long as the Mass lasted, he capered and tumbled and sprang till he fell fainting upon the ground, whispering, 'Lady I can do no more today but I will come back.'

"Every day this tumbler returned to the crypt and did his service according to his lights. And it became known among the other brothers that he went there, yet none knew what he did.

"Now, in the course of time, one of the monks, who blamed him in his heart for neglecting matins and vespers, stole down to the crypt and kept watch. And he saw him perform all somersaults, tumbler's tricks and dances. 'By my faith,' muttered this monk, 'he dances and leaps while we are at prayer or at work. Would that the other monks might see him. How they would laugh to watch him killing himself by tumbling.'

"And he smiled and was merry. But when he saw how the tumbler fell to the ground with weariness and begged the Queen of Heaven not to despise his service, he felt sorrowful.

" 'I believe,' he thought, 'that he does this in good faith,' and he went to the abbot and told him.

OUR LADY'S TUMBLER

" 'Son,' said the abbot, 'speak to no one of this matter and we will go together and watch, for it may be that this service is pleasing to God.'

"Quietly they followed the tumbler into the crypt and stood in the shadow of a pillar that he might not observe them. Soon he began to leap and caper, to walk upon his hands, to stand upon his head and turn the somersaults of Metz and of Champagne, the Roman somersault and the somersaults of Spain, of Brittany and of Lorraine. All this he did with such eagerness that he fell fainting to the ground.

"The abbot watched and as he did so, he saw descending from the roof a glorious Lady in a robe of blue, gleaming with gold and precious stones. All around her were angels and archangels who came to the tumbler and comforted him and raised him in their arms while our sweet Lady fanned him and wiped his face with a white cloth.

"Four times the abbot and the monk went to the crypt and watched the tumbler. And the abbot was joyful for he knew that this good man did his service for the glory of God and that it was pleasing to God.

"Within a few days the abbot sent for the tumbler and said, 'I bid you answer me truly. You have been with us a long time, both winter and summer, tell me how you serve God and in what way you earn your bread.'

"The tumbler was shame-faced. Believing that all had been discovered, 'Sire,' he said, 'I can do nothing that is right. Let me depart.'

" 'I bid you tell me how you serve,' said the abbot again.

"Weeping, the tumbler told him what he did in the crypt, then, thinking that he would be turned away, he fell on his knees and kissed the abbot's feet in farewell.

"But the abbot raised him gently. 'Brother,' said he, 'God grant that you stay with us as long as we deserve your presence. Fair brother, all I bid you, now, is that you perform your service openly.'

"The tumbling brother was overjoyed, and so cheerfully and

ceaselessly did he perform his service, by day and by night, that he fell ill.

"His illness was long and he was much troubled because he could not be busy about his tumbling and dancing, and he felt that he was neither earning his bread nor working to please God. Yet he was too weak to rise.

"As his illness grew worse, the holy abbot came with the monks each hour to chant by his bedside, until, at last, his soul left him and his body was buried with great honour as though it were the body of a saint.

"Thus died the minstrel who cheerfully tumbled for the Glory of God."

"Are you awake or asleep?"

Redcap opened his eyes.

"All those different somersaults," he sighed. "I wish I could do so many. He was clever."

"Yes," said the monk, "but I doubt if he was thinking about that."

He chuckled, looking sideways at Redcap, but there was no mockery in his laughter. There was something comfortable and friendly about it.

"I wish I could stay here for a few days," said Redcap, "and hear more stories about tumblers who became saints."

"Encouraging," said the monk, "isn't it? But I am afraid I have no other story like that. In fact, I only heard it a short time ago."

His face had grown serious and Redcap waited, watching him.

"I am too hasty in my judgments," he said. "That is sinful. I was told this story by one whom I judged too soon."

"Yes?"

"A minstrel came to the gate and stood outside with the beggars when we were feeding them. I gave him a bowl of soup, thinking he did not deserve it, and I said to him, 'A man of your age would do better to think of praising God than of roaming the streets singing light songs, leaping and juggling.' Very ill-spoken, I was, when I rebuked him."

"Then I suppose he was a wicked minstrel?" said Redcap.

"There are idle vagabonds and bad men roving through the country and I, in my hastiness, judged him to be one of them. But while I was scolding him, the Lord Abbot passed by. 'Brother Martin,' says he looking into these black damson eyes in this old pudding face, 'who is this stranger? Bring him in.' My old black damsons seemed almost to fall out of the pudding. 'Father,' said I, 'this is a minstrel, not a God-fearing man.' 'How do you know?' asked the abbot. 'By his trade,' said I, turning up this bit of lemon-peel called a nose. 'Stranger,' said the abbot, 'come in and tell Brother Martin a story that he may judge whether you be evil or not.' "

"And he told you about Our Lady's Tumbler?"

"Ay, and when he had finished the good abbot said, 'I pray you, stay with us and teach Brother Martin that story until he has it by heart — and in his spirit.' "

"And that's how you know it," said Redcap.

"Yes — and a new sum it was for me to reckon. One wise abbot plus one wandering minstrel plus one fair tale: total one humbled monk — to wit myself. Old Pudding Face owes much to that green stranger."

Redcap leapt from the straw bed.

"It was Red Eric," he cried. "How long ago, oh how long ago was he here? Please, please!"

"A few days ago," said the monk bewildered, "but boy . . ."

"I know him. Brother Pudding Fa—, Brother Martin, we are looking for him, Nial and I. He's my uncle."

"So that is why I thought I had seen you before. It's the hair and the look in the eyes."

He laughed with delight, his very cheeks shaking.

"Of course you must go after this good uncle and since must is must, there's no time to be lost, but have a care of that cough on your journey. Come, I will take you to the door."

Redcap's heart was thumping. Red Eric was near. Surely,

he would find him now. In his excitement he scarcely saw where he was going and was startled when the monk unlocked the wooden door at the top of the steps where he had, a short time ago, been so sick.

"Goodbye," said the monk, shaking him by the hand. "Those somersaults — I hope you will do them *in the right way.*"

"They're difficult," said Redcap as he ran down the steps. "Oh — thank you for everything."

He turned and waved. "Pudding Face" still seemed to be chuckling and Redcap thought that he saw him wink.

Why?

But he had no time to wonder. He had begun to run, eager to find Nial to tell him about Red Eric. Then he stopped.

Coming along the road towards him were Fulk and Nial. Fulk had the stick in his hand and Nial was looking anxious.

Redcap dragged one foot after another, trying not to look as though he was dawdling. He braced his shoulders, and wished he was feeling stronger and better able to take whatever punishment was coming to him, but he had been so battered in the fight that he did not think that he could bear much more although he supposed that he deserved it. After all he had done his tumbler's act when Fulk had forbidden it. He stopped to cough and his head throbbed badly but he went to meet Fulk, determined to make no excuses.

"And *now* . . ." said Fulk.

"I — am — sorry," said Redcap.

"You'll be sorrier still in a minute," said Fulk ominously.

"I — I know." Redcap pushed back the bandage from his eye so as to see Fulk better and the crooked mouth wavered for a second.

A helpful look came over Nial's face. He took off his peaked hat, made a bow to Fulk and bustled up to him fussily.

"Will I hold the little switch, Master, while you beat the young boy?" he asked. "For a task like that 'tis best not to be burdened with over many things in your hands."

"I'll put it across *your* back, if you don't take care," answered

Fulk, and, grinning at the impudent face beside him, he tossed the stick over the monastery wall. "Come, boy."

Nial fell behind and Redcap walked along beside Fulk.

"I have a quick temper," said Fulk after a few minutes' silence. "But why need you provoke it so often? Be careful or we may both be sorry."

Redcap nodded. He saw a fleeting look of sadness in Fulk's face and he felt, suddenly, that he had let him down and he longed to make up for disappointing him.

"Hold that," he said, tearing the bandage off his head and pushing it into Fulk's hand. "I promise never to do the tumbler's tricks unless you tell me, and when I do I'll always try as hard as this. Look."

And with no thought of himself but his mind intent upon pleasing Fulk, he did four of the most difficult somersaults, including one which he had never before been able to master.

"Gloria alleluia!" said Fulk with awe in his voice.

Redcap stopped short. *Gloria alleluia?* For the glory of God? Had he begun to understand? He had not wanted to show how clever he was, he had only wanted to please Fulk.

To make another person happy, was that one of the things that the monk had meant when he said that one should do things for the Glory of God?

"He must have meant that," said Redcap, seeing the pleasure in Fulk's face.

"Who meant what?" asked Fulk but Redcap, unaware that he had spoken aloud, said, "Nothing, I was thinking."

"And I am thinking that we must bind up your head again. Listen Redcap, you did those somersaults better than I have ever seen them done and perhaps at our next stopping place I will let you give a performance, but I want you to rest till you are stronger. Do you hear?"

"Yes."

"Then be a good boy, Redcap."

(Something echoed in his mind. *"Be a good boy, Redcap."* *"Husband, take that frown off your face."* How long had he been away from home? Did his parents miss him as much as he missed them? He shook away the thought.)

"Keep still while I tie the bandage." Fulk's fingers were fumbling with the knot. "Redcap! Your neck is damp with sweat and your forehead is burning. Are you feeling ill?"

"My head aches."

"Then you had better come and rest. The pieman says that if we stay in the fair-ground tonight we can lie under his long table by the wall. That will give us enough shelter if it rains. You must keep warm! 'Tis easy to catch a chill when one is feverish. We'll double your own blanket under you and put Jack Piper's over you."

"Doesn't Jack want his blanket?"

"No."

"Where is he?"

"In the pillory."

"*Fulk!*" Redcap stood still. His face had turned white. "Because of me and the fight."

"You seem unaware that you also kicked the guardian of the fair," said Fulk coldly.

Redcap's jaw dropped.

"Jack," continued Fulk, "was arrested for permitting a breach of the peace. He was sentenced by the Mayor at the Court of Pie Powder."

The Court of Pie Powder — the court of *pieds poudreux* or dusty feet, given this name because so many travellers came to the fair — Redcap had heard about it. That was where people who cheated by having false weights and measures or by putting bad materials in their goods, were punished. That was where brawlers and cutpurses were sentenced.

"But it wasn't Jack who fought and kicked, *I* did."

"They said that he was responsible."

"Fulk, they mustn't put him there. He's lame. Fulk, please tell them it was my fault and I must stand in the pillory, not Jack."

"Too late. Now lie down and I'll cover you with his blanket.

No one will hurt Jack. He will be uncomfortable, nothing more. It's only for one night."

"But he's lame."

"Listen, Redcap!" The crooked mouth was beginning to turn down at both corners as it always did when Fulk was getting annoyed. "You are to lie down and try to sleep and not to talk. You must rest or you will fall ill on the road and put us to greater trouble. We all have to leave early — before the fair opens."

"But why aren't we staying? It goes on for three days."

"We have been dismissed."

"Because of me?" whispered Redcap.

"Yes," said Fulk shortly.

Redcap crept under the pieman's table, pulled the blanket over his head and turned his face to the wall.

XXII

FEVER

*In which Redcap has a strange dream and finds himself back
with a kind friend*

R E D C A P tossed his head from side to side, sipped some
water with a bitter taste, which someone was holding to
his lips, and wished that faces and scenes would stop
floating in front of his eyes.

Once he screamed, "It's Gaptooth. Go away. Go away!"
but someone soothed him and gently patted his hands. That
could not be Gaptooth.

Everything near him seemed to be moving and he had a
strange feeling that he was in a bed and that Brother Pierre
was standing over him, wiping his forehead and giving him
something to drink. But the monk's face did queer things. It
grew wide, then narrow, then spun quickly round and round
like a top and turned into the back of Nial's head which receded,
slowly, until it was no bigger than a robin's egg.

Redcap shut his eyes tightly so as not to see, but he could
not close his ears and snatches of conversation were wafted
towards him, now in low tones, now louder, now as though
they were remote but drifting nearer from somewhere in the
past.

"I was wrong entirely, I should have taken him home that
very day," said Nial's voice, "but he had a way with him."

"It was my fault." This sounded like Fulk. "I let you
persuade me too easily because I thought he would earn money
for us."

Then dim and far away, like an echo in the distance, came
his mother's half-whisper, "Be a good boy, Redcap."

"He is my responsibility." Was that Jack Piper? He had
said something like that to the fair-guardian after the fight,

but it sounded like Red Eric and Redcap half opened his eyes. A figure in green seemed to be bending over him. It had Red Eric's eyes but the face slowly changed to a grinning freckled one and a voice jeered, "Tumbler! Tumbler!"

"For the Glory of God," shouted Redcap, sitting up wild-eyed.

He felt a cool hand touch his forehead and a pair of firm strong arms bore him gently back till he was lying down again.

The bad dreams returned.

He was under the pieman's table crying softly so as not to wake Nial and Fulk, who were asleep beside him. Jack Piper was in the pillory and it was his fault.

He must find Jack. He did not know how, but he must sit by him and rub his lame leg and then seek the guardian of the fair and ask if he might stand in the pillory in Jack's stead. The fair-guardian would be only too glad to put him there. After all, it was not Jack who had kicked his shins and tripped him. It was Redcap, and the guardian would see the justice of punishing the right offender.

He stood up and Rex, who was lying at his feet, shook himself, wagged his tail and licked Redcap's hand.

How hot it was.

He had never felt so hot before. Why was his chest hurting and his head aching? That freckled boy was a savage fighter.

He passed his hand over his mouth. His lips were dry and the palms of his hands wet. It ought to have been the other way about. Perhaps he really was a changeling as he had told the robbers in the wood, that day.

Never mind. That was an unpleasant thought and what was it Nial once said about unpleasant thoughts being bad company? In any case it did not matter very much. The important thing was to find Jack.

Carefully he stepped over Nial and Fulk, and, with Rex padding along behind him, made for the city gate.

It was dark and there were very few stars but the fair-ground was lighted by torches of burning pitch and people were still moving to and fro or talking in groups. No one noticed him, and, if they did, they were not curious and he reached the city gates unmolested.

Even here no one spoke to him, and, although during fair time the night watch was doubled and the citizens had to hang lighted lanterns in front of their houses, the city gates were kept open longer for the convenience of the merchants.

Redcap slipped through. The gate keeper was sitting on the ground playing dice with another watchman by the light of a lantern. The shadows of their moving hands throwing the dice looked like giant spiders on the ground. Redcap quickened his steps.

"Who was that?" asked one of the men.

"Maybe some 'prentice lad, keeping late hours," answered the other. "If his master is sitting up for him, the meeting will be painful. Your play!"

Redcap went on. He passed through one narrow street after another, noticing that most of the windows were shuttered as though the citizens had gone to bed. He tried to go quickly but he felt dizzy, almost as though he were walking in his sleep. He was looking for something. What was it? Why had he forgotten?

He stood still with his hands pressed to his forehead, thinking, and Rex waited, looking up at him and wagging his tail.

Oh yes. Yes, of course, he wanted to find the market square where Jack Piper was standing in the pillory. It would probably be in the middle of the city. He must try not to forget what he was doing but his head kept turning like a wheel, there was a sound of rushing water in his ears and although he had been so hot a few minutes ago, now he was shivering.

He turned a corner. Rex gave a little yelp of recognition and dashed away.

The market square was in front of him. It was dark and deserted but a lantern fixed to the top of the pillory made a pool of light which revealed Jack's pale drawn face. Through the holes in the board nailed to the pillory, the minstrel's head and wrists were locked. His body sagged and his knees were slack, as though he were supporting his entire weight by his imprisoned neck. Around him on the ground there were egg shells and cabbage stalks, and his clothing was spattered with mud, which showed that he had been pelted.

"Jack," cried Redcap, in his heart, but the word never left his lips and he ran forward and knelt at the old man's feet, chafing the lame leg and trying to take the weight of the body on to his own knees.

"Jack," he said, "speak to me. I have come to rescue you. Jack."

The old man made no sound. His eyes were closed in his white face. He might have been carved in stone.

Redcap stood up, seized his belt and shook it.

"Jack," he said and now he was shouting at the top of his voice, terror robbing him of all control.

"Jack! Jack! JACK!"

Once again two strong gentle arms were forcing him to lie down. A quiet voice said, "Jack is quite safe," and someone was dabbing his brow with a soft wet cloth.

He went on dreaming.

Rex was licking his forehead.

He looked up and by the light of the lantern saw that he was lying at the foot of the pillory staring into the pale still face of Jack Piper.

He struggled to his feet. He knew that he must find the guardian of the fair or someone and say that Jack had fainted and was dying. But where could he go, and what would happen if he left Jack?

He bent down and patted Rex.

"Good dog," he said and pointed at Jack. "On guard."

Rex thumped his tail on the ground and sat alert, very close to the pillory.

HE MIGHT HAVE BEEN CARVED IN STONE

K   R.R.A.

"I am going for help, Rex. Stay *on guard* till I come back."

He set out again, but a little snuffling whine and pattering footsteps followed him and when he turned his head, Rex was half way between him and the pillory, looking first at one and then at the other.

"Bad dog! Go back at once. On guard!"

Rex whined, then, with his tail between his legs, he slunk away and sat by Jack with a long snuffling sigh.

As he walked once again towards the city streets which led out of the market, Redcap turned once or twice. Rex was still at the pillory, sitting stiffly upright, and with a sigh of relief, he passed on till the dog and the motionless man whom he was guarding were out of sight.

He felt himself trembling but he knew that he must keep his senses alert and find someone. If he could reach a tavern there might be people there, who would come to the rescue. He could explain that he was to blame and not Jack, and they might be willing to go to the guardian of the fair and ask him to release the minstrel. No one would let a guiltless man die in the pillory.

Was that an inn, over there on the right?

Yes, a lighted lantern showed a bunch of evergreens over the doorway.

Redcap tried to run but his feet felt as though they were in deep, sticky mud and he seemed to be pulling himself along.

At the door of the tavern he swayed.

Suddenly he gave a cry. Two hands with fingers of steel had gripped him from behind and a voice said, "So ho, my little changeling, we meet again! Turn ye round!"

"Let me go," gasped Redcap.

"What? Has our little No Bones forgotten how to vanish like smoke?" said the voice, and Redcap found himself staring into the evil face of Gaptooth, the robber.

"Let me go!" he begged, "please let me go. Jack's dying and I want to get help."

"Not so fast," leered Gaptooth. "Let me see if you have

anything in your purse! Over you go, No Bones," and he tucked Redcap under one arm and pulled the wallet off his belt with the other.

"Ho ho ho!" he laughed, waving the bride's garter and the silver pin which Redcap had put there for safety. "So our No Bones *has* learnt to steal. Well, well, Squint *will* be pleased. He will have an apt pupil. You can rob a merchant at the fair as well as I can, eh? So we will work together."

"I'm not a thief. You're hurting me. Stop!"

"Not so loud," hissed Gaptooth, gripping Redcap so tightly that he gave a cry of pain.

"Who is there?"

The door of the tavern burst open.

"Let go of that child."

Someone strode out. There was a blow and Gaptooth crashed to the ground with Redcap under him.

Out of the tavern surged young men and old.

"What has happened? Who is it?"

"Seize that man! Now move aside. There's a boy on the ground. Have a care!"

Redcap felt himself grasped firmly.

"It's Gaptooth," he cried. "Go away! Go away!"

Once again, someone was soothing him and patting his hand and a quiet voice which seemed to come from a long way off and yet reach his heart was saying insistently, "You are quite safe. You would know it if you were to say, 'Into Thy hands I commend my spirit.' Try to say that after me, mon petit. *Into Thy hands I commend my spirit.*"

With an effort Redcap murmured the words.

He dozed, then, and felt himself floating away, rocking gently to and fro. There was music somewhere, too. It seemed quite near.

Then the dream came.

This time he was being carried.

275

The swift strides of a tall man were swinging him along. He felt the cool night air on his face and he was lulled by a song:

> A woman is a gladsome thing
> They do the wash and do the wring!
> Lullay, lullay she doth thee sing.
> And yet she hath but care and woe.

The words died away and the singer shifted him to the other arm.

"Are you asleep?"

Was he? Redcap felt neither asleep nor awake. He wondered whether he was alive or dead. He knew that he had fallen somewhere and struck his head so hard against the cobblestones that, for a while, everything had grown black. And now?

Now he kept hearing Red Eric's song. Was he simply remembering it or was someone singing? There it was again.

> To unprize woman it were a shame
> For a woman was thy dame
> Our blessed Lady beareth the name. . . .

The footsteps came to a halt.

A bell rang. A door opened.

"Brother, I have brought you a sick child."

He felt himself transferred to another pair of arms.

Darkness crept around him, then, numbing his body, stealing into his heart and into his mind and he knew nothing more.

"Tiens, that is better. A sweet sleep and no fever."

Redcap opened his eyes.

He was lying on a straw mattress in a small white-washed room and Brother Pierre was looking down at him. He tried to sit up but his limbs would not obey him and the monk put out a restraining hand.

"You must lie very still and in a few days you may sit in

276

a chair with a pillow behind your back. That will be pleasant, hein?"

"Is Brother Pudding Face here?"

"He has gone to the kitchen to fetch a bowl of fine chicken soup for a sick boy."

"For me? Am I sick?"

"You have been ill for five days. The brothers have been praying for you and now you are getting well."

Redcap moved restlessly.

"I want to see Nial." A look of distress passed across his face. "They haven't gone without me? Brother Pierre, they haven't left me? They were dismissed from the fair. I must go after them. I must . . ."

"They will come to you. When you have drunk your soup and had another sleep, Nial will see you. But only for one minute, just to shake you by the hand and say, 'Ha, good-day, mon vieux!' Then you have another sleep, yes?"

"Did I have adventures?" asked Redcap. "I keep remembering and forgetting. I don't know what was a dream and what is true."

He looked distressed, moistened his dry lips with the tip of his tongue, and Brother Pierre put an arm behind his head, raised him and gave him another sip of the bitter water.

"I think I shall tell you what happened," he said, "and then you will not be troubled. I am told that the big minstrel put you to sleep under the pieman's table at the fair."

"I can remember that. And I can remember that he came to bed and Nial and Rex and after that everything seemed to be floating about— and — and now I am here. Is *this real*?"

Brother Pierre smiled.

"This is real, but certainly! Under the pieman's table you fell asleep and you awoke with a high fever. When people are very ill, they do not know what they are doing. I think you crept from under the table and went into the city."

"Jack — was — in the pillory," said Redcap slowly, still trying to remember.

"That is so, and from what you said in your fever, we think that you went to find him and the little dog followed you."

"Then Gaptooth caught me."

Redcap turned a pair of terrified eyes on Brother Pierre, who patted his hand.

"He will not find you again, that bad one. He was stealing at the fair and they have put him in the prison. Someone brought you here and left you with us. And now, when you are strong enough, your three friends will come and see you. You are safe, mon petit, and so is Master Jack. He is no longer in the pillory."

So Jack was free and the other two minstrels not far away. That was good.

But Red Eric? In his dream (or had it really happened?) he thought that Red Eric had found him. He had heard him singing. But what had Brother Pierre said? *Someone brought you here and left you.* Had Red Eric gone again? Redcap felt so tired and weak that he dared not ask, lest the answer should be "Yes, he has gone." He did not want to hear it.

Brother Pierre saw that something was troubling him.

"Shall the good Nial give you your soup?" he asked. "I see him at the door."

Redcap's eyes brightened and he looked round.

"How many more frights will you be giving me?" asked Nial. "Another few days like these and I shall be destroyed entirely. Take a sup of this, now," and he began to feed Redcap with a spoon. "Fulk says, 'Tell that rascal to get well for we have need of a tumbler,' and Jack Piper sends you his love."

"Please Nial . . ."

"No blethering! If you talk, this doctor monk will have my life's blood and I'm not wanting my latter end to overtake my middle age. 'Tis unnatural."

He put Redcap back on his pillow, lightly pulled his red forelock, and went away.

In a few seconds Redcap was fast asleep.

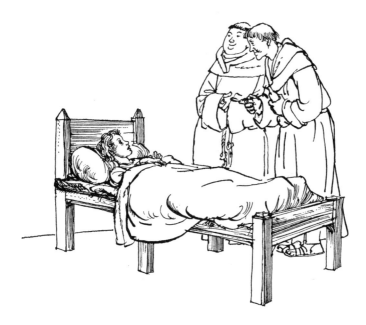

XXIII

TRYING TO GET WELL

*In which Redcap is given some parting presents and spends
five lonely days that end in a surprise*

SLEEPING, sipping unpleasant medicine from a horn
spoon held to his lips by Brother Pierre, sleeping once more,
drinking strong chicken broth, then sleeping again: that
was how Redcap's time was spent.

He did not know how long his illness had lasted for he had
lost count of the days. He only knew that when he tried to sit
up, supported by Brother Pierre's arm, his body felt as though
it were filled with sand and had neither bone nor muscle. His
hands, too, looked thinner and he could see the blue veins
under the skin like the markings in the pale petals of the
cuckoo-flowers which grew in the fields.

279

"How did I fall ill?" he asked.

Brother Pierre shrugged his shoulders, "Who knows? They tell me that you stood for hours in a moat, up to the chest in water, and that chilled you and left you with a cough. Afterwards you may have become over-heated and overtired, it's hard to say. But now you lie in bed, you sleep, and little by little you grow better. Is it not so?"

Redcap felt that he was getting stronger for he was no longer feverish except, sometimes, at night, but his slow recovery troubled him. The minstrels, he knew, had been anxious about him, and because they had been dismissed from the town, the good abbot had taken pity on them and had allowed them to help in the fields and in the garden in return for their food and a lodging in one of the barns. But this could not last much longer and soon they would have to take to the road again, and Redcap was determined to work hard and repay them for their loss of time.

"As soon as we set out," he said one day to Nial who was sitting at the foot of his bed, "I shall show Fulk that I haven't forgotten anything. I shall do all my somersaults, every day, and then when we come to a village or a town, I shall earn enough money to make up for being ill and keeping you all here. After that, we shall have a feast and buy new clothes and red leather shoes."

"Hmm!" said Nial, "you are not, by any chance, counting your chickens before they are hatched? There was a man who did that, once. If I remember rightly, he was of a frugal nature. Scraping and saving every little thing, he was. One day, he saved a morsel of butter from his supper and put it in a honey-jar and lying down to rest his bones, he looked at the jar and said to himself. 'Butter is sold at a high price; if I save a little each day, I shall surely make a fortune.' Then he bethought him of what he would do with his fortune. First he would buy a pig, then a sheep, then a cow. And in his mind he saw a herd of pigs and a flock of sheep and many fine cattle. These he would sell and buy the biggest farm in the land. But a farm would need more than one pair of hands to work it. Well, it was a fine thing, surely, that he had a grand young son, very strong and willing. If the boy worked well, he would give him half the profit from the farm. But suppose he were idle? What then? 'I'll teach him, the young good-for-nothing,' shouted the man and seizing a stick, struck the honey jar such a blow that it broke into pieces and the butter fell into the dirt. So maybe 'tis a foolish thing to say what you *will* do before you are sure that you *can* do it!"

He looked at Redcap who was lying on the bed with his arms behind his head.

"You are not listening at all," he said. "Your thoughts are like birds flying far away."

"Nial," said Redcap, "when are we going? All the time that we stay here, Red Eric will be getting farther and farther away."

"Are you thinking of the ends of the earth, again?" asked Nial.

"When Gaptooth found me in the city and I fell under him, I dreamt that Red Eric picked me up and brought me here and I saw him leaning over the bed. Then he went."

"The abbot says that he did bring you here."

"And I've lost him again," said Redcap hopelessly. "I don't think I shall ever find him."

"Wheest, be easy now," said Nial. "You are not trusting me. Am I not telling you over and over again that I will help you to find him? Am I a poor creature that breaks his word?'

"No."

"Then cease fretting. If you are not strong and healthy enough to seek him, I will be doing it for you."

He stood up and went across the room to the door. "Remember that," he said, "for there's no knowing what may happen to divide friends, but a promise must never be broken. Go to sleep, now."

He closed the door after him, leaving Redcap alone, but the boy could not sleep. He knew that whatever happened Nial would keep his word but what had he meant when he said that friends might separate? He and Nial were friends.

"He wouldn't leave me," thought Redcap, "he couldn't. What did he mean?"

Next morning, he understood.

Brother Pierre had pulled his bed near to the long narrow window and had propped him up with pillows and now he was looking out across the monastery grounds.

The sky was pale and a mist was rising from the monks' fishpond so that only the tops of the trees could be seen, their delicate tracery of branches etched against the sky, their trunks seeming to rise without roots in mid-air. Redcap wondered whether they felt as though they were floating. Since his illness, he had sometimes a strange feeling that he was hovering above the ground, but this, Brother Pierre had told him, was weakness after fever.

What would happen if he remained weak for so long that Fulk became impatient? In his mind's eye, he saw the small irritable frown that came and went when the minstrel was annoyed, and the crooked mouth, turned down at each corner with no vestige of a smile.

He turned his head restlessly and saw Fulk in the doorway. The minstrel's eyes were observing him kindly but he had an air of determination as though he had made up his mind to carry out some purpose from which he would not swerve, and he reached the bed in two strides, his crooked smile twisted upwards.

"Your eyes," he said, "are still a little too large for your face. They look as though they might drop out if you were to turn a somersault."

Redcap shook his head. "I could show you," he said, "only Brother Pierre says that I mustn't get out of bed until he tells me."

"Ah," said Fulk and looked at him without speaking for a second or two. Then he sat down on the edge of the bed.

"I wanted to talk about that," he said.

Redcap waited. Fulk was opening the leather wallet which hung on his girdle and was pulling out of it something which looked like a piece of cloth.

"When I was a minstrel in a great house, I wore my master's badge. I still have it but I may not wear it, now, because I no longer sing for him. I am a wanderer. Now, you have been my tumbler...."

Redcap's face glowed. This was praise, indeed, and he felt proud and happy.

"And so I have a badge for you," continued Fulk, and he handed Redcap an oval-shaped piece of white cloth. Sewn on this was a fragment of black woollen material, shaped like a boy standing on his head. The figure had a red hood and a red patch and around it embroidered roughly in linen thread were the words "Fulk, his Tumbler".

"One of the brothers in the scriptorium traced the letters for me," said Fulk. "I told him what to write and I sewed my stitches over it. Do you know what it says? You once told me that you could read."

"Our priest taught me," said Redcap. He pointed to the letters, spelling the words aloud, then looked up, smiling shyly but with joy shining in his eyes. "Fulk, his tumbler — and — it's . . ."

"It is you — and when you wear it, everyone will know that you are my tumbler — *even when we are not working together*."

Redcap fingered the badge lovingly.

"When are we going?" he asked.

Fulk crossed one leg over the other, uncrossed it, stood up and walked towards the door and back again.

"I came here to tell you about that," he said. "Jack Piper and I . . ."

"Here comes Jack," said Redcap. "Jack, look at my badge! Now everyone will know that I am Fulk's tumbler."

Jack examined the badge, carefully and seriously.

"It's a speaking likeness," he said, "but there's one thing

283

lacking. There should have been a knife and a ball in one corner to show that you are a juggler, too. And very soon you will be a piper for I have cut you a whistle from a piece of wood."

Redcap held out his hand to receive the gift, put it to his lips and blew a wavering blast.

"You must practise, when we have gone," said Jack. "Then one day, if we meet again, Fulk will add a pipe to your badge."

The whistle dropped from Redcap's hands and Fulk stooped to pick it up.

"I have promised to go with my company to a wedding," he said with embarrassment, "and we must not be late. We go today."

Redcap began to get out of bed. "I must dress," he said.

But Jack put him back on the pillows and Fulk shook his head.

"Listen, Redcap. We cannot take you. We have stayed here so long that we must make the journey quickly. Even if we were to push you in the handcart, your strength would fail."

"It wouldn't," said Redcap, "and — and — I am your tumbler. You said so."

"I shall always think of you as my tumbler but we cannot take you with us."

"Then you'll come back for me?"

"Once we set out we cannot come back. There are many places which we must visit, and here you will rest and grow strong."

Redcap gazed, unblinking, at Fulk's face. The world was growing desolate and he could not speak.

"The good monks will care for you," said Jack Piper. "You will be in better company with them than with us."

"When you are well and strong again, they will know what to do with you. You need have no fear," said Fulk.

But Redcap was afraid.

"Where's Nial?" he asked, then desperately, "Nial will not leave me. He's my friend."

"I know," said Fulk, "but he is my minstrel and I need him. Long ago he promised to follow me and sing in my company for a year. The year is not yet over and Nial does not break his word."

That was true. Nial, himself, had always said so, but where was he?

"He will be coming to say goodbye to you very soon," said Jack as though he had read Redcap's thoughts. "I am an old man and I know that goodbyes are difficult things at the best of times, but you are his friend so you must not make it *more* difficult for him. He is bound to Fulk, and Fulk has given his promise to sing at this wedding and at other feasts, so Nial must go with him."

"I could come too. I'm nearly strong again."

Fulk shook his head. "Not strong enough," he said gently.

"I can make myself strong. I promise to walk fast even if I'm tired."

"You must believe me, Redcap. It is not possible for us to take you."

Redcap's voice rose querulously. "I can keep up. I know I can. If you would only let me try."

Fulk's crooked mouth was set and his eyes unsmiling. He pulled the cover off the bed. "Now stand," he said, "and walk across the room."

Jack Piper put out a hand.

"Leave him alone. Now, walk."

Redcap took two or three steps. His knees trembled and his legs felt like water. He put out his arms to keep his balance and Fulk caught him and lifted him back into bed.

"We are going, now," he said. "God keep you and bring you speedily to health."

He held out his hand and Redcap put his own into it but he did not look at Fulk and he could not speak. Fulk shook the hand and said nothing, too. Jack nodded kindly, waited for Redcap to say something, then went out.

The room was empty, now, and the world seemed empty, too.

Redcap did not move. For a long time he lay on his back with his eyes closed.

"Nial," he whispered, "Nial, why don't you come?"

"Will you open your eyes and look at me, then. Am I not here, sitting still as an image and thinking you were asleep."

"You're leaving me."

"It's the last thing in the world I want to do. But we'll be meeting again for I never lose sight of my friends even when I'm away from them."

"We were going to find Red Eric, together," said Redcap with difficulty, "and now . . ."

"I shall seek him and I have not lost hope so let your heart rest. Fretting has never helped anyone, yet."

"Must you go?"

"You know that I must, if not, wouldn't I be staying with you?"

"What shall I do, when you are gone?"

"Everything that Brother Pierre bids you. And I'm telling you we shall meet again. It may not be yet awhile but I have no mind to lose you, Redcap. One day you and I will be sitting like two old cronies saying, 'Do you remember . . .' We will so!"

Redcap clung to Nial's hand, despair in his heart. From somewhere at the back of his mind a thought seemed to be moving, trying to reach him but it was dim and far away.

"Have courage," said Nial.

The thought came, then, crystal clear. He remembered the hawk who had lost her courage. She could be given medicine and set in the sun and her strength of heart would return. But Red Eric had told him that if a man's courage began to ebb, no medicine in the world could help him. He must call up something that was hidden deep down in himself.

Whatever this inner strength was, he needed it, now, for Nial was going. He was standing near the bed with Rex beside him, and his face was troubled.

"If you believe me when I say that we shall meet again, will you wish me God speed?" he asked.

Redcap felt his courage slipping away. He must not let it go. With an effort as though he were pulling the words from some great depth, he looked up at Nial.

"God speed," he said huskily.

"Thank you," said Nial. "You have a stout heart and I am proud to know you, I am." He looked down at Redcap's pale face. "You'll be having a message from me, one of these days," he said and Redcap saw that he was smiling as though he had some gay secret which he wanted to tell but must keep for a few days longer.

"You will not be long alone," he added. "On guard, Rex."

The door was closed softly and Nial had gone.

Redcap buried his face in the pillow, and Rex sat, bolt upright, beside the bed.

Redcap must have dozed for an hour before he became aware of a sound of whimpering, short snuffling sighs and whines.

He remembered then that Rex had been left "on guard" and it slowly dawned upon him that the dog, whom Nial loved so dearly, was his parting present.

Fulk had made him a badge, Jack Piper had given him a whistle, but Nial had left him the treasure which he prized most in all the world. Rex had been Nial's companion ever since he was a puppy. Nial had taught him his tricks, shared his bed and his skimpy meals with him, often giving the dog the larger portion. Wherever he went, Rex went, too. They were always together, day in day out. And now as a token of friendship, Nial had left his beloved comrade with Redcap.

The boy let his arm fall over the edge of the bed and waited for a wet tongue to lick his hand but nothing happened and he opened his eyes.

Rex, with his tail between his legs was standing with his nose against the closed door.

"Here, Rex!" called Redcap.

The dog's tail wagged feebly, then dropped once again.

"Stand at ease!" said Redcap. "You're off guard. Come here."

Rex turned his head for a second then pressed his nose against the door.

"He wants Nial," thought Redcap. "So do I."

"Rex," he said. "Good dog! You'll stay with me now and some day he'll come back. Here, Rex."

The dog pattered up to him, put his front paws up on the bed, gave a short bark and pattered back to the door.

"He'll be lonely without Nial," thought Redcap. "Poor fellow!"

Then suddenly it came to him that Nial would be lonely without Rex, that his parting present was a great sacrifice, too great for one friend to allow another to make.

"Wait," he said. "Wait, Rex."

Slowly he put first one leg and then the other out of bed and with great care stood unsteadily upon his feet. He began to move, at first deliberately and then with tottering steps till he reached the table, clung to the edge, and, keeping his balance by touching the wall, arrived, shakily, at the door.

"Go seek Nial. Find your master," he said and lifted the latch.

Like an arrow from the bow, Rex shot into the garden, ran sniffing the ground and was lost from sight.

"Brother Martin will let him out," thought Redcap, "and he will find Nial before dark. Nial will know why I did it. It's like sending him my love."

With the same slow care, he wobbled back to the bed and lay there, panting from the exertion.

He felt glad and sorry by turns, and wondered crossly whether he was happy or miserable. He was only sure of one thing. Nial would be pleased, but for himself the days would be empty and time too slow.

The days would be empty and time too slow.

Indeed, five days seemed to Redcap as long as ten and on the fifth afternoon when Brother Pierre came in with his horn spoon and his jug of medicine, the boy sighed so deeply that the monk put the tray on the table and shook his head.

"It is," he said, "a sad thing for those who care for the sick to be greeted with mournful faces. You do not like my medicine, mon petit, yet it would be pleasant for me if you were to smile and say perhaps, 'God keep you'."

"God keep you," said Redcap hastily.

"And you, too," said the monk in more leisurely tones. "Am I right in thinking that you find yourself lonely. Yes?"

Redcap nodded.

"It is now five days since the big minstrel and the old man and the good Nial left you. And the little dog who would have been a comrade, he, too, is gone."

"He wanted Nial more than he wanted me."

"That is so. A dog loves his master. When he reached the minstrels and jumped on his master, wagging his tail, the good Nial must have understood. I think he would say to himself, 'It is a message of friendship from the boy.' And he would look as I have often seen him look — merry and pleased."

"I'm glad I sent him," said Redcap.

"It was a good message. And now, my son, you must take your medicine quickly. The father abbot has sent for you. He has a message from Messire Nial."

He filled the spoon and Redcap, who did not like the smell, held his nose, and swallowed quickly, eager for Nial's message.

"And now," said Brother Pierre, "as you cannot walk so far I shall take you on my back and set you on your feet when we reach the door of the father abbot's chamber. You will knock and say, 'May it please you, Father Abbot, I have come for Nial's message.' See, I will tie this blanket around you. So. Now put your arms around my neck. So. We will go."

Slowly they made their way along the stone corridor across a garden path to the abbot's lodging.

At the door of his room Brother Pierre bent down so that

Redcap could slide off his back without effort. Then he left, saying over his shoulder:

"Knock and then lift the latch."

Redcap obeyed.

"May it please you, Father Abbot," he said, "I have come for Nial's message."

"Enter."

Redcap pushed open the door and went in.

RED ERIC WAS STANDING BY THE WINDOW.

XXIV

THE ROAD OR THE FORGE?

*In which Redcap recovers his strength, takes to the road with
Red Eric and has to make a choice*

TIME was racing, now.

One day moved swiftly to another, which seemed
scarcely to have begun when it was over. Redcap forgot
the long tedious hours which he had thought would never end,
and lived each new moment with delight, for Red Eric was his
constant companion and their friendship deepened as time
passed.

Each day, too, Redcap grew stronger. He was allowed to
walk in the monastery gardens with a sleeveless sheepskin
coat over his old clothes, which were threadbare, and a pair
of pointed leather shoes made by one of the monks and reaching just above the ankle, for he had grown and his hose, too
short for him now, had worn away and were footless.

"How did Nial find you?" he asked Red Eric one day.

"When we parted after the wedding, I told him some of the
places which I might visit but nothing that I said was certain
for my feet carry me where they will and if I meet a stranger
whom I like, I go with him."

"Then how did Nial know where to look?"

"He traced me through people whom he met on the road.
For two days and two nights he walked, hardly sleeping,
leaving the others a long way behind."

Redcap's eyes opened widely.

"Did Fulk really allow him to go alone? He was *bound* to
Fulk for a year."

"I know," said Red Eric, "but Crooked Smile wanted him
to find me for your sake and he knew that Nial would come

back according to his bond, so when they were on my track, he wished him God speed and a quick return."

"Where were you, when he found you?" asked Redcap.

"I was resting by the wayside and I saw him come limping along the highway towards me. At first, I didn't know him at that distance. Nial always has a spring in his feet but he had walked for two days and two nights and was almost as lame as Jack Piper. I was sitting on a great stone with the old horse browsing on the grass by the ditch when Rex bounded up to me and Nial followed. 'It's yourself,' he said, 'never was a man gladder to see you in all his born days.' "

Redcap smiled as Red Eric spoke with Nial's voice and copied his way of talking.

"He sat down beside me," said Red Eric, "and told me who you were and rounded on me, too. 'And why would you walk away in the night,' he asked, 'with the young child lying at death's door and yourself his lost uncle?' "

"But you didn't know you were my uncle."

"No. So I said. But Nial would have no excuses. 'And why wouldn't you know,' he asked, 'and himself the spit and image of yourself?' 'Come to that,' said I, 'why didn't you know if you saw the likeness?' ' "

Redcap was enjoying himself. He could picture the scene, Nial tired out and humorously cross, and Red Eric bridling because he thought that he had been stupid.

" 'Man dear,' says he, 'you put your best leg forward and hitch a couple of wings to your heels and get you back to that monastery. And I would take it kindly, I would, if you would cease acting like a minstrel without a care in the world and would behave yourself like an uncle with a nephew to mind.' "

"So you came."

Red Eric laughed. "I came quickly," he said. "Had I wasted a minute, upon my soul, I believe he would have dragged me on the end of a rope."

"I wish he had," said Redcap.

"Oh do you! And why should you wish me to have been put into such an unpleasant and humiliating position?"

"Then Nial would have been here, too. I would like to have him near always and always."

"He's your friend, isn't he?"

"Yes."

"Then whether he's beside you or not, he's near. That's the wonderful thing about having a friend. Even when you and he are at the opposite ends of the earth you take him with you everywhere. You will never lose Nial, and if you and I separate you will not lose me."

Separate? Redcap's face grew still. Then he spoke, with an effort, his eyes fixed on Red Eric's face.

"Are you going, too?"

"All my life, I am coming and going. Whether we separate or not will depend upon you and what you really want to do. As soon as you are well, shall we take to the road together?"

Redcap's eyes brightened.

"Please," he said, "Oh please! I don't cough any more and I can sing with you and get money. May I be your tumbler?"

"I thought you were wearing Fulk's badge."

"Oh — yes — I forgot." He frowned for a minute. "Does that mean that I'm bound to Fulk like Nial?"

Red Eric's eyes twinkled and once again he had a fleeting look of Redcap's father. He put his hand to the leather belt around his waist and opened his wallet.

"I feel sure that I have Fulk's leave to hire his tumbler," he said seriously and gave Redcap a silver ring. "Now here's needle and thread. We will sew the ring to Fulk's badge and when you meet him again, he will understand what has happened."

Very gravely he stitched the ring securely beside the figure of the boy on the cloth badge. Then he sewed badge and ring to Redcap's hood.

"With Brother Pierre's permission we will seek a blessing from the good abbot and depart within a few days. The horse has been shod and well fed so you can ride behind me," said Red Eric. Redcap had scarcely enough patience to wait for Brother Pierre to pronounce him fit for the road.

At last the day of their departure had come and Redcap, who had been so eager to set out, now found it hard to bid farewell to all the good monks who had been so kind to him.

Never before had he noticed how wise and gentle were the eyes of the stern old abbot who blessed him and Red Eric. He put a friendly hand on the boy's shoulder, saying, "If ever you pass this way, pull the bell rope and we shall make you welcome."

Brother Pierre, seeing the badge sewn to the scarlet hood, tapped it with his forefinger.

"Tiens," said he, "this cloth boy, he must always stand upon his head. Never can he put his feet to the ground. But you, mon petit, must leave all such antics to him for a few weeks. The good uncle and I have talked on these matters and you will do as he advises, is it not so?"

"But I'm his tumbler," said Redcap.

"There is a time for all things," said Brother Pierre, "and the time that follows sickness must be passed restfully. Ride the good uncle's horse, sing only when he bids you and tumble not at all, and each morning you will awake feeling stronger, until, one day, prrt! you will be running like the little dog Rex. And now, au revoir."

"Goodbye," said Redcap, "and thank you."

"I shall remember you in my prayers," said Brother Pierre gravely. "Would it be too much if I were to ask you to remember me in yours?"

Redcap shook his head. It would not be too much but he did not know what to say. It seemed strange to him that a good man like Brother Pierre should ask a boy to pray for him but he knew, now, that whenever he set foot in a church he would remember the monk who had watched over and comforted him when he was ill and miserable.

"I don't think I could ever forget you," he said and slowly followed Red Eric to the side doorway leading to the road, where Brother Martin stood under the elm tree holding the minstrel's horse.

The fat old "pudding face" was looking very solemn.

"Goodbyes," he said, "are a hard sum, a very hard sum. One monastic house plus two redhaired minstrels equals a pleasant visitation. Multiply the answer by one horse, subtract the two minstrels and the result is 'goodbye'. Divide the answer into two parts and you get 'God be with you'. Am I correct?"

Redcap grinned at him.

"Ho ho ho!" laughed Pudding Face, "you're laughing at me. Don't deny it. I delight in it! Laughter," he wiped tears of mirth from his eyes, "laughter directed against oneself is the finest medicine! Ho ho ho! Now up with you!"

He lowered one of his hands. Redcap put his foot on it and sprang into the saddle behind Red Eric.

"You're a joke, Pudding Face," he said, and giggled.

And the old monk, still chuckling and winking, waved till they were out of sight.

For a few minutes they rode in silence until Redcap, peering over Red Eric's shoulder, noticed that the minstrel's thoughts were far away and that he was riding with a slack rein, allowing the horse to choose its own path.

"Red Eric," he said.

"Well?"

"Is Peter taking us the right way? You're not telling him."

"He knows."

"But is this the way you want to go?"

"Yes. He knows me so well that he feels what is in my mind. There's no need for me to speak to him. I had a donkey, long ago, and he used to do the same thing."

"Would he stop without your pulling the reins?"

"Yes, if that was what I wanted. Watch him. I think I'll walk for a while and let you ride."

In a few seconds Peter stood still without any sign from Red

Eric, who dismounted and began to lead him while Redcap sat in the saddle.

"I think if a horse knows his master well, he often understands what he wants and what he is feeling. Columkille's horse was like that. Do you remember?"

But Redcap did not know the story and to while away the time Red Eric told him.

"Columkille lived in Iona in a monastery of small grey stone cells. It is said that once when he called the people to prayer, no one came. Only an old lame donkey strayed into the church and stood there patiently waiting and Columkille, ready with the word of God, preached to the donkey who stayed till the last 'amen' then trotted away.

"There was a horse in Iona, too, they say, who had more understanding than many a human soul.

"It happened one day, when Columkille was old and ailing, that he and his servant Diarmait went to bless the monastery barn and the corn that was in it. And when he had given his blessing, Columkille, weary and bowed down with age, left the barn and sat for a while by the roadside to rest. And he was joyful for he knew that very soon the labour of his life would come to an end and he would be in everlasting peace.

"As he sat there, the old horse, whose task it was to carry the milk cans, came up to him and put its head upon his breast. And from the creature's eyes great tears dropped slowly and it made grievous sounds as though it were lamenting.

"Diarmait, seeing this, came up and would have driven the horse away but Columkille forbade him, saying: 'Let the beast alone for it loves me so dearly that it must needs pour out its grief on my bosom. You, Diarmait, are a human being, able to think and to reason, yet you know nothing of my approaching end save the little that *I* myself have told you: but to this dumb beast the Creator has given the knowledge that its master is about to leave it for ever.'

"And he blessed the old horse, who had understood his thoughts."

"Tell me some more," said Redcap and in his mind's eye he saw Columkille with a face half like Brother Pierre's and half like the old abbot's, and a voice like Nial's with the gaiety grown old.

And so on the road time passed happily, with Red Eric telling stories and singing songs and Redcap joining in or listening silently.

They wandered through towns and villages, sometimes sleeping under cover, sometimes camping by the wayside and seldom spending more than a night in any one place. Often the days were sunny and occasionally cold and wet, but Red Eric was an experienced wanderer and he always managed to find a sheltered nook so that Redcap was in no danger of getting chilled.

Gradually the evenings grew shorter and darkness came earlier. The mornings were misty and the trees bare, and in the woods and fields there was a smell of damp earth. Autumn, with its quick changes from cold to warmth and from warmth to cold again, was slowly turning to winter. The afternoons were dull and the sky grey until sudden bursts of sunshine flecked the roads with pools of light, and lent gleaming magic to the hedgerows.

One day late in November, Redcap, astride the horse, drew three deep breaths, quickly, one after another, inhaling the keen frosty air and feeling that he was well and as strong as he had ever been. He slipped off Peter's back.

"Look," he said and he ran forward, sprung upon his hands and lightly turned head over heels. He was about to do it again when he noticed suddenly that they had turned into a lane which he recognized. He stood still. He knew it as well as he knew his own name and for a minute his heart seemed to stop beating.

It was the lane where he and the boys of his home-village used to play leapfrog when they were free from their tasks of scaring birds from the cornfields or helping on the land.

He turned to Red Eric, with a question on the tip of his tongue. The minstrel had flung Peter's reins over his head and slung them around his own arm.

"I see you know where you are," he said, "and now I want to talk to you."

"You are not going away?"

The great upward rush of joy which had flooded his heart when he had recognized the lane was slowly turning to dismay.

"Are you going to leave me, here?"

Red Eric stood still and Peter began to crop the tufts of grass that grew by the wayside.

"I shall only leave you if you want to stay. And if you stay I shall come back one day to find a singing smith in the village. But you must choose, Redcap. If you want the road, the road you shall have and we'll share the wandering life, the cold, the poverty and the danger."

"When I'm with you, I forget those difficult times," said Redcap. "Take me with you."

"When I ran away I was almost a grown man," said Red Eric, "and even then I little knew what the life of the road was like. You are a child, and know still less. When were you born?"

"When the great elm in the village was struck by lightning. The priest said that was about nine years ago."

"No more than ten years old," murmured Red Eric half to himself. "You would learn much at home and much on the road," he said aloud, "and so when we reach the edge of the village I shall leave you to make up your mind. I shall come back and sit here by this clump of trees till the moon rises. If you come to me then, the open road will be our home. If you stay behind, we shall still be together."

"But how?" asked Redcap, for home was pulling him and so was the road.

"You and I are friends, just as you and Nial are friends. Nothing can really part us. But come, boy, or the sun will set before we reach the end of this lane."

They walked on, in silence, Redcap kicking at the stones and Red Eric leading Peter and whistling softly.

At a bend in the lane they came to the outskirts of the

OLD JANET

village, and at the edge of the wise woman's wood someone was sitting with her back towards them on the trunk of a fallen tree. A cat was walking up and down rubbing itself against her skirt and a jackdaw was perching on her shoulder.

It was old Janet, and the familiar sight swept all troubling thoughts from Redcap's mind and he laughed up at Red Eric.

"Look! Shall I go up softly and surprise her?"

"Has she ever been surprised?" asked Red Eric, and immediately old Janet, without turning, called, "I have been waiting for you, these two hours and more."

Redcap ran up to her, joyfully.

"How did you know?" he asked.

For answer she stretched out her two arms as she had always done and he pulled her to her feet as he used to do but now it was easier for she seemed lighter and more like a fallen leaf than ever.

"Taller, paler, thinner, wiser," she said, peering into his face. "What have you learnt in your wanderings, Redcap?"

"Stories and songs and juggler's tricks."

Old Janet looked at him silently but he knew that she was laughing, for her eyes twinkled and her body quivered as though the laughter had been hidden away, deep down inside her and came scampering up when something unlocked it.

"You have learnt much more," she said and she placed her two hands on his shoulders. "If you cannot put it into words today, as time goes on you will find out what it is." She turned to the minstrel. "And you, Red Eric?"

"I am still learning," he said.

She waited, bending her old head back as far as it would go so as to see the face of the tall man, smiling down at her.

"Janet," he said, "whenever I come and leave I give you a present."

"So you are leaving once more, obstinate redhead! Well, what have you brought this time?"

"Maybe a singing smith. Maybe the same old song."

He stooped, kissed her hand as though she had been a queen, smiled at Redcap and said, "I shall be waiting." Then he mounted and rode away, singing his song.

THE ROAD OR THE FORGE?

A woman is a gladsome thing
They do the wash and do the wring!
Lullay, lullay, she doth thee sing
And yet she hath but care and woe.

Redcap shaded his eyes, with his hand, gazing after him, and, as the green-clad figure grew more and more remote until it became a part of the twilight and of the darkening wood, the song, too, drifted away like the evening breeze.

Redcap stood watching and listening. Somewhere out of sight Red Eric would be waiting till the moon rose. Should he follow?

He turned to seek help from old Janet but the wise woman had gone and he was alone in the lane, with the open road in one direction and his home in the other. He knew, now, that he must decide for himself and that whatever way he chose would need all that inner strength which Red Eric had told him about when they had spoken together of courage.

To go home meant losing Red Eric. To follow him meant losing his home.

For a minute he strained eyes and ears to catch a glimpse and an echo of the red-haired minstrel whom he had sought for so long and had found at last. Was he to let him go?

He turned towards the village. It was growing dark and doors and shutters were closed, but little by little, their framework appeared delicately traced by the light from fires and lanterns inside the cottages.

He looked first at them, then at the dark lane which led to the open road, then back again at the village.

He knew which was the door of the forge by the brightness of its outline. Suddenly it opened and a great square of rosy light illumined the path which led to it.

Redcap caught his breath and stood without moving, gazing at it. Slowly its friendliness stole into his heart, seeping through his veins and filling his whole body with its own warm glow.

Crying, "I've come back! I've come back!" he ran towards it.

NOTE

In the fourteenth century, the time of our story, the wandering minstrel was a well-known figure. Sometimes, like Green Stranger on page 204, and Jack Piper on page 244, he made verses on the spur of the moment to suit the occasion, but more often he sang songs which had been passed by word of mouth from father to son, changing a little with each generation until they were written down. Most of the songs in this book were first written on parchment in the fifteenth century, but the words may have been known long before this.

The stories, too, passed from generation to generation. Some of those which you have read here came to Europe from the Far East through such people as Aesop, the slave, who was telling stories to the Greeks six hundred years before the birth of Christ. Nial's tales of *Big from Afar* (page 99) and the *Poor Man and his Butter* (page 280) are examples. St. Gerasimus and the Lion, called here *The Soul of a Lion* (page 38), was written in Latin by one of the early Christian teachers more than thirteen hundred years ago. *Columkille's Horse* (page 296) is an old story too. We know about it because it is told by Adamnan, an abbot of Iona who wrote the life of Columkille, and died in 704.

St. Benno, who had the adventure with the frog (page 232), lived to be a very old man and died in 1106. Perhaps he knew about *Alfrad's Donkey* (page 190) whose story is in a Latin poem of the eleventh century. Jack Piper would not have known the English translation given in this book because it was made by my sister, Eileen Power.[1] I put it here because I thought you would like it, and I am sure that Jack would have liked it too.

Learned monks and friars knew many such tales, which the minstrels borrowed. For instance, the Wise Woman's story of

[1] From *Medieval English Nunneries*, by Eileen Power (Cambridge University Press).

NOTE

the *Abbot's Jackdaw* (page 24) was written by a monk of Clairvaux, that of *Willy Gris* (page 213) by a Grey friar. A chronicler, writing a "history", puts against the date 1138 the story of the *Changeling Monk* (page 156). *French Roland and the Ordeal* (page 183) was part of a sermon given by a Dominican friar who died in 1312. And the beautiful story of *Our Lady's Tumbler* (page 259) had long been known and loved before it was put into rhymed couplets by Gautier de Coincy, a thirteenth-century monk.

In those days many a story taught a lesson of good manners and of common sense. A fourteenth-century knight called Geoffrey de la Tour Landry, who fought in the Hundred Years War, collected stories which told how women should behave (see pages 128 and 146) and wrote them in a book for the education of his daughters. In the fifteenth century they were printed by Caxton, who set up the first printing press in London, but doubtless the knight had heard them from his mother and his grandmother, who probably learnt them from her parents.

Moral tales were enjoyed by young and old, but courtiers and knights preferred the more romantic stories, like the *Grey Palfrey* (page 195), which came through France to England, where French was at one time the language of the court. *Bisclavaret* (page 63), too, was a favourite. It was written in verse by a lady called Marie de France who is said to have lived at the court of Henry II. We are told that she lay awake many a night, making her rhymes, and "know ye," she said, "it is no light thing to tell a goodly tale".